*This book is dedicated to my son Christopher.
Who, since he was a little boy, has been a wonderful example of
how to act like a man.*

JACK FROST

A DETECTIVE JACK STRATTON NOVEL

CHRISTOPHER GREYSON

GREYSON MEDIA

Novels featuring Jack Stratton in order:

**AND THEN SHE WAS GONE
GIRL JACKED
JACK KNIFED
JACKS ARE WILD
JACK AND THE GIANT KILLER
DATA JACK
JACK OF HEARTS
JACK FROST**

Also by Christopher Greyson:

PURE OF HEART

THE GIRL WHO LIVED

ISBN: 1-68399-081-1
ISBN-13: 978-1-68399-081-9

JACK FROST

A DETECTIVE JACK STRATTON NOVEL

CHRISTOPHER GREYSON

GREYSON MEDIA

Novels featuring Jack Stratton in order:

AND THEN SHE WAS GONE
GIRL JACKED
JACK KNIFED
JACKS ARE WILD
JACK AND THE GIANT KILLER
DATA JACK
JACK OF HEARTS
JACK FROST

Also by Christopher Greyson:

PURE OF HEART

THE GIRL WHO LIVED

CONTENTS

1

BEWARE OF FALLING ROCKS

With his legs dangling forty-five feet above the floor of the indoor climbing gym and less than ten feet to go till he reached the top, Jack wasn't about to stop now. He'd already scaled all the other courses today, and every muscle was burning, but this was the highest peak and the most advanced course, and he was determined to conquer it. He was going on assignment soon; he needed to shake the dust off his mountaineering skills or he was toast.

Jack reached for the far climbing hold and grabbed it with his fingertips. His long legs swung out as he released his toehold. He hung by just his fingers, his body swinging above the mats below.

He looked down at Alice, who had finished the last of the intermediate climbs and nervously watched him from the gym floor. "You're getting a little high there, darling," Alice called up to him. Since their engagement, she'd taken to calling him darling. Jack didn't mind, though it seemed a bit old-fashioned. Pretty and petite, she looked all business in her climbing harness, her hands on her hips. She was still trying to figure out a way to go with him; he was sure of it. The way she fit with him and completed him, and wanted to be with him no matter what he was doing or where he was going, were only a couple of the astonishing things about his fiancée.

But Alice wouldn't be accompanying him on this assignment. Jack would be undercover and flying solo.

He reached wide for a climbing hold and grabbed it. When he released his toehold, he hung by just his fingers until he found another cranny for his foot. He pulled himself higher, his sweaty body flat against the rough wall, but now he was stuck. The next hold was too far out for Jack to reach, even with his long arms. He should probably double back and take a different route to reach the top... but where was the fun in that?

"Don't!" Jack's conscience and Alice called out at the same time.

He didn't listen to either of them.

Instead Jack let go with his left hand, let his body swing back and forth, and flashed a quick grin at Alice before swinging himself toward the far-off grip and letting go completely.

For a moment, he was suspended in midair fifty feet above the gym floor. It was as good as flying, and so was the thrill—he hadn't realized he missed it so much.

His left hand closed around the targeted climbing hold, but he was sweaty, and his fingers slid across the slick plastic. Then his pinky and ring finger slipped off altogether. Still, he managed to maintain his grip, if only with three fingers, which was far better than lying on the mat below in failure.

One last climbing hold before the top. He'd have to rock back and forth to get near it. His sweaty hand was slipping.

Alice gasped. The sound ripped through him like buckshot. Jack's blood ran cold as a feeling he hadn't known for a very long time sliced through him.

Fear.

And that was his critical mistake. Fear was his kryptonite. He lost concentration. His mind, at first focused solely on the next hold, leaped instead to thoughts of his future and everything he now had to lose. As if he were catching a glimpse of the life he wished for, his eyes opened wide, taking it all in: Alice, and all his plans and dreams.

His fingers unfurled, and he fell like a stone, clawing the air for the climbing wall, just out of his reach, as he plummeted. Jack heard Alice scream his name, saw some people far below snapping to attention, and tried not to look at the thin mat forty feet below, which would do nothing to cushion his fall.

He shot his feet straight out in front of him, as if he were sitting on a floor, arched his back, and propelled himself toward the wall. The last-ditch effort engaged the friction plate and cam on the belaying device, and he knew it had worked when the safety harness dug into his groin with a sudden jerk. He spun slowly like a watch on a chain as his belayer lowered him to the floor.

"That was awesome, man," the twenty-year-old fellow adrenaline junkie yelled. "You looked like freaking Batman, flying through the air!"

Jack grinned.

"You are *not* going to do anything like that ever again, Jack Stratton, or you'll… I'll…" Alice's lip trembled, which was *never* a good sign. Her big green eyes blazed, but the fire went out as they welled up with tears.

"Yeah, man. She's right," said the belayer. "You try that on the mountain, and dude, you'll die."

ALICE CRIES FOUL

Jack leaned back in his chair. "Do you know when I'm going on site?"

"That question is at the *top* of my list."

They were the first to arrive in the drab conference room. The long oak table had six chairs pulled up to it, but Jack didn't know how many people would be attending. He poured himself and Alice each a glass of water from the pitcher in the center of the table, straightened his tie, and sat down again next to Alice, whose excessively good posture in front of her laptop screamed, *I wish I were anywhere but here.*

It had been a bumpy ride since being forced out of the Darrington PD, but he'd come a long way. He didn't love being a bounty hunter and private investigator as much as he had being a cop, but it paid the bills. And when this opportunity came along to provide undercover security and do some investigation—with a little extra risk thrown in—he didn't hesitate.

Alice was clacking away, completely engrossed, and biting her lower lip, a sure sign she was nervous. This meeting was important to both of them; it would be their first big insurance investigation, and they wanted to get it right.

He leaned close and whispered, "We're going to nail this, don't worry. You're locked and loaded." He nuzzled her neck and drank in the sweet lilac scent of her favorite perfume.

She let out the breath she'd been holding and nudged him with her shoulder. "Get serious, Jack. They'll be coming in any second."

Their relationship had had its bumps, too, from knowing each other when she was just a kid in foster care at Aunt Haddie's, to Jack's taking her in as a tenant, to their becoming investigative partners, and now… engaged to be married, but they were working on building a new, wonderful life together. This new insurance niche could provide steady work and a solid foundation to build their dreams on.

The case was interesting. Jack would be working undercover on the set of the hit show *Planet Survival.* An accidental death had occurred during filming a year ago, and it had recently been followed by a threat on the lives of the remaining crew. There was no concrete link between the two events… but that was part of what the show's insurance company wanted Jack to find out.

He had to admit he was intrigued by the idea of being on the set of a TV show, especially a big production like this. *Planet Survival* was the leading program in the "competitive reality survival" category. Contestants risked life and limb battling with each other for a spot in the next episode. The contestants' only goal was to survive—

both the competition and the hazards of nature. And that was the appeal of the show, really. The competitions were deliberately dangerous and harrowing to watch. Viewers at home couldn't get enough of these brave—and slightly crazy—contestants going head-to-head. Each of the show's seven seasons so far had been filmed in a different exotic locale, from remote tropical islands to treacherous frozen mountains. Most slunk home after defeat, but more than a few had ended up in the hospital. The one person who survived would get a boatload of cash, endorsements, and the coveted title of Supreme Planet Survivalist.

And despite the dangers inherent in filming a show like this, *Planet Survival* had managed to accumulate success and dodge tragedy for its entire run—until now. After the accidental death of a crew member, production had been halted mid-season, for the first time in the show's history.

By the time they'd gotten the go-ahead to resume filming, winter was over, and they'd had to wait to start production again. Which led to them being here today.

The door opened, and Brian Strickland entered. As the son of the owner of the insurance company, Brian was the heir apparent. He'd just been promoted to acting vice president, and he seemed as eager as Jack to make sure this deal ran smoothly. Jack and Alice had spoken with Brian several times over the phone, but this was their first time meeting in person. He was short, with a bushy mustache, a comb-over, and a thousand-dollar suit. He held the door open for an attractive black woman, who glanced down at her watch and frowned as she entered.

Jack rose from his chair and extended a hand across the table. "Good morning. I'm Jack Stratton, and this is my business partner, Alice Campbell."

"Pleasure to meet you, Mr. Stratton." The woman shook Jack's hand and then Alice's. "Leah Coleman. I'm the executive producer of *Planet Survival*. Call me Leah."

Her conservative black jacket and slacks would have fit in well at any Fortune 500 company, but Jack felt, along with the strength of her grip, some hardworking calluses. Simple diamond stud earrings complemented her subtle champagne eye shadow, dark eyes, and deep-brown skin. She wore her black hair short. And she smelled as expensive as she looked. Chanel No. 5.

Brian ran a hand over his head to make sure his hair was still shellacked in place. "Since *Planet Survival* is the biggest policy McAlister Insurance has ever written, we've assigned Alice and Jack to your policy, Ms.—ahh, Leah. They're our best investigators."

Leah looked from Jack to Alice then back to Jack, sizing them up.

Jack pressed his knuckles against the table. He hated lies. The only reason he and Alice were the company's best investigators was because they were the company's *only* investigators. And, to be honest, this was their very first job for McAlister. Then there was their youth, which had to add to Leah's skepticism. Though people always assumed he was older, Jack was only twenty-seven, and no one meeting twenty-two-year-old Alice for the first time could possibly guess how seasoned and tough she was. But they needed this job; the trick was to make hunger look more like determination than desperation.

Brian took a seat at the head of the table. "Well, shall we begin?"

The others sat as well, and Leah set her coffee down. "Confidentiality is paramount, given the show's renowned success and the special circumstances surrounding this very unfortunate accident. They've both signed the nondisclosures?"

Brian turned as white as a ghost, and began blinking as if sending a distress signal to a passing ship. A few more seconds passed while he cleared his throat and rifled through his papers.

"We signed all thirty-seven pages," Jack assured her.

Alice added, "We understand completely. Privacy is a core value of our organization—a cornerstone of our business."

"We've taken a number of steps to preserve your anonymity," Brian said. "The papers all reference Blue Stone, LLC, and there's no mention of *Planet Survival* or any of its affiliates."

Leah folded her hands neatly on the table. "And those steps are greatly appreciated. But I still don't understand this latest request for *additional* security. We run a completely closed set. We resumed taping four days ago, and everything's running smoothly, except for the fact that while I'm here, my show is going on four thousand feet above us *without* me."

Brian held up his hands in a gesture of apology. "I appreciate that this presents an additional burden on your production, but I think it's called for." He picked up a remote, the lights dimmed, and the television on the wall behind him came to life. "This is the note that was pinned to your lodge door."

A handwritten note was projected onto the screen. The blue letters were boxy and easy to read:

THE WRATH OF THE MOUNT MINUIT IS UPON YOU INVADERS. ONE LIFE WAS REQUIRED FOR YOUR DESECRATION LAST YEAR. HOW DARE YOU RETURN TO THIS SACRED LAND!! LEAVE NOW OR YOU NEVER WILL, AND KANIEHTIIO MOUNTAIN WILL BE KNOWN AS ONEKWENHSA MOUNTAIN!!

"Alice did some research and identified those names as Native American. Iroquois, to be exact," Brian said. "The last line translates to 'If you don't leave now, the snow mountain will be called blood mountain.' It's a *direct* threat against the 'invaders'—which clearly refers to *Planet Survival*'s production team and cast. Due to the substantial insurance policy that my company is carrying, I must insist that additional security measures be taken to ensure the safety of those insured."

And your investment, Jack wanted to add, but he kept his mouth closed.

"We talked about this, Brian," Leah said. "We agreed that on-site security would be too disruptive to the show."

Brian smiled. "That's why I propose that the security go undercover. They'll pose as a new crew hire."

"The crew is bare-bones. It's part of *Planet Survival*'s allure. I don't know how anyone you add would be able to blend in." She tipped her head toward Jack and Alice. "And adding *two* people is completely impossible."

"We're not looking for two slots, just one. Jack is ex-military, with stellar mountaineering skills." Jack hoped that wasn't another lie on Brian's part. "He has the rappelling and climbing experience necessary for this detail. I'm sure you can figure out some job he can legitimately do without letting on what he's *actually* doing," Brian said, seemingly pleased with himself.

Alice turned to Leah. "Actually, I think it would be a great idea if both Jack and I were on set."

"Impossible." Leah crossed her arms. "I'm struggling to think of a plausible role for Jack."

Brian opened a folder and put his hand down on the thick stack of papers inside. "In the spirit of open communication, let me reiterate that the policy *does* contain an observation clause. This is not a request; it's a requirement for coverage."

Leah eyed Brian for several moments, like a poker player assessing the table. Then she folded her cards and spoke. "When would this *observation* start?"

Brian turned to Jack. "How soon can you be ready?"

"I'm packed and ready to go," Jack said.

Leah held up a hand. "Slow down. Getting a waiver through the union will take some time." She took a sip of coffee, hiding a faint smile behind the rim of the cup. "At least a few weeks."

"I already checked on that," Alice jumped in. "You can use the 'local contractor' clause of the contract and hire us as nonspecialist local contractors. You won't need a waiver." She glanced at Brian. "Jack and I are a team. We can work something out." Jack backed his partner up with a nod.

Leah pointed at the policy. "The policy states 'observer.' *One.* I don't care who, but there will only be one." The muscles in her delicate jaw tightened as she clenched her teeth.

Jack tapped Alice's leg under the table. She had always been his fiercest protector, and he knew it was driving her crazy that she'd have to stay behind. But this job would help pay for their wedding.

"That'd be me," Jack said.

Leah swallowed her irritation. "Send me his contact information. I'll get the paperwork processed and be in touch." Rising majestically, she nodded around the table at no one in particular. "I have to get back. I can't miss any more production time."

Brian stood, holding his hand over the stack of papers like it was the nuclear button and he was ready for launch. "I'm sorry, but there will be no production without an observer on-site. This is nonnegotiable."

Leah drew in a long, jagged breath, then nodded. Jack understood the squeeze Brian was putting on her—production downtime gobbled up profits, so she'd have to move quickly, despite her reservations about the plan. "Give me the afternoon to get it done. I'll send someone down to get him tomorrow morning. Ten o'clock. Agreed?"

Brian nodded. "Tomorrow, then."

"But I have to make one thing perfectly clear before we begin this *observation*. He stays in the background, does exactly what I say, and in no way impedes my show or interferes with my people."

"I understand perfectly." Brian shook her hand in agreement. "Jack is a professional and will be discreet."

Leah turned to Jack. "Bring cold-weather survival gear. I'll have my assistant email Brian a list of the other things you'll need."

Jack nodded but kept his poker face on. Internally, he was grinning from ear to ear.

As soon as the door closed behind Leah, Alice turned to Brian. "I still think it would be best if Jack and I work together on this."

Brian picked up the remote and tapped it against the oak table. "You will. Just not in the same location. I need you back here, spearheading another aspect of the investigation. In light of the threatening note, the earlier death needs to be reevaluated. We're reopening last year's accident claim."

Alice perked up and gave Jack a look that was invisible to Brian but signaled to Jack her giddy excitement for a new case.

Brian dimmed the lights again and pressed the remote. The TV began to play the footage from the accident. Jack and Alice had already seen it, of course. It had all been caught on tape. Well, *almost* all of it.

First the iconic north face of Mount Minuit. A helicopter swung into the shot, with Gavin Maddox, *Planet Survival*'s shameless, showboating host, in full ski gear, suspended from the end of a rope. The helicopter set Maddox down on the slope, and when he gave a thumbs-up, the helicopter rose and began to fly away.

That's when everything went wrong.

As the helicopter rotated around, a section of snow on the cliff face beneath it gave way and then the whole slope began to slide, picking up ice chunks and spewing plumes of snow. In a heartbeat, the peaceful mountain scene had become an unstoppable wave of destruction. An avalanche.

The camera panned, following Maddox frantically skiing away from the crumbling wall of snow, until spruce trees and a small hill blocked the shot and all you could see was a white wave flattening the trees as it swept down the mountainside, crushing everything in its path. The camera jerked back and forth, searching wildly for the host, who appeared a moment later, skiing triumphantly away from the path of destruction.

Several crew members ran into the shot then, shouting and pointing. One woman sank to her knees and dropped forward with her head to the snow.

Brian hit pause. They'd already seen the bulk of the video. The real tragedy of the avalanche hadn't been caught on camera. Charlie Parker, a crew member, had been filming from a different vantage point behind the ridge, directly in the path of the avalanche. He never stood a chance.

Brian cleared his throat. "Our original accident investigation blamed the avalanche on wash from the helicopter's props—and that's still the most likely explanation. But with the delivery of that note, we're obligated to reexamine the evidence." He had a hard drive that included hundreds of hours of footage, evidentiary reports, OSHA reports, and interviews with everyone on that mountain. "That's what I want you to work on, Alice."

"Great!" Alice gushed. "If everything's on a portable drive, I can take it with me and go with Jack and do the work up there."

Brian shook his head. "I'm sorry. Not on the mountain. There is no Wi-Fi and the only phone service available is via satellite phone. Besides, this is extremely sensitive information. The *last* place we want it is anywhere near the very people we're investigating."

"Alice," Jack said, "Brian's right. It makes sense for you to work the investigation from down here."

Though Jack agreed with Brian, it was for very different reasons. Brian was concerned about pushback from Leah and putting the undercover nature of the operation at risk. Jack was concerned about the love of his life and her safety. With an active threat against "invaders," not to mention the occasional rogue avalanche, he wanted Alice safe and sound and as far away from that mountain as possible.

Alice's green eyes grew wide and her lips pressed together. She'd clearly expected Jack to back her up on this.

Brian, apparently oblivious to the growing tension in the room, excused himself to retrieve the hard drive. "I'll be right back."

"Jack, I can't believe you!" Alice said when he was gone. "Why did you agree with him?" She gave Jack no time to answer. "You *need* me up there, and you know it. I've been training so hard I can climb faster than most monkeys! I'm really ready, totally willing, and super able to help you on this. We're a team. C'mon, we can think of something before he gets back."

Jack put his hands on Alice's shoulders, looked her straight in the eye, and said, "We *are* a team, but this is for the best. I need you to trust me on this and stay put, okay?"

She didn't respond, and Jack knew from experience that her silence didn't necessarily mean she agreed; but maybe it meant she'd trust his judgment on this.

Brian walked back in and handed Alice a portable drive. "That's everything we've digitized. It includes the background checks we ran on everyone on the mountain at the time of the accident and just prior. But I want you to dig deeper."

"How can you be sure you know who was on the mountain?" Jack asked. "What if someone climbed up another way?"

"That part's simple. There are only two ways up, gondola or helicopter, so we know who came and went. The only people up there were eight crew members, five competitors, and a researcher who mans the weather observatory."

"Are all of them back on the mountain now?" Alice asked.

Brian shook his head. "Not everyone. Mack Carson, the helicopter pilot, died on vacation last month."

Jack noticed Alice's slight frown and shared her disappointment. Witness statements were sometimes only as good as the investigator's questions. Now that the pilot was dead, they couldn't get in any additional questions of their own.

"Fortunately, we'd already gotten his sworn statement concerning the accident," Brian went on. "It's on the hard drive. And Carson wouldn't have been back anyway. McAlister didn't renew the show's helicopter insurance policy for this location, so *Planet Survival* will have to rely on drones for aerial shots now."

"How did the pilot die?" Jack asked.

"Climbing accident. The whole crew is a bunch of adrenaline junkies and extreme sport enthusiasts. Any downtime they get, they scatter to the four winds to base-jump off buildings, run with bulls—you wouldn't believe the antics." Brian raised an eyebrow at Jack. "Do yourself a favor and don't catch that fever. There's a reason the premiums for those activities are so high. Statistically, those people don't live long."

Alice cleared her throat and cast a sideways glance at Jack, doubling down on Brian's warning without saying a word. "Brian," she said, "can you please email me all the information you have on Mack?"

"I'll do it right now. Jack, can you be ready to go in the morning?"

"Sure. I'll just need the gear list that Leah said she'd email over."

Brian said he'd check on it, and they concluded the meeting. In less than an hour, Jack and Alice had gotten not one but two jobs.

Alice waited for Brian to leave. "Jack, I don't have a good feeling about this." Her beautiful eyes pleaded with him to find a way for her to go with him.

There wasn't a way—but he couldn't blame her for trying. He knew how *he'd* feel if *she* was the one going up a dangerous mountain and someone had threatened to kill everyone on it.

"Don't worry, Alice," Jack said. "We're a team, remember?"

3

BREATHING IS A MUST

Jack held open the door for Alice and followed her inside the apartment. His senses immediately buzzed with alarm. *Something's off.* Usually, Lady would bowl them over, begging to go out. But she wasn't at the door waiting for them.

He flicked on the light, and Alice gasped.

Jack's hand flew to his gun.

Perched on the edge of his leather recliner was an extremely beautiful Asian woman. She sat calmly, balancing a teacup in one hand and stroking Lady's head with the other. The enormous, 120-pound King Shepherd lay at the woman's feet, gnawing on a new dog bone so big it looked like it originally belonged to a dinosaur.

"Good evening, Officer. Alice."

"Kiku." Jack took his hand off his gun. Like gears jamming, his muscles struggled against his mind as he ordered his body to stand down and the sweat to stop rolling down his back.

Alice gave a tight smile and a quick wave.

"I've already become acquainted with your dog." Kiku scratched behind Lady's ear with her long red nails, and the giant dog's thick tail drummed the floor with a happy beat.

"Lady?" Jack shook his head in disbelief. "The great watchdog that would never let a stranger into my house, unless that stranger happened to bribe her with the thighbone from a *T. rex*? Where'd you get that thing, the natural history museum?"

Alice laughed, revealing the deep dimple that melted Jack every time he caught a glimpse of it. No matter the pressure of the situation, Alice always had his back; that was one of the things he loved most.

Kiku set down her cup and rose, her black evening dress shimmering. "Lady likes me. We are kindred spirits." She smiled broadly, revealing sharp canines. "It has been far too long, Officer." Her eyes traveled slowly over Jack's body, then finally locked on his face. "I see you are well." There was a lilt to her voice that made Jack's cheeks flush.

"Life's good, thanks. You stopping by on the way to the opera?"

Kiku's four-inch stilettos clicked on the wood floor as she strolled over and stopped well inside Jack's personal space. Her perfume smelled of an unknown flower, but it was like a good drink—once you have a sip, you want more.

"I have another visit to make later this evening. Forgive me if I am overdressed. Would you care for me to remedy that situation?"

"*I* wouldn't." Alice's brunette ponytail swung back and forth like a metronome.

Jack laughed. "What brings you by, Kiku?"

Kiku's gaze shifted to Alice for only a fraction of a second, but for a trained police officer it was enough; it confirmed Jack's suspicions.

"You two have been in touch with each other?" Jack said. He crossed his arms, stared at his fiancée, and waited for the answer.

"Actually…" Alice squirmed. "I asked Kiku for a favor."

Jack looked at Alice in utter disbelief. Dealing with Kiku was like walking into a lion's den. And doing it without thinking it through first was as bad as having a steak in your pocket when you went in. "Please excuse us, Kiku." Jack took Alice by the elbow and marched her to the bedroom and shut the door.

"Are you out of your mind, Alice?" Jack whispered. "Kiku is *Yakuza*."

"She's still our *friend*, Jack." Alice picked up a hairbrush off the bureau.

"Being a Japanese mobster makes her our *long-distance* friend." Jack started pacing. "That's how this friendship works. I can't believe you reached out to her without talking to me about it first."

"You would've said no way, Jack. Besides, *you* asked her for a favor not long ago." Alice's beautiful eyes hardened.

"Yes, I did. It was the only way to bring that child molester back from Thailand."

"And she did it, right?" Alice leveled the hairbrush at his chest.

"Yeah, she brought him back. In *two different boxes*," Jack whispered loudly.

"Maybe he was dead when she found him."

"Oh, come on. Look, I like Kiku. I owe Kiku. But she's dangerous." Jack stopped pacing. "Wait a second, what was the favor you asked for?"

Alice sat on the side of the bed. "I need her to find out who killed my family. I'm too close to it to think clearly, and you're too close to me. I was afraid what you'd do if you found the killer."

Jack's stomach tightened. "What *I'd* do? Did you miss the part about the guy who hurt you coming back here in pieces?"

"This is different. I'll make Kiku *promise* she won't kill them."

"And you believe her, but you don't believe me?"

Alice tapped the hairbrush against her leg and stared up at him. "It's not that—"

There was a knock on the bedroom door, and Kiku opened it a crack. "Excuse me. With these thin walls, I can hear every word of your conversation. There is one fact that both of you are neglecting to consider in your deliberations."

"Which is?" Jack opened the door the rest of the way, and Kiku stepped in.

"Alice has asked for my assistance, but I have not yet said that I will provide it."

Jack didn't know whether he felt relieved or indignant. Ambiguity was only one of Kiku's specialties.

"I'm sorry." Alice tossed the hairbrush onto the nightstand and walked back into the living room. "This isn't going very well. Let's sit down and I'll try to explain." She held her hand out to the recliner and sat on the well-worn couch.

Kiku took the offered seat. Jack leaned against the doorframe. Lady was still munching on her bone.

"When I was seven," Alice began, addressing Kiku, "my parents and my twin brothers were killed in a head-on car accident. When I was in the hospital, a nurse told me that the other driver died in the crash. I don't know if she was trying to protect me because I was just a child or if she was misinformed. But when Jack and I were in Florida last month, Jack tracked down a friend of my mother's."

"I was trying to help Alice learn more about her mom and to spare her the disappointment if it was another dead end," Jack added.

"My mother's friend had some photos of my family, and she also told Jack that the other driver didn't die in the accident. The scumbag fled the scene. The truck he was driving was stolen. All these years, the police haven't been able to find him."

Kiku closed her eyes and bowed her head for a moment. "My sincere condolences for your loss." She turned to Jack. "You are the detective. And there is little on the internet you cannot uncover, Alice. Why do you two need my help?"

Jack looked at Alice. He wanted to hear her answer, too.

"Because I'll kill the man if I find him," Alice admitted as she started to shake.

Jack took two long strides over to the couch to place a comforting hand on her shoulder.

Kiku traced a fingernail down her jawline. "But that is an empty threat. You are not a killer, Alice." She spoke nothing but the truth here, as usual, and they all knew it. "However, as demonstrated by Jack's protective reaction—he is more than capable of killing the man, and he *would* find him."

Alice's green eyes caught his, the golden flecks sparkling with a look of love, admiration, and understanding Jack had never known before her. "I don't want Jack to have to make that choice. You know he doesn't count the cost to himself—it's who Jack is." She leaned forward to plead. "But Kiku, you're not too close to this. You can promise me you won't kill him, and I know you won't."

"Kiku promised me that once before," Jack said, giving Kiku an intense look.

"No, Jack," said Kiku. "You asked that I bring a child molester back to the United States. I did exactly what you asked of me. You never specified he was supposed to be breathing."

"You *knew* I didn't want you to kill him."

"Did I?"

He felt his stomach knot. He wished he'd specified "breathing," and now wondered if, subconsciously, he didn't ask on purpose. Kiku's cold stare reinforced her words. She was a mercenary, a skilled hunter who killed her prey at the end of the hunt. That was her job, and Jack had known that when he asked for the favor.

Alice broke the awkward silence. "Kiku, I need your help—we need your help— and I trust that when you give your word, you will honor it. Will you find the man who killed my family, and if you locate him, will you allow him to live to stand justice?"

Kiku sighed and smoothed an invisible crease in the black silk along her thigh. "What you're asking me to do will not ease your pain, Alice. Pain from your family's death is separate from seeking justice for them. Even if I do find him, only you can address the former."

"What I can't live with is my family's murderer walking around free. I live with the pain of their absence every single day! I'm forced to live with it." Her voice broke and her lip trembled. "Kiku, my brothers were practically babies… Will you help me?"

Kiku had been calm and silent, her porcelain hands folded in her lap. Her gaze shifted from Alice to Jack. As usual, he assumed she could see inside his head. "My apologies, Officer, but yes, I will help Alice."

Jack took a deep breath. "For the record," he said, "this time, breathing is a must."

4

NOT WORTH JACK

Alice parked Jack's prized Charger in the parking lot and left the engine running. The slope of Mount Minuit rose up before them. At its base, at the far end of the parking lot, two men and one woman were loading equipment onto the gondola that would take Jack up to the filming location.

"Please, can't we talk to Brian again? I don't like you going up there without me."

Jack shook his head. "We've been through this. We're going to divide and conquer and get this case done twice as fast. You're going to be crazy busy and tied to your laptop. You won't have time to miss me."

Jack had Alice's back just as much as she had his, but they had both read the disclaimers. Anyone on the production site needed to be able to climb, for real.

"I can climb. You taught me."

"C'mon, Alice, Pete's Pike is an indoor climbing gym. They won't count that as experience." He lightly ran his fingertips over her knee. "Even if they did, Leah was adamant. Only one person on the set." They could really screw things up for Brian, too, and for any future in the business if they breached their contract in any way.

"Have you figured out how we're going to communicate?" This was a real problem. The contract Jack had signed said absolutely no cell phones were allowed on the production site. And even if he could have smuggled one up there, he doubted there'd be a signal. Leah had a satellite phone and was supposed to check in with Brian daily.

"Brian said we'd be able to update each other during his calls with Leah."

Alice took his hand in both of hers. "It's a good thing I'll get to talk to you every day. I'm going to be worried; I can't help it. Aunt Haddie and your folks stood in your way of ever climbing this mountain for a reason: to try to keep you in one piece."

They both craned their necks to see the awesome mountain ahead through the windshield. Its beauty was breathtaking; severe gray stone, crystalline ice, and white snow, all frosted by a lavender haze spreading across the morning sky. Jack had to admit the frozen peak was stunning but intimidating. Known locally for its weather station, Minuit attracted climbers from all over. But only ones with top-notch ice axe skills dared to ascend the treacherous elevation to the notoriously sheer summit. The dangers on the mountain were legendary, and several daredevils had lost their lives. The climbing conditions posed a threat on their own, but unpredictable weather could turn even a leisurely hike at lower levels into a harrowing fight for survival.

"When's the last time you climbed? Eight years ago? And was it ice?" Alice must have realized that her mountainside manner needed a little adjustment. "I'll ride Lady up there if I have to."

Jack chuckled. "I'll be fine. You're going to be with Kiku. You're the one we should worry about."

Alice was right. It *was* a dangerous job, and that was part of the fun. Jack was looking forward to getting back out on the rock face, where his life depended on his wits and the strength of his fingertips. In the military, on the force, in a situation like this—it served him far better to be excited about the mission than to fear it. Fear saps the strength in the muscles…unless you convert it into psychological fuel.

"Ah, Kiku… She did promise to be on her best behavior." Alice stroked the back of his hand with her thumb. "The timing of her visit isn't great, smack in the middle of our first job for Brian, but I am glad she's willing to help. But seriously, be careful."

"Of course, I will be. The only one *not* promising to behave and be careful is *you*, my darling."

"You called me darling! Just like your dad calls your mom!" Alice threw her arms around Jack's neck and kissed him.

That's why she's been calling me 'darling.' Now it made perfect sense. Alice admired his parents' love for one another as much as he did. They both must have picked up the habit from them.

They got out of the car and walked to the trunk, their breath fogging in the crisp mountain air.

"Well, you already dodged two bullets," Alice said with resignation. "I caught the weather report and the storm front coming down from Canada has slowed. There's another one heading up the coast, but it's supposed to miss us completely, too."

"See? Nothing to worry about." Jack tugged the hundred-pound duffel bag out of the trunk and laid it at his feet. He faced Alice and smiled. "And I have some good news."

Which he had deliberately saved for this moment. He knew this mission was hard on Alice, and he wanted to leave on a positive note.

"My father thinks his cardiologist is going to give him travel clearance. My parents will be in Hope Falls in six weeks."

"Does this mean you're fine with a little chapel wedding?" Flecks of gold sparkled in her eyes.

Jack sighed theatrically. "Well, ever since I was a little boy, I've dreamed of a lavish wedding in a grand cathedral, with a full orchestra, and a flock of doves released when I enter. But those dreams—"

Alice swatted his arm, laughing.

"Of course I'm okay with a small wedding." He pulled her close and kissed her. "I'm just glad you said yes."

She wrapped her arms around his neck and pressed her lips and chest against his, both vulnerable and imperious.

"I love you, Jack Stratton. Come home to me."

He forced a smile, but the words stabbed him right through the heart—exactly the same words that Kelly, his first girlfriend, had said to him in the airport before he deployed to Iraq. In an instant, all the memories, all the feelings, and all the pain of war blasted through him.

Come home to me.

When Kelly had said it, he was sure he would. But the Jack who made it back wasn't the same Jack who'd left. Part of him died in Iraq with his best friend, Chandler.

"I will," he said. "I love you, too."

Jack set his jaw, opened his eyes, and turned away quickly. The already heavy Army-issue duffel bag felt like an anvil as he walked toward the gondola, gulping air like a drowning man breaking the surface of the water. All of his therapist's suggestions for dealing with PTSD echoed in his head, but he shoved them aside and concentrated on putting one foot in front of the other, soldiering on.

Two men were struggling with a tarp-covered crate the size of a refrigerator. One was tall, lanky, and reminded Jack of Abe Lincoln—if the president had had a neck tattoo, nose ring, and a soul patch in place of a beard. The other looked to be in his late thirties and was built like a dump truck. He was five inches shorter than Jack but his shoulders were broad, and judging by his crooked nose, he'd been in a fight or two.

"You the new gofer?" the stocky man asked in a thick Australian accent, lifting his square chin.

"I am."

"Well, don't just stand there gawking. Dump your gear and help this candy boy with his end."

"All the weight's on my side," Abe protested. He shifted over so Jack could get a handhold on the huge crate.

Jack set down his duffel bag, and between the three of them they managed to lug the box into the gondola. As they lowered it, Abe's side slipped, and the crate hit the metal floor with a tremendous bang.

Abe jumped back like he'd dropped a bomb. And when the Australian pulled off the tarp, Jack understood why.

Warning labels in multiple languages covered the crate, but the one in English was good enough for Jack—*DANGER: EXPLOSIVES.*

The Australian ran a hand over his sweaty forehead and through his dirty-blond hair, graying at the temples. "Thanks for the help. I think this guy gets scrawnier with every job. Name's Ollie. This here's Abe."

Son of a gun, I called it! Jack wasn't the only one who had noticed the resemblance.

"Jack Stratton. And the next time you ask me to move explosives, give me a heads-up on what we're moving."

Ollie scoffed. "Aw, they're just big firecrackers. Avalanche charges. That mountain's as pregnant as a two-week-overdue momma. She's ready to pop all on her own; this stuff just lets us say when." He eyed Jack up and down. "Leah said you're US military?"

"I was. Army."

"That where you learned to climb?"

"Yeah."

"You can spot for Abe then." He pulled out a walkie-talkie. "Don't know what's wrong with your military, but I've never known one of you who knows how to *really* climb. Not even a Ranger. If you want real training, join the Australian Defence Force."

Jack swallowed a comeback and went back for his bag. Abe followed him out of the gondola.

"Ignore him," he said, tipping his head back toward Ollie. "He busts on everyone. Ollie's about as approachable as a porcupine. Just don't get on his bad side."

"Let me guess, Ollie's one of the guys I report to?"

"The gofer's low man on the totem pole. You report to everyone, dude. Go-fer this. Go-fer that. I should know, I was a gofer before I got promoted to camera work. Ollie is the other cameraman, and he gets really pissed when we have to haul boxes and stuff, but that's half the job. And the gofer has to do the jobs *nobody* else wants to do."

Jack took an instant liking to Abe. He looked to be a couple years younger than Jack and when he wasn't being bullied, he was open and smiled easily.

Jack hefted his duffel while Abe grabbed a three-foot-wide crate and rocked it awkwardly onto his shoulder.

"When do we head up?" Jack asked.

"Now. We just came down for these crates and you."

Abe stepped aside at the gondola's door so a young woman in a glossy new winter jacket could get on first.

"Thanks, Abe." She extended a hand toward Jack. "I'm Bree."

"Jack Stratton." He shook her gloved hand.

"Did you get enough batteries?" Ollie asked.

Bree nodded and patted her backpack. "I got ten packages."

"Ten? You shoulda got twenty." Ollie smirked. "Here's a tip for you: all those little microphones that are always on need lots and lots of batteries."

Abe shot Ollie a look that Jack interpreted as *Ease up.*

Bree tightened her lips and adjusted the faux fur collar around her head. "Yeah, well, everybody forgets stuff." To Jack she added, "In season three, we were in the Alps, and Charlie forgot his wind muffs for the microphones. We looked for a whole day in this little Swiss village—lots of cheese, but no wind muffs. We finally found someone who fashioned one for us out of an old jacket collar. It worked sweet, and it totally saved our jobs." She and Abe were laughing at the memory, but Ollie killed the moment.

"Leah should have fired both of you for that one." He moved over to the intercom and yelled into the mic, "Everyone's on board! Bring us up!"

Glancing back at the Charger, Jack saw Alice still idling, waiting, as he knew she would be. She'd probably wait there until the gondola disappeared into the clouds. Jack drew in a long, deep breath, as if to swallow the space between them, and held it for a second, savoring her one more time.

"Congratulations, Bree," Abe said. "I heard they gave you a promotion to lead audio official. I wish you got it under different circumstances."

A dark storm cloud passed through Bree's eyes. "Thanks." She grabbed the handrail as the gondola jerked forward.

"How much did they bump your pay?" Ollie asked. He wiped the corners of his mouth like he was eager to chew on the answer.

"You know we can't discuss pay; it's against union rules." Bree set down her bags and leaned against the railing.

"Who's gonna know? Besides, I'm due for a raise and I'm asking as soon as an opportunity presents itself. You don't have to tell me a number, love. Just get me hand-grenade close. Twenty percent?"

"You should ask Leah to double your pay." Bree grinned. "But let me know before you do so I can put my headphones on to block out the screams."

Abe pointed at the avalanche charges. "Yeah, we won't even need these explosives. Leah's shrieks will bring down the mountain."

Jack chuckled.

Ollie shot him a dirty look, but Jack met his glare head-on. Jack's cover was playing the part of a gofer; he was supposed to keep a low profile and observe—but Ollie was a bully, and Jack was already tired of keeping his mouth shut.

"Well, just wait until *you* got a question that *you* need an answer to," Ollie said to Bree, turning a splotchy red and pointing his finger inches from Bree's face. "When that time comes, I bet you'll wish you'd told me. Unless you think you won't have any questions, you being so experienced in your job and all, Miss Fancy Pants." Ollie brayed at his own joke and the other occupants of the gondola, embarrassed, looked at each other and came to a silent agreement to let it go one more time and not call Ollie on his bull.

Jack gave Bree a reassuring smile, which she returned.

"I'm not risking my job and the wrath of Leah to help you get a raise," she said. "Seriously, stop asking me. You're getting annoying."

"Whatever. But I see which side your bread is buttered on. Who did you come to when Gavin's microphone stopped working? Me." Ollie thumped his hand on his chest for emphasis. "Like I said, wait till next time you need something. No more Mr. Nice Guy."

"Hey, Bree, you can ask me if you need anything," Abe offered.

"Fat load of good that'll do you," Ollie huffed.

"Thanks, Abe," Bree said pointedly.

Budding romance between Abe and Bree? Certainly no love lost between Bree and Ollie.

Jack looked down at the parking lot falling away behind them. Alice had gotten out of the car and was waving back and forth.

Ollie whistled. "Is that yours? Just say the word, and I'll turn the gondola around and bring her up with us. As long as she agrees to keep us *all* warm—"

Jack grabbed the handle of the door and yanked it partially open. The chilly wind blasted in. "Say another word about my fiancée and we'll see if the ADF taught you to fly," he yelled over the racket.

Ollie wiped his mouth with the back of a callused hand and stepped back. "Don't go getting all touchy." He held his hand up, palm out. "Just havin' a little fun."

Jack waved back to Alice, then slid the door shut. All they could see from the windows now was white mountain face or infinite blue sky.

Silence reigned in the gondola for a minute, then Bree brushed her light-brown hair away from her face and turned to Jack. "Engaged, huh? Congratulations. When's the wedding?"

"Right after we're done filming."

"What will you do on set?"

"He's the gofer." Ollie eyed him up and down. "Leah said you went to film school. Trying to be the next Spielberg or something?"

"I want to get an idea of what TV is like behind the scenes," Jack said.

"Oh, and maybe this could be your ticket to Hollywood." Ollie rolled his eyes. "You'll really *go places* with this job." He put one hand on his hip and stuck his arm out, trying his best to imitate Leah. "*Go* over there and get me that tape. *Go* stand over there and hold that mic pole." He burst out laughing. "Get it? Go places?"

Abe groaned, and Bree shook her head.

"I'm the sound woman," Bree said. "I handle all things audio."

"I figure, on a show like this, you must have a dozen cameramen," Jack said. "How many do you have?"

"Two. I'm camera two," Abe said. "Ollie's camera one."

"What? How?" Jack asked. "I've seen the show. It looks like you shoot from fifty different angles, so you must have fifty different cameras."

"We do," Ollie said. "But the rest are all remote-controlled, mate."

"We set up dozens of them all over the mountain and in the camps," Abe said. "The unmanned cameras are less intrusive."

Ollie scoffed. "They're cheaper. It costs a hell of a lot less for plastic and lens on a stick than a person. Then Harvey can get whatever shot he wants."

"Harvey's the control room operator," Abe explained. "You should see his setup. It's like being on the starship *Enterprise*."

"Yeah, he's in the captain's chair, and we get the grunt work," Ollie grumbled.

"Aw, c'mon, they use you for the important shots," Bree said.

"They *use* us, all right," said Ollie. "We're about as disposable as those cameras. If Leah really wants a shot, she'll have us dangling over the edge. They don't care about losing a camera *or* a cameraman." Ollie stared at Jack. "And especially not a gofer. Keep that in mind, mate. Up here, your life's not worth *jack*."

Yeah, I've heard that one before.

"Hey, what's that?" Abe walked over to the door and pointed.

On a large, flat boulder about twenty feet away was a long, thick red line with a circle underneath. Someone had taken the trouble to scrape the snow and ice off the boulder to expose its surface. The whole thing had to be six feet across—very large, very red, and very angry.

"Stupid graffiti even up here," Ollie grumbled. "I'll have to tell Harvey to keep that out of the shot."

Abe turned to Jack, his face serious. "Did Leah tell you that some nut job made some threats against the crew?"

"Death threats," Bree added.

Jack nodded.

"Don't go on about it; you'll be scarin' the greenie." Ollie walked over to the other side of the gondola and sat on a crate. "It's all a big ado, nothin' to it. TV draws crazies like ants on a dropped doughnut."

Jack turned back to look out the window. "I think we should take any threat seriously. Especially this one."

If you knew the symbol, it was a clear warning. He'd seen it during Alice's research for Brian. It was the Iroquois symbol for death.

5

HOMEY

The gondola crested the last ridge and a two-story, L-shaped building came into view. Apart from a few Alpine touches, like painted wooden shutters, the heavy, boxy cement structure had all the warmth of a Russian gulag and screamed government building. It was like being back in the Army.

"Homey, huh?" Abe said. "It was a World War Two Army training base."

"Until some sap bought it thinking he'd turn it into a ski resort," said Ollie. He looked out at the ridge. "Four thousand feet of witches' teeth. The rock's splintery, and it'll cut you to ribbons if you ain't careful. Worthless for climbing, too." He turned back to Jack and fixed his gray eyes on him. "Piece of advice, mate. Check your anchor *twice*. You don't, and we'll be scooping you up with a spoon." He laughed.

Jack didn't respond but made a mental note. *Anchor twice or die once.*

"Uh-oh." Abe pointed. "Get ready for your talk."

Jack followed the line of Abe's outstretched arm. Leah Coleman had stepped out the front door of the lodge and was heading straight for them. Though she'd traded in her pumps and business suit for a fur-lined parka and ski pants, he saw the same take-charge, no-nonsense demeanor she'd shown in Brian Strickland's office.

"Leah gives all the new crew a rundown of the rules," Bree explained.

"She lays down the law all right," Ollie said. "Which reminds me. I forgot. I have to pat you down. Arms out."

Jack glanced at Abe, who gave a quick nod. "Leah made Ollie security. He's got the power."

Jack held his arms out, and Ollie frisked him. "Do you have a phone, camera, or any other type of recording device on you or in your luggage?"

"No."

"Any weapons?"

"Nope." Jack smirked.

"What's the smart-ass grin for?"

"In my gear, I have an ice ax, crampons, and a utility tool that I'd sure as hell classify as weapons. But we'll just call them tools, right?"

Bree quickly hid her smile.

"Do you have a gun?"

"No."

Ollie opened Jack's duffel bag and rifled through it. When he was done, he grunted, then turned to Bree. "Your turn," he said, a smile slowly spreading across his face.

Jack's jaw tensed.

Bree held her arms out. "I have Human Resources on speed dial if your hands so much as hesitate."

"Oh, I take no pleasure in this, love." Ollie's hands traveled down Bree's body. "I'm just doing my job. Now turn around." He winked at Abe, but the lanky man shook his head and turned his back.

Ollie opened one of the shopping bags in her backpack. "You bought a lot of stuff."

"Batteries and some personal things."

Ollie went through a second bag and lifted out a pair of panties.

Bree grabbed the underwear and the bag. "Go ahead, search my tampons." She lifted out a large package of feminine products and held them under Ollie's nose.

The gondola settled into the shack with a bump, and Abe pulled the doors open.

"Now I understand why you're so cranky," Ollie said. "Like I said, just doing my job."

Bree pushed by him as Leah walked up. Leah gave Bree a quick hug and then leaned back, keeping both hands on Bree's arms and staring into her eyes. "Good to see you. Are you okay?"

Bree nodded. "I'm good, really."

"No hugs for us?" Ollie said. "That doesn't seem right, does it, Abe?"

"Knock it off, Oliver," said Leah. "Get the gear into the back room. We're having a production meeting before lunch. I'll see you all there in an hour."

Leah held out a clipboard. "Fill these out."

Jack glanced down at the stack of papers and raised an eyebrow.

"Safety waivers," Leah explained. "Everyone's got to do them."

He'd already filled out all the paperwork at Brian's office, so he didn't know if these were more for show. He waited until the others were out of earshot, initialing the mountain of pages as they clumped in their heavy boots toward the lodge.

"Someone spray-painted a boulder halfway up the gondola route. Another threat. A thick line with a circle underneath it. That's the Iroquois symbol for death."

"You're sure that's what it means?"

"I'll have to check with Alice"—*she won't like hearing this*—"but I'm positive."

"Did the crew see it?"

"Yes."

Leah frowned. "Bree gets flustered easily."

Leah herself seemed unfazed.

"Death threats have a way of doing that. Ollie said he was going to let the control room operator know about the symbol so he can avoid it in shots. Can you tell Harvey to get a few pictures of it instead?"

"Why?"

"I need to record it and I didn't have any way of taking a picture." Jack held up the clipboard. "Do I really have to initial these?"

"No, but we need to make you coming on board look real, so… keep signing."

After another minute, he handed the papers back.

"Follow me." Leah tucked the clipboard under her arm and turned on her heel. Jack grabbed his duffel and fell in step beside Leah as she headed to the lodge. He couldn't get a read on her. Was she bored by the death threats? Did she think they were a joke, all in a day's work on the set?

"You're in 104. We've got a full day, so I'm going to make this short. You've met Ollie, Abe, and Bree. They're eyes and ears. Camera one, two, and sound. Got it?"

"Yes."

"You'll meet the rest of the crew in the production meeting. The contestants are scattered over the mountain in their own camps. We keep them separated. We also have half a dozen emergency shelters on the mountain. Each is equipped with medical supplies, blankets, and a radio. They're off-limits to contestants unless there's an emergency."

A gust of wind swept down the side of the mountain, picking up snow and creating a faint wave in the air that shimmered in the sun. *Beautiful but deadly.*

"We've marked several trails around the mountain. Green flags are the main route back to the lodge. Orange, blue, and yellow flags lead to the contest sites. The mountaintop is perfect for taping. It's a plateau, but there are several cliffs that we use for challenges. Stay the hell away from the slopes on down. We've marked the crest line with red flags. Any contestant who crosses into the danger zone is out."

"For a reality survivor show, you sure have a lot of rules."

"You can thank your insurance company for most of them," Leah grumbled.

Above them, what sounded like a thick piece of glass snapping in two echoed off the building. Jack shot forward, slamming Leah into the front door, pressing his body against hers and covering his head with one hand as a huge icicle shattered into big chunks on the steps where they had been standing just a split second earlier. A brick-sized piece careened off the concrete and smashed into Jack's calf.

Leah let out a muffled cry.

"Are you hurt?" Jack asked as he felt his leg for damage. He'd probably have a large bruise on his calf, but looking at the large, jagged ice chunks scattered around his feet, he was grateful the icicle hadn't split his head open.

"I'm okay. You?"

"Yeah, but that could've been real ugly." Jack stepped back and looked up. The wide base of the icicle was still clinging to the roof in front of the second-story window. He couldn't be sure, but the window blinds appeared to be moving. "Is anyone up there?"

Leah glanced up and shook her head. "That room is empty. I'll have to have Ollie and Abe clear any other icicles over the doorways."

Jack continued to stare at the window. His attention had been on Leah as they walked up to the lodge. Was the window open when they approached the building? Why would a window be open in this weather? Smoker? He sniffed for cigarette smoke but didn't detect any in the frosty air.

"You sure moved fast." Leah kicked the largest chunks of ice off the steps. "Most people would have looked up when they heard the icicle break. One that big could kill you."

Jack wasn't most people. War had conditioned his reflexes; bombs and bullets had a unique way of doing that. Today it had saved his life. Tomorrow a car backfiring in a parking lot might send him diving for cover. Either way, it wasn't something he wanted to explain, or felt he could explain to her, so he simply nodded.

Leah pulled open the lodge's big front door and they entered the warmth of a great room with a fireplace in the back. In front of the hearth, two large couches formed an L, and four mismatched recliners were scattered about haphazardly. In an alcove to one side was a round table surrounded by chairs. There was no one there now, but they could hear sounds from the back—Ollie bickering, thuds, and clatters.

"Only the crew are allowed in the lodge. This place has almost fifty rooms, so we each get our own. The control room is on the second floor. Kitchen is past the main room. Men's showers are downstairs, women's upstairs. You're down here."

Jack followed Leah down a dimly lit hallway. Her blasé reaction was puzzling. Her emotional temperature was chillier than any icicle.

Leah pointed down the narrow passage. "We've all taken rooms at one end of the building or the other, beside the stairwells, because these end rooms are larger than the ones in the middle." She shoved a door open. "Here's yours."

Jack wondered what the "smaller" rooms looked like. *Luxury lodge?* His dorm room at the police academy had been twice this size. Yet someone had managed to cram in two twin beds and two bureaus. A second door was on the side wall—probably leading directly to the staircase.

"Put your duffel bag down and your arms out."

"Ollie already frisked me."

"That's why I'm doing it again. I run a tight set. Arms out."

Jack held his arms out, and Leah frisked him. Her hands traveled over every inch of his body, then she turned his pockets out. This kind of treatment would be unnerving to most folks, but not Jack. Between the police force and the Army, he'd frisked more people than he cared to count. Something about Leah reminded him of that time in his life; she had yet to say the word *please*, and frisking him didn't seem to bother her at all.

"You didn't bring a phone?" Leah asked, a bit surprised.

"Nope. It was on your list of banned items."

"I didn't think you'd read it, let alone comply." She went through his duffel thoroughly, removing everything and laying it out on the bed. "Sorry about all this. We can't take any chances. Any leaks from the set could tank the ratings."

Well, there was a *sorry*. Wonder of wonders.

"Have you had an issue with that?" Jack asked, stuffing his pocket lining back into his pockets.

"Not since I took over." Leah stared down at his gear and nodded, apparently satisfied that he hadn't brought any contraband. "I'm going to pair you with Abe to start. Stick by him and stay out of the way of everyone else unless I tell you otherwise. These guys know what they're doing."

"So you've all worked together before?"

"Seven seasons. Same elite crew every year. The show is so specialized, it would be a nightmare trying to swap in anyone new. And we have to run lean; it costs too much to bring on new members. That's why it's going to be next to impossible keeping you a secret."

Ah, the profit motive. Maybe that was what made her tick.

"I'm sure you'll manage. Just stick to the truth. A local guy you had to bring on."

"I'm going to treat you the same as everyone else. No outside communication of any kind. No talking to contestants unless it relates directly to your job. And your job is to do whatever you're told to do."

"About that. It would be easier if I reported directly to you."

Her eyes sparkled. "You're the gofer. If a crew member needs something, anything at all, you do it. Got it?"

Jack nodded. He got it. She didn't want him here.

"No drinking. No smoking. Breakfast is at five forty-five. Lunch is at noon, dinner is at six. I have a studio breathing down my neck to wrap this season up, so we'll be shooting around the clock. Grab sleep when you can, because you won't know when you'll get it again."

"Understood."

"Don't forget to drink a lot of water today to get acclimated to the altitude. Take an aspirin, too. The production meeting's in forty-five minutes in the great room."

"Will do, thanks."

Leah's hand hesitated on the doorknob. After a moment, she turned back to Jack. "Remember to be careful. We move fast, but... being on a mountain is dangerous. Running around filming a TV show makes it potentially deadly. The most important thing to remember is to focus on yourself first. I know it's your job to be watching other people, but if you forget about where *you* are, it could cost you your life."

6

RESEARCH

Still haunted by the image of the gondola slowly disappearing into the fog, Alice took a seat in front of her laptop and gazed out the apartment window at the distant mountain.

She tried to shake it off. *Jack can take care of himself. He always has.*

No, that wasn't true. He *hadn't* always taken care of himself. She'd been a big part of helping him out of his last few jams. A reel began to play in Alice's mind. Jack's mother's kidnapping, his father getting shot, the alligator...

She closed her eyes tightly. *Please, God, keep Jack safe.*

Lady's cold, wet nose nudged her hand. Alice scratched behind her ear, and Lady drooped her head across Alice's lap with a little whine.

"I miss him too, Lady. But we're not just going to sit here feeling helpless. Let's get to work."

She had already plugged in the hard drive Brian had given her. She flexed her hands and pulled up the official accident report from last year. She split the computer screen down the middle, with the report on the left and a blank spreadsheet on the right. In the spreadsheet, she listed the names of the eight crew members, the five contestants, the helicopter pilot, and the meteorologist stationed at the weather center.

She would look into all of them eventually, but she wanted to start with the victim on that fateful day. Charlie Parker.

She opened the profile the insurance company had compiled. At the top of the file was a photo. Charlie had been a handsome young man with blue eyes. He was listed as six feet tall, but in the photo, he sat with his shoulders rounded, making him seem smaller. Shy. He was only twenty-seven years old. The same age as Jack.

He's fine. She stroked Lady's silky ears and was rewarded with a contented snuffle.

Charlie's résumé was brief. He'd attended college and majored in music history, but dropped out of school in his junior year to take a job with *Planet Survival* as assistant sound designer; promoted to sound designer the following year. His obituary listed mother, father, and a sister as survivors, all living in Boise, Idaho.

Alice flipped past the autopsy photos to the summary. The cause of death was listed as suffocation. *That can't be right.* But it made sense when she read that Charlie's avalanche locator beacon had been knocked off, leaving Charlie trapped under the snow for two hours before they found him. And by then he was dead. Suffocated by snow.

Alice shivered and flipped back to an earlier page in the insurance company report. For determination of the settlement with Charlie's family, Charlie was found partially negligent because his locator beacon wasn't properly attached to his harness. *Way to go, punish him again, why don'tcha?*

She went through the details of the accident, carefully reconstructing it. She created a map and marked the placement of each person. The contestants and the weatherman were easy—none of them were anywhere near the accident site. Mack was flying the helicopter that dropped Gavin at the foot of the ridge. Harvey Guppy, the control room operator, was back at the lodge. The rest of the crew was waiting two hundred yards downslope for Gavin to ski down and present the show's introduction. Charlie Parker was directly downhill from the drop-off area, running camera three. The initial investigation questioned why the soundman was running a camera at all, but *Planet Survival*'s small crew had a history of crew members filling in for many different jobs.

Sad to say, Charlie's camera might provide the clearest view of the accident. She pulled up the video log and scrolled down to find the video captured by camera three that day, but there was nothing listed, only a note explaining that Charlie's camera was never recovered.

Alice grabbed a notecard off the table and wrote *Camera Three Footage* on it, along with a star. This was the second time she'd wanted more information and hit a dead end—she couldn't reinterview Mack Carson, the helicopter pilot, and now the camera with the best angle of the accident was missing.

Something else was missing, too: Leah Coleman. Alice checked her map again, but there was no location marked on the mountain for the producer at the time of the accident. A quick check of Leah's brief deposition provided the answer. Leah wasn't on the mountain at all that day; she'd gone into town for a doctor's appointment. Reading between the lines, Alice got a better understanding of Leah's brusqueness—she was lucky she still had a job. The transcript of Leah's testimony read like that of a ship captain who was sound asleep when the iceberg hit.

Alice laid down her pen and gazed outside once more. She could no longer see the mountain, obscured by silver-gray drizzle. But she knew Jack was out there, and she wanted to join him in the worst way. She thought of a hundred excuses she could use for showing up on set but dismissed them all. Jack had asked her to trust him on this and stay put. Alice didn't like it, but she knew he was right. She growled in frustration.

Lady replied with a growl of her own.

7

JACK RABBIT

Jack had just finished unpacking—or rather, putting away in the bureaus what Leah had so thoughtfully unpacked for him—when there was a knock at the door.

Abe stood in the doorway, a big grin on his long face. "Leah asked Ollie and me to check out a camera on the watchtower. Up for a tour? I've got a feeling you'll like this."

"Sure." Perfect for both his *Planet Survival* jobs, unofficial and official. "We're not taping the contestants or anything?"

"There's a challenge in two days, so today and tomorrow are rest days for them. Harvey's babysitting the contestants with remote cameras, making sure they don't break any rules. Mostly it'll be shots of them sleeping."

"Do we have time? There's a meeting in an hour."

"Plenty of time. Leah pushed the meeting back and wants us to check out the camera. She said we can have the meeting when we're done. Don't forget your goggles."

Jack followed Abe down the hallway. He was surprised when they walked past the front door and continued down the opposite corridor toward the side exit.

"Ollie's meeting us out by the generator," Abe explained.

They stepped outside into a cement courtyard swept clean of snow. To their right, on a cement platform, sat a boxy generator. Stacked against the building to their left was a bunch of metal storage boxes and wooden pallets. At the opposite side of the courtyard stood three snowmobiles. Ollie sat perched on the center one, completely ignoring Leah's no-smoking policy.

"Sure took your sweet time." He took a long drag and blew the smoke toward Jack. "Know how to ride?"

Jack grinned. He loved snowmobiling. "Sure do."

"Great. If you can't keep up, the blue and yellow trail leads there." Ollie laughed and tossed his cigarette.

Jack straddled one of the snowmobiles and turned it on. The deep hum of the powerful engine brought a smile to his face.

Abe pointed down at a bulky backpack. "You're supposed to carry the tools, Ollie."

"The gofer can do it." Ollie cranked the throttle, drowning out his laughter, and drove away.

"I've got it," Jack said. He hopped off the snowmobile, swung the heavy backpack over his shoulders, and got back in the seat. He pulled his goggles down, gave Abe a thumbs-up, and shot forward. The front of the snowmobile lifted slightly, and Jack's hands tightened on the grips.

Ollie was already fifty yards ahead and pulling away fast. Jack fought the urge to race after him. He knew that was exactly what Ollie wanted him to do. The man was trying to get under Jack's skin. But this was a job, and Jack was a professional.

Ollie looked back and held up a hand. He was far enough away that Jack couldn't see the finger he was raising, but he was pretty sure Ollie wasn't giving him a thumbs-up.

Jack clenched his jaw. Maybe he didn't have to be *entirely* professional.

The snowmobile roared as he tightened his grip on the throttle. The weight of the pack pulled him back in the seat, so he leaned forward and low. The rear tread of the snowmobile shredded the layer of ice covering the snow, kicking up a plume of white behind him.

Alice had made Jack watch lots of video footage of the mountain before he left, but the pictures didn't do it justice. It was breathtaking. He felt more like he was on another planet than a mountainside. He was a kid playing explorer, and he loved it. Some people hated the unknown, but the challenge of discovering its secrets fired Jack up. Had he been born five hundred years earlier, he would have headed straight for the nearest harbor and the fastest ship to take to the seas.

The trail, marked by colored poles, ran in a wide arc, gradually sloping upward. Ollie was up ahead—Jack was catching up to him quickly—and Abe was far behind, riding with his back straight and his head up, looking like he was taking a leisurely ride and leaving the racing to Ollie and Jack.

Ollie disappeared over a ridge, and as Jack crested it a few moments later, he saw Ollie parked and waiting for him.

"So, you do know how to ride." Ollie pointed at a tower atop a ridge rising in the distance. "It's five hundred yards to the watchtower, mate. I'll bet you a hundred bucks I make it there first."

Jack was about to offer to double it, then reminded himself that he was on the job. "No thanks."

Ollie stared him down until Abe pulled up.

"Why are we stopping?" Abe asked.

"I offered the newbie a chance to make a few bucks, but you know what they say about those ex-Army guys. Or were you really in the Army? USO maybe?" Ollie laughed. "What about you, Abe? A hundred bucks says I'm the first person to the next tower."

Abe shook his head. "I like keeping my money."

"Tell you what, gofer," said Ollie. "I thought you were shaking because it's cold, not 'cause you're scared. I'll spot you a five-second head start and give you two-to-one odds."

A long list of reasons to keep his mouth shut ran through Jack's mind, but he pushed his internal warnings aside. He looked at the marked, winding path up to the tower, and smiled. "Tell you what, Oliver. I'll spot *you* a five-second head start. I'll give you two hundred if you win. And if I win, only Abe gives me orders on this shoot. You'll have to keep your big trap shut."

Abe whistled low, then snickered.

Ollie broke a chunk of ice off his snowmobile and fired it at Abe's head, but missed by two feet. "What are you, a sheila? Shut up." He glared at Jack. "Deal."

"You're going to take the head start?"

"Bet's a bet," Ollie sneered.

Abe shook his head. "This was a bad idea, my friend. Ollie can ride. You're going to lose two hundred bucks, and he's going to give you even more crap jobs."

"You can be sure I will," Ollie said with a laugh. "Just time him, Abe."

Ollie waited until Abe took his glove off, pulled his jacket back to reveal a watch, and nodded.

"Go!" Abe said.

Ollie gunned it up the trail.

Jack focused on the slope in front of him. The trail Ollie was taking looked like the safest way to go. But there was another path, off to the left, and it looked a lot faster—and definitely much riskier. There was a tricky patch of icy rock before he'd even get to the path, and then he'd have to make it up an even steeper incline, but if he could pull it off, it looked much more direct than Ollie's route. The only question was whether he had the skills. It had been a long, long time since he'd been on a snowmobile.

"Go!" Abe shouted.

Jack revved the throttle. Horsepower ignited testosterone, which built deep in his gut and escaped his lips in a loud war whoop. He felt fully alive, and he loved it.

He leaned low over the handlebars and raced for the first ridge. The moment of no return loomed. He cut hard to the left and headed directly for the rocky area covered in ice, swept clean of snow by the wind. The snowmobile shot up like a jet, metal scraping against rock like a banshee shrieking into battle.

Jack fought the instinct to hit the brake. That would press the front end down and push the skis against the rocks—and that was the last thing he wanted. Instead he rode the throttle, revving the engine and pulling up on the handlebars to keep the front end up as much as possible. He slid sideways for twenty yards before the snow thickened once more. Jamming back the throttle, he added horsepower to momentum and chewed up the snow-packed slope.

It was working. He let out another excited war cry as he rocketed upward.

After a minute the snow cover grew increasingly difficult to navigate. The rear tread struggled for traction, caught, and bucked. Jack wrestled to hold on, leaning in toward the slope, trying to shift the center of gravity of the machine to the side of the tread so the metal could cut into the snow and find a grip.

But it wasn't enough. The tread was still slipping, and Jack was losing speed. He gunned the throttle and yanked hard on the handlebars. Metal clashed with ice, and the machine snarled like a beast and struggled up the slope.

Giving it one last blast, Jack crested the ridge and gunned it straight for the tower. Glancing over his shoulder, he saw Ollie thirty yards away on his right.

Jack was almost to the base of the tower when he saw something shiny flash, something strung across the trail ahead of him.

There was no time to think. He jammed on the brakes and pulled the snowmobile almost onto its side, stopping in a shower of snow just a couple of feet away from the thin metal cable stretched across the path—right where his neck would have been.

Ollie's snowmobile roared closer.

"Stop!" Jack jumped off, waving his arms.

Ollie leaned forward, trying to steer around Jack and win the race.

"STOP!" Jack bellowed, stepping directly into his path.

Ollie pinned the throttle back and Jack dove, slamming into Ollie, and both men crashed to the ground. Jack's goggles were ripped off his head as he tumbled along the snow.

Ollie's snowmobile skidded forward a dozen yards before slowing to a stop.

"Are you dodgy in the head?" Ollie yelled as he scrambled to his feet, yanking out his climbing ax and leveling it at Jack.

Jack rolled his shoulder back, getting the kink out. "There's a wire across the path." He pointed as he picked his goggles off the ground. "It would've taken your head right off."

Ollie slowly walked forward and tapped his ax against the metal cable. Jack noticed that his other hand trembled as he rubbed his throat.

They both turned around and blocked the way as Abe's snowmobile thundered up.

Abe skidded to a stop. "What happened? Who got here first? You two aren't fighting, right?"

"A guy-wire came loose from the tower." Ollie followed the wire down to the tree it was stuck in. "Jack saw it hanging across the path."

"Oh, wow, he saved your life."

"You're as much of a drama queen as Gavin. I would have seen it." Ollie tugged angrily on the wire until it came free.

"After it decapitated you." Abe rolled his eyes. "Hey, it's still connected to the footing."

"They went overkill on the guy-wires on this tower," Ollie grumbled as he coiled the wire and set it down. "We can reconnect it later if Leah wants it hooked back up."

"But how'd it break free and end up in the tree?" Abe asked.

Ollie shrugged. "Bad luck, I guess."

Jack didn't say anything, but he wanted to know the answer to that question too. He didn't believe in luck. Between the icicle at the lodge and now this, Jack was starting to believe the events were more than just happenstance.

Abe's smile returned. "Hey, Jack, looks like you won two hundred bucks. Is that why you saved his sorry butt?"

Ollie stopped halfway to his snowmobile. "Have you lost your mind, too?" He gestured back down the slope. "His hot-dogging it could have cost the production a brand-new snowmobile!"

Jack grinned. "Is that Australian for congratulations?"

"You didn't stick to the trail."

Jack shrugged. "That wasn't part of the bet. It was about who could get to the tower first, and you had a head start. I'm sure Abe remembers the conversation."

Ollie ran his hands through his wiry hair and glared at Abe. "There's no way he waited five seconds."

Jack started to answer, but Abe cut him off. "He waited and I timed it. He beat you fair and square. Don't even think about trying to get out of the bet. You do, and I'll tell everybody, you welcher."

Ollie pulled out a cigarette and lit it. "Me, go back on a bet?" He shrugged. "What for? It's not like I'm out anything."

Jack decided to extend an olive branch. "Look, we're good. I know you've got a job to do, and so do I. I just don't want you busting my chops the whole time I'm here. Where'd you learn to ride? And don't tell me the Australian Defense Force."

Ollie actually cracked a smile. "I took a detail once in Germany. Baumholder. You?"

"My father got me a snowmobile when I was twelve. I lived on it every winter until I could drive."

Ollie rolled his eyes. "I got hustled by a joey."

"It's about time." Abe laughed.

"Don't judge a book by its cover," Jack said. "I'm not just a pretty face." All three men erupted in laughter.

They spent the next half hour troubleshooting the camera on the tower. When they were done, Ollie lit a cigarette and waved Jack and Abe over.

"Let's give you the thirty-second bird's-eye view, Jack." He pointed back the way they had come. "That's home base."

Jack could just make out the roof of the lodge in the distance.

Ollie pointed in a different direction. "That huge tower over there? Between those two trees? That's the weather station."

Jack peered at the tower covered in satellite dishes. "That thing's huge."

"Five hundred feet," Abe said. "We piggyback our radio and video feeds off it and then beam them back to home base."

"The guy at the station is a real nut job." Ollie let smoke drift slowly out of his mouth. "Last year he freaked out when we set up a camera in one of the trees. He said we screwed up some mating zone for a thrush or something."

"Yeah, and you should have seen him about the snowmobiles," Abe said. "He went totally bananas on Leah. Ask Harvey to show you the tape. I wanted him to put it on YouTube."

Ollie pointed at a path that ran alongside a steep cliff. "That's the trail to Grandma's House and Grandma's Field."

Jack had seen the long, wide field in video footage a dozen times. "Grandma's House" was the challenge they were getting ready to tape when Charlie died.

"What's the deal with using nursery rhymes for the names of the contests?" Jack asked.

"That was some executive producer's brilliant idea. Some stupid promo a fan won and now that's how we roll. Each season, the contests all follow a theme."

"I kinda like it," Abe said. "One week we did a contest called 'Over the Hill and Through the Dale.' All the contestants had to climb over a cliff and then race on snowmobiles."

"Tell me about Grandma's House."

Ollie pointed with his cigarette. "We set up this ridiculous plywood German cottage that was Grandma's House. It was just a façade but from a distance it looked pretty darn good. The contestants were supposed to rappel down a cliff and then cross an open stretch of field to reach it. Sounds easy, right? Except Ryan and Leah brought in a pack of Saint Bernards. You know, the huge rescue dogs? They would play the part of the wolves."

"It would have been so over-the-top," Abe said. "I wish we hadn't had to cancel it. They were going to have the contestants put on those big protective suits, the ones the attack dog trainers wear. Saint Bernards are too nice to attack someone, so they were going to put bags of dog treats on their waists. If a dog got to a contestant before they reached the cottage—that player got eliminated."

"No one would have made it," Ollie said, shaking his head.

"Guess we'll never know," Abe said.

Because of the accident.

Ollie flicked his cigarette. "The accident happened right when we started shooting. From now on, no more shooting in Grandma's Field. Out of respect. You know about the accident?"

Jack nodded. "Yeah, I heard. You guys were there?"

"We don't talk about it." Ollie cast a warning glance Abe's way.

"Why not?"

"Leah's rules. Ask her. Anyway, there's your tour. Now for the real reason we dragged you out here. You're gonna help us set up for the event." Ollie jabbed a finger at the slope leading to the cliff face. "That's where the 'Jack and Jill Slalom Challenge' is happening, day after tomorrow."

"The contestants have to reach the top of the cliff, grab a pail, and bring it back down," Abe explained.

"But we have to make sure it's safe for the contestants to get there. See that slope to the right of the hill?" Ollie pointed. "The snow has built up too high on that ridge. There's no way we can have an elimination contest with an avalanche hanging over everyone's head. Have you ever seen an avalanche?"

Jack shook his head.

Abe's long face paled and his eyes darkened. "It's like something out of a nightmare. Seriously, it's like the mountain comes alive, and it's ticked off."

Ollie nodded. "If you even *think* you hear one—run."

Jack had seen video of avalanches, including the one here on the mountain that had killed Charlie, but still… he couldn't deny that part of him wanted to see one live. Video was one thing, but it never came close to the actual experience. Ever.

"If it doesn't slide on its own by tomorrow morning, we'll have to help it down," Ollie said, looking off into the distance.

"Help it down? How?" Jack asked.

"Blast it down, mate."

8

A TRAIL GONE COLD

Kiku parked her red Lexus in front of a ranch house at the end of a tree-lined cul-de-sac.

Alice removed her seat belt. "Thanks for coming with me."

"You are most welcome." Kiku zipped up her cropped leather jacket. Though they were on Alice's mission, Kiku was in the driver's seat, in more ways than one. "So, we have arrived at the house of Detective Clark, of whom Jack speaks so highly." The seventy-year-old detective was a friend of Jack's father, so Jack had known him since he was a boy. Alice had met him several times for dinner.

Alice reached for the door handle as a big question flashed like a neon sign in her head: *ARE YOU READY?* She hadn't fully realized until now that when she fell in love with Jack, she would have to open herself to him entirely, and that when he insisted they had to unlock the mysteries of her past, it would mean exposing herself to others, asking for help, and stirring up nightmares. She couldn't remember ever feeling so confused and yet so determined.

Kiku put her hand on Alice's wrist and tightened it. "Once we get out of this car, you will embark on a path I do not think you will be able to escape."

Alice had an honor code of her own. She had to press on. She needed answers, and she owed it to her family to find out what really happened to them.

"I understand." She took in one last deep breath of luxury vehicle and Kiku's orchid-like perfume. "Do you want to wait here for me?"

Kiku found this quite amusing—her laugh was high and bright and somewhat disconcerting as they both exited the car.

The neighborhood was typical suburbia. Three men were out and about, and all of them stopped what they were doing to look over at Alice and Kiku. Alice thought at first it was because of the car—it was out of place in the modest neighborhood, or even in Darrington, for that matter—but then she realized they weren't gawking at the flashy car. Or at her. Their eyes followed Kiku, her dark hair spilling around the white fur collar of her slim jacket, strutting down the walkway like it was a catwalk—head high, shoulders back, hips swaying—and raising the temperature all around.

Alice rang the doorbell. The door was opened by a tall, silver-haired man in a button-down shirt and khakis. "Good morning, Alice." His manner was controlled but his eyes were kind. He nodded politely to Kiku. "Ms. Inuzuka."

He only briefly scanned Kiku's body. Alice wouldn't have blamed him for looking longer, but Detective Clark was different, an old-school gentleman.

"It is a pleasure to meet you, Detective Clark. Please call me Kiku."

"Derrick." He stepped aside and held the door open.

As they entered the gray-shingled house, Alice noticed Clark waving a hand dismissively at his neighbors, and then saw all three men giving Detective Clark a double thumbs-up.

"Your neighborhood is charming," Kiku said as she walked into the open living room.

The home wasn't exactly what Alice had expected. Given the house's classic exterior, the style inside was surprisingly modern. Her eye followed the herringbone pattern in the wood floor through the airy, open kitchen and past the sliding glass door to a gorgeous winter view of a small river winding through woods behind the house. What wasn't surprising was how neat and organized everything was; the detective was retired Army and law enforcement, so Alice had expected nothing less.

"Can I offer you something to drink?" Clark's deep voice rumbled.

"Maybe later, thank you," Kiku replied.

She seemed to be studying the detective's face, and Clark didn't wilt under her gaze. In fact, he seemed to be studying her, too. Jack had taught Alice that watching someone was a lost art, and most people found it disarming. It was a technique he had learned from Detective Clark. Alice felt like she was watching two prizefighters sizing each other up.

Finally, the detective held a hand toward the kitchen. A manila folder waited for them on the table, where they all took a seat.

"Kiku, I understand you're a private investigator."

"Yes. I am also a friend of your protégé, Jack Stratton."

"Protégé?"

"His word, Detective."

"He thinks the world of you and he'd be here if he weren't working," Alice added, wishing Jack were sitting next to her.

"I've known Jack since he was a kid, but I couldn't find any information about you online."

Kiku smiled. "That's a good thing. I consider myself a *private* investigator."

Clark chuckled, a deep rumble. "I haven't heard it put like that before. But seriously, I'm not in the habit of helping people I don't know."

Alice shifted uncomfortably in her seat, but Kiku seemed relaxed and poised. "You and I are both helping the same man."

"Actually, the favor is for me," Alice said. "And Kiku is helping us."

Clark's fingers drummed on the manila folder as he stared into Kiku's dark eyes. Alice knew he'd sat across the table from people from all walks of life, many of them guilty criminals lying right to his face. His expression tightened and his eyes narrowed.

Kiku said, "Nothing I say will convince you to assist me, except perhaps this: Jack trusts me, and he is asking you to do the same."

Clark nodded. His fingers stopped drumming, and he pushed the folder over to her. "I'm a bit old-fashioned, so I printed everything out. It's not much. I also put the files on here for you." He handed Alice a thumb drive.

Alice exhaled. "Thank you, Detective Clark."

He nodded.

"What is your opinion regarding the car accident?" Kiku asked.

"My opinion?" Clark leaned back and ran a hand through his well-groomed gray hair. "Jack just asked me to organize the facts. I didn't have anything to do with the initial investigation. It wasn't in my jurisdiction."

"Organized facts lead to an opinion, do they not?" Kiku said.

"They do." His gray eyes darkened.

Alice wondered how many dark scenes those eyes had studied. There seemed to be a sadness in their depths.

Kiku waited and Alice held her breath.

Clark shrugged. "My opinion is, you should be looking into it. Someone should."

"Why?" Alice asked with trepidation.

"A few reasons. The first is simple: the case wasn't solved. I don't like open cases and unanswered questions. But it's not just who was driving the stolen truck that bothers me. The case was assigned to Joe McLean—he's a detective over in Westford—but there was nothing in his report beside the initial findings. He did the preliminaries, and then… there's nothing after that."

"*Nothing?*" Alice asked in disbelief. "My whole family was killed. There had to be some sort of follow-up." She tapped the thin folder. "Are you telling me this is all the information?"

"I mean exactly that. There's only his initial report. It could just be a computer foul-up or misfiling. I already put a call in to Joe—I know him from a while back. I'll talk to him, get his read on it, and I'll get back to you."

"Well, thank you, Detective." Alice cleared her throat in an attempt to regroup and hide her frustration. "I appreciate your help."

"Anything for Jack. And for you, Alice. Congratulations again on your engagement. You couldn't have chosen a nicer family to join. The Strattons are good people."

"I agree wholeheartedly."

The interview seemed to be over, as Clark got up, still studying Kiku closely, and wished them good luck.

Alice and Kiku said their goodbyes and headed back to the car. The gray sky had darkened, and it felt colder now. Kiku met Alice's eyes.

"Do you trust him?" she asked.

Though Alice had hoped for more from Clark, he'd shown her the trail into the unknown, and she had to take the first step. She nodded firmly.

"Why?"

"Because Jack does."

9

ALL CHARGED UP

Jack shut the water off and stepped out of the shower. He'd gotten up before everyone else and was pleasantly surprised that there'd been hot water. His sore shoulder and bruised calf were both reminders to stay on guard. Especially given that Leah, the only other person on this mountain who had full disclosure, did not share Jack's opinion about the severity of the situation.

He stood on the cold tiles and pulled a towel from a hook on the wall. He had a penchant for long, hot showers—a simple luxury he truly enjoyed after his days of quickie showers in foster care at Aunt Haddie's and many missed showers in the Army—but today he needed the heat to ease his sore muscles, and knowing that outside was all ice and snow made it feel twice as good. Jack whistled as he dried his mop of dark hair and stepped toward the sinks. All the heat was driven right out of his body and he saw his eyes widen at the message that the steam revealed in the foggy mirror.

YOU'RE DEAD

* * *

"You need to pull the security footage and see who wrote the message on the mirror." Jack stood in Leah's room, his hair still wet and his shirt clinging to his back.

"We don't have cameras in the bathroom."

"Then pull the footage from outside the bathroom."

Leah crossed her arms and glared at the floor.

"You have security cameras inside the lodge, right?" Jack did his best to keep his voice low.

"No, we don't have any cameras *inside* the lodge. The contestants aren't allowed inside the lodge, so they weren't needed."

"This isn't about film footage for the show," Jack said through gritted teeth. "You've had *direct* threats against the *crew*. You told Brian there were—"

"There *were* security cameras inside the lodge at that time," Leah fired back unapologetically. "I didn't lie to Brian. I just didn't inform him of my decision to utilize the cameras elsewhere. I have a show to run."

"You have a crew to protect."

"That's *your* job." Leah jabbed a finger at his chest.

"That is *our* job, Leah. Do you really need to be reminded that we're on the same team?"

Dark eyes blazed at him.

"We need to work together. The risk level has gone from yellow to red. That note on the mirror wasn't a prank, okay? Whoever is making threats isn't just on the mountain, they're close—dangerously close. The notes, the icicle, the guy-wire… you have to admit that things have gone from bad to worse. This time they came *inside* the lodge." Jack pointed at the floor for emphasis.

"Those were accidents. The guy-wire came loose in the wind. It's a portable tower and the wind up here is fierce. I agree that the note on the mirror looks like another threat, but killer icicles and decapitating wires? Now, *that's* some must-see television." She turned away, unable to hide her scorn.

Was Leah trying to make light of the situation to avoid cancellation of the insurance policy and keep the show filming, or did she really not fathom what was going on around her?

"There is an undeniable and present danger posed by the notes alone. You need to inform the cast and crew." But even Jack's best detective voice—clear, concise, and authoritative—had little effect.

"They're all aware of the threats, but I'll tell them there've been more. But I do it my way. One-on-one. I don't need everyone running around afraid."

Jack ran a hand through his damp hair. "I don't think you get it. These threats are following an escalation pattern. Whoever is making them is getting bolder, and that means they're more likely to act, if they haven't already. This guy is getting the nerve up to do something. Everyone should be afraid."

* * *

The crew had gathered in the lodge's main hall. Ollie and Abe were on a couch with Bree. Abe introduced Jack to Harvey, the control room operator, a chubby man who filled up a big leather chair, his feet on a matching leather footstool; he was tapping away on an iPad.

"Why isn't Gavin here?" Jack whispered to Abe. "Shouldn't the host be present for the planning meetings?"

"His Highness can't be bothered with lowly production meetings," Abe joked.

Bree chuckled and gave him an elbow in the ribs. "Careful."

"That's another rule." Abe bumped Bree's shoulder but looked at Jack. "Don't say anything about the king or it's off with your head." He drew a finger across his throat for emphasis.

"And they dock your pay," Bree added.

"Speaking of losing your head," Abe said, "Leah wants us to replace that guy-wire tomorrow."

Jack nodded.

Leah walked to the front of the room and clapped for attention. "Listen up, everyone. I'm not saying this twice. By now you've all met Jack Stratton. He's a local climber who's serving as our new gofer. Don't take advantage of Jack or I'll send you rolling off this mountain myself." Her eyes traveled around the faces in the room but stopped on Ollie. "I mean it."

Ollie shrugged.

"Tomorrow's the slalom cliff climb, affectionately dubbed the 'Jack and Jill Slalom Challenge.' In the morning, we're shooting the opening."

"There's been a slight change in plans." This from a man coming down the stairs in jeans, a red T-shirt, and a backward-facing baseball hat. "A couple of slight changes, actually." He held his index finger and thumb close together and smiled sheepishly.

Leah took a deep breath and closed her eyes. "Ryan, you promised this morning that everything was set in stone. It's too late—"

"See, I ran those changes by Gavin, and he thinks—"

Leah slapped her hand against her thigh. "Gavin's the *host*, not the director. I thought that was your job."

"It is, but—"

"But nothing, Ryan. We agreed on the opening."

Harvey lowered his iPad. "Let's hear him out."

Ryan smiled smugly and made a motion like someone shooting a gun as he winked at Harvey.

Leah crossed her arms and waited.

"So, instead of starting the show with the memorial—"

Bree leapt to her feet. "You're not cutting Charlie's memorial!"

"That's crap," Abe chimed in.

"I'm not cutting it," Ryan said. "I just thought of a better segue. We open with Gavin—"

"No more Gavin stunts," said Leah.

"It's not a stunt." Ryan moved to the center of the room. "It's more of a dramatic walk-on, with the drama coming from a drone shot. Picture this: the drone sweeps over the jagged peak of Mount Minuit. Rising higher and higher, it clears the crest and then zooms down until it locks on a close-up of Gavin. He'll lead into the tribute for Charlie, and after a minute we'll fade into the behind-the-scenes shots of Charlie. It's brilliant."

Ollie laughed. "It's just more face time for Gavin."

"Fine." Leah waved a dismissive hand. "But nothing more than a walk-on."

Ryan grinned. "Agreed. Trust me. It'll be powerful." He turned to Bree and added, "And moving. It will honor Charlie, I promise."

"We've got one problem." Ollie picked at a fingernail. "There's a bad snow ledge built up near the contest slope. We need to clear it first."

"Great," Leah muttered. "How long will that take?"

"We have to place the charges by hand," Ollie said. "But it's a short hike. An hour, tops."

Leah checked her watch. "All right. We'll set up the gates for the slalom afterward, so you'll need to go now. Take Abe and Jack with you."

Ollie looked over at Jack and grinned. "Hope you like explosives, 'cause we're going to have a blast. Get it, gofer?"

The meeting broke up, and Leah waved Jack over. "Before you say anything, I'm going to fill the crew in on the new threats, but one-on-one—not in a meeting like that, with all the drama queens."

"Do it today, Leah," Jack said firmly.

She sailed past Jack's comment. "Come with me. There'll be no time tonight for a call, so Brian agreed to switch it to this morning."

Jack followed her to her room, where she pulled out her sat phone to call Brian. Jack was surprised that Leah took the initiative to relate the new threats and the incidents with the icicle and guy-wire. The two of them spoke tersely for several minutes regarding the best way to proceed. Leah held her position that the notes were still just toothless threats meant to intimidate, and in the end, Brian agreed to stick to the original plan and let her keep her shooting schedule.

Satisfied that she had won the argument, Leah covered the receiver and lowered her voice. "Okay, Jack. Touch base with your partner, but keep it quiet and brief."

Jack took the heavy phone. "Alice?"

"Jack." She said his name like she wanted to climb through the phone and curl up in his lap, and it made him smile. "You need to be careful. I don't agree with Leah and Brian. I've got a feeling this guy is just getting started."

"Me too." Jack walked over to the window so he didn't have to see Leah drumming her fingers impatiently. "How are the background checks on the cast and crew coming?"

"So far, no big red flags." Alice ran down what details she had. "I heard some bad news about those storms and now I'm really worried."

"Did the meteorologists change the forecast?" They had a huge weather station on the mountain—did she know something they didn't?

"I ran into Mrs. Sawyer, and she said her hip is acting up, which means we're going to get clobbered."

Jack rubbed his eyes, half amused, half worried. When he was a patrolman, Mrs. Sawyer's joint pain was more reliable than any weather forecast. It had taken only a few times getting drenched in a surprise downpour for him to learn that if she said it was going to rain, he'd better pull out the foul-weather gear.

"I'll be fine." Jack practically whispered so Leah would not hear him say, "Please make sure you go to the store and get what you need for you and Lady before everything is wiped out."

Leah twirled a finger. "Wrap it up."

"I've got to…" He trailed off. No matter how he tried to phrase it, he couldn't figure out a way to tell Alice he was going to go start an avalanche. "I've got to go prep the challenge course."

His voice was way too upbeat and an uncomfortable silence grew on the other end of the line. She'd picked up on it for sure. He could picture her standing there, full lips pressed together, right eyebrow arched high in disbelief.

"And there's no call tonight," Jack said quickly. "I'll touch base with you tomorrow."

"I love you, Jack." He glanced up at Leah. Alice had broken their rule that they were going to keep their relationship under wraps.

"You, too."

"Don't take any stupid risks up there," she blurted out.

"Okay, talk to you tomorrow."

Jack hung up the phone and stared out the window. Technically, he hadn't lied. But he had a feeling Alice would disagree. To her, purposely starting an avalanche would almost certainly count as a stupid risk. His reflection stared back at him and he remembered the message on the mirror: YOU'RE DEAD.

10

SUPERFAN CLUB

Alice tried to focus on the report of the National Transportation Safety Board that explained the effect a helicopter propeller had on nearby objects—known as prop wash. But the material was dry, and her thoughts kept drifting back to Detective Clark. Had he called the detective from Westfield yet? Had he found anything?

She jumped at a knock on the apartment door. From the way Lady happily padded to the door, Alice could guess who it might be. Mrs. Stevens, their landlady, had fallen in love with the giant dog and she spoiled Lady rotten. She brought her treats, took her on walks, and volunteered to dog-sit. It was hard to believe there was ever a time when Mrs. Stevens and Jack didn't get along, though Alice did remember that time... She and Jack were getting to know each other again—as adults—amid the confusion and pain of their first case together, the disappearance of Michelle, Chandler's sister and their foster sister. Mrs. Stevens had displayed an excessive fondness for rules, while Jack had a violent allergic reaction to most rules. Thankfully, after Alice and Lady became tenants, too, and they moved into a bigger apartment in the building, Jack broke fewer rules, the need for his apology gifts became rare, and they had all grown genuinely fond of one another.

Lady whined as Alice opened the door. Mrs. Stevens stood in the doorway with two plates covered in aluminum foil. Her bob of red hair bounced back and forth in synch with Lady's tail. "There's my *baby*. I've got a treat for you." She looked up at Alice. "And something for you, too."

Mrs. Stevens walked into the kitchen, and Lady followed after, her whole rear end swaying back and forth. Mrs. Stevens placed one plate on the counter. "For you, Alice, there's a plate of chicken, stuffing, and mashed potatoes. And for my sweet little girl"—she looked down at the giant King Shepherd, who returned her gaze adoringly—"chicken and pumpkin!" She pulled off the aluminum foil, revealing a heaping mound of mashed pumpkin topped with sliced chicken.

Spoiled rotten, both of us!

Lady sat on her haunches and let out a bark that shook the apartment's thin walls.

"Use your inside voice, Lady." Mrs. Stevens smiled warmly and set the plate down by the kitchen counter.

Alice's ears were still ringing as Lady began to wolf down the food. "Thanks, Mrs. Stevens."

"Oh, I'm happy to do it. I was just making myself some lunch when I thought of

Lady's upset stomach. They say pumpkin's great for that, and Lady loves it, so..." Her eyes widened as she spotted something on the counter. "You have a *Planet Survival* pen!" She picked it up and turned it over in her hand. "Don't tell me you're a fan, too!"

Alice's mind raced. Her researching the show was supposed to remain secret. She must have picked up the pen with the materials Brian had given her. "I sure am."

Mrs. Stevens clapped her hands together and did a bit of a happy dance. "I'm a superfan. We can watch the new shows together! I *never* miss an episode. Did you get the new knit hat? They sold out online in under two hours. I have the exclusive sweatshirt from last season. I'll wear it next time I come over. I added a little lace around the collar to dress it up a bit."

"I'd love to see it." Alice glanced at the bedroom door to make sure it was closed. She was using the bedroom as an office, and the last thing she needed was for this "superfan" to find out she was investigating her favorite show.

Lady noisily lapped up the pumpkin, scooting the plate across the floor.

"I can't wait for the continued season," Mrs. Stevens said. "I read on the PS forum that they're taping it right now! My money's on Frida."

"Frida? The German climber?"

"Yes, she's amazing. Fearless. And she's been climbing her whole life. Her parents own a lodge in the Alps. She'll win, I just know it." Mrs. Stevens set the pen back on the counter. "If they had just listened to her... who knows."

"What do you mean?"

"You know... with the accident? Frida was the only one looking in the right place for that poor man."

"Back up. How do you know this?"

"The TV special. You saw it, didn't you? When they announced that the show was going on hiatus, they ran a special on the accident. I recorded it."

Alice didn't want to tell her that sitting on a hard drive in the next room was the raw footage of that special. She hadn't reviewed the video yet; it was still on her to-do list. There were hours of footage to go through, in addition to all the research.

She closed her eyes and rubbed the bridge of her nose. *I'll never be able to get through it all.*

"Oh, I have to go!" Mrs. Stevens threw her chubby hands in the air. "I'm baking a half dozen pies for my niece's bake sale. Let me know if you want to watch the special. I'm so excited about the show's return, I'm going to binge-watch the first part of this season again. We could have our own little superfan club!" She gave a little wave over her shoulder and hurried out.

Alice stood staring at the closed door.

I do need help going through all that footage...

Her phone beeped, and a new email notification appeared in the middle of the screen. It was Brian, getting back to her about the helicopter pilot, Mack Carson. It contained an attachment, which she looked at first: McAlister Insurance's letter to *Planet Survival* notifying them of nonrenewal of their helicopter policy.

Then she read the email. Most of it was uninteresting, but the last line...

Alice's legs began to shake. She wanted to call Jack and tell him to be *extra* careful, but she couldn't. Not right now. She'd have to wait until tomorrow to speak with him during their prearranged phone call.

She read the last line of the email again, and the uneasy feeling that had begun to form in her stomach grew.

Mack Carson had been killed in an avalanche.

11

WHITE FLASH

Jack trudged behind Abe and Ollie across the plane of snow. The blue sky had deepened in color but remained cloudless. It was hard to believe that a storm was brewing.

They reached the edge of a snow-covered field that stretched out like a soft comforter. Jack inhaled the crisp mountain air and admired the winter splendor. He pictured Alice building a snowman and Lady tearing through the fresh snow. He tolerated winter; they loved it.

Ollie grabbed Abe and spun him around. "Crouch down, beanpole, so I can open your pack."

Abe obediently squatted down. "Why do I have to lug them? You're the one who has special training on this stuff. It's *your* job to transport them."

Ollie opened Abe's backpack, which was filled with bright orange and yellow boxes. "It's my job to set them off, not carry them. And Leah put me in charge," he added. Though Ollie had become slightly less obnoxious since Jack first arrived, there were still no visible cracks in the man's world-class ego. It was not a quality Jack would have sought in a partner on any assignment, let alone a dangerous one, and he remained wary.

"Here you go, Jack." Ollie held out a neon-orange container the size of a tissue box. Jack took a giant step back.

Ollie snickered. "Man up, Jumpin' Jack."

"There's nothing to worry about," Abe said. "You can bash that thing off a rock and it won't go off. We used to toss them out of the helicopter."

"Yeah, when we had one. Lost the whirlybird due to budget cuts." Ollie spat and wiped his mouth. "This show's a ratings monster, yet all they do is cut back funding more and more each year."

"I thought you stopped using the helicopter because the pilot died on vacation." Jack was careful not to mention the insurance policy not being renewed.

Ollie's eyes narrowed. "And where'd you hear *that?*"

Not careful enough. Jack tipped his head to the side, pretending he was trying to remember. "One of the guys mentioned it when I asked how I was getting on set. I figured you used a helicopter, but he said you weren't using one for the rest of the season. I asked why and he said the pilot died."

"They could've hired another pilot," Ollie said.

"They can't replace Mack," said Abe.

JACK FROST - 43

Ollie made a sour face. "Everyone's replaceable. Hell, if they could save a buck, they'd replace all of us. They replaced Mack with a toy plane and they replaced Charlie with a broad." He apparently didn't have a high opinion of Bree—or maybe he just didn't like that she took over from Charlie.

"How'd the pilot die?" Jack asked.

"The Zugspitze did him in," said Abe.

"That's a mountain in Germany, right?"

"Yeah," said Abe. "Mack said it was calling to him, 'Climb me, climb me.' He talked about going for a long time. He was really looking forward to it. And then we had the break in filming, and he finally got his chance." Abe cleared his throat and wiped his eyes. "He got caught in an avalanche."

Mack Carson was killed in an avalanche?

"You sure ask a lot of questions," Ollie said. "This ain't no quiz show. We've got work to do." He tossed the avalanche charge at Jack, snapping him out of his trance.

Jack caught the box and glared. "Talking beats standing around watching the snow melt."

Abe laughed and took the charge from Jack.

"Let's get this done, you pansies." Ollie sneered. "I'll do the first couple to show you how it's done. Four should clear the whole field, and then we'll set up for the contest."

"How do you set them off?" Jack asked.

"Each one has its own remote code." Ollie pulled out an electronic device the size of a large walkie-talkie with a display screen. "We dial a charge's code into this remote, place the charge where we want it, press the button on the remote when we are ready, and ten minutes later—boom."

The three of them climbed atop a large, flat rock and surveyed the problem area. The snow all looked the same to Jack, but Ollie whistled.

"That's a disaster just waiting to happen. Well, it's showtime, ladies."

Ollie read a number from the side of the charge, then punched it into the remote. Three beeps sounded from the charge, and a light on the side flashed bright green.

"Green means it's armed." Ollie heaved the box across the snow. "Red means it's countdown until it goes boom."

"Red means run," Abe said.

Jack nodded, taking in the critical information. Simple enough.

Ollie started walking. "We'll place four, spread across the area, then set a ten-minute countdown. There's not much black powder in them, but you don't need much to get the snow moving when it's ready to go. We just gotta give it a little push."

"Harvey's rigging a drone to plant them," Abe said. "That'll make it easy-peasy. Safer, too."

Jack pictured a drone flying overhead carrying an explosive, and it didn't make him feel safer. He had seen plenty of machines break down in Iraq; the sand wreaked havoc with machinery. What would snow, ice, and bitter cold do? And if the drone *did* crash with explosives…

"Did *you* know Mack was going climbing?" Abe asked Ollie, snapping Jack back to the conversation.

Ollie shook his head. "He still owed me five hundred bucks. Lying sack of crap told me he didn't have it, but he goes to climb the Zugspitze?"

"Well, it *was* his dream climb," Abe said.

Jack wasn't surprised Mack hadn't shared his dream with Ollie.

"He would have paid you back later," Abe said, kicking at the snow.

"Guess we'll never know now, will we?" Ollie sneered.

Jack heard a faint sound coming from Abe. He grabbed the tall man's arm. "Hang on a sec, guys," he said. "Listen."

The muffled electronic chirping sound was coming from inside Abe's backpack.

"Crouch down," Jack ordered.

"What are you doing?" Ollie snapped.

Jack lifted the flap of the backpack and peered in.

Dozens of red lights glowed on the devices inside.

"Damn," Jack muttered.

"What's wrong?" asked Abe.

Ollie saw the red glow coming from Abe's backpack and swore.

"Can you shut them off?" Jack asked.

"Shut *what* off?" Abe's voice had risen.

Ollie pulled out the remote trigger and looked at it. "What the hell? The timer's running." He ripped off his glove and started wildly pushing buttons. "We've only got one minute."

"The charges are on? In my pack?" Abe shrieked. "GET 'EM OFF ME! GET 'EM OFF ME!" He started clawing at his backpack.

Jack fought down his urge to run for cover. He grabbed Abe's pack and pulled one strap loose, but Abe's twisting and turning knocked his hands away.

"The bloody thing won't shut off!" Ollie shouted. He looked at Abe, his eyes wide, and shook his head. Then he turned and ran.

"Get it off!" Abe slipped his other shoulder out of the shoulder strap, but the waist strap was still fastened. The pack tipped and hung down his long legs.

Jack snapped open his utility knife, seized Abe's belt, and sliced the pack off. Abe tumbled forward and fell face-first into the snow. Not two feet away, the charges' lights cast a glow that turned the snow blood-red. The beeping seemed to grow louder. Jack knew that just one of these charges going off in his face could kill him; with a dozen going off at once… there'd be nothing left of him or Abe.

He grabbed the backpack and pulled back his arm to fling it away, just as the sun crested the ridge and the sun's reflection off the snow blinded him.

White flash!

For a moment the world froze and Jack was back in Iraq. He saw Chandler holding the little girl wearing the suicide vest. He knew his friend was about to die, and he was helpless to do anything except watch.

The girl looked at Chandler and smiled. She thought he'd saved her life. But Chandler realized that she'd just killed her would-be savior. And Jack saw it. In that second, the last second of his life, Chandler knew he was about to die. And Chandler responded by doing what he always did: he thought of someone else. He looked at the girl in his arms and smiled.

White flash!

Jack blinked wildly, trying to see through the white-hot blaze of snow while the backpack buzzed like an angry hornets' nest.

"Throw it!" Abe screamed.

Everything was moving in slow motion. *How much time do I have?* Jack fought down the panic tearing at him. He heaved the backpack as far as he could.

"Get down!" Jack yelled.

Abe's eyes were wide and he was shaking.

Jack tackled the lanky man and dragged him down into the snow just as a huge explosion shook the ground. Jack waited until the blast echoed off the rocks and then glanced over his shoulder to see a pillar of snow shooting high into the sky. Air rushed in and out of his lungs, and he forced himself to focus on that fact. He was breathing, he was alive. Sweat and melting snow ran down his face. His hand shook as he wiped his eyes.

"You saved me. I can't believe it. You saved me." Abe was as pale as a ghost and babbling, clearly in shock.

The sound of the explosion was still resounding off the mountain. To Jack, each echo was as loud as a starter's pistol, and the sound was building to a thunderous roar, instead of dying down.

Confused, Jack looked back at the column of snow, slowly drifting to the ground like an early-winter snowfall that brought with it the possibility of a snow day. But the rumble growing louder...? Jack had been around enough explosions to know that this wasn't normal.

Abe stopped babbling and cocked his head. His throat tight with fear, he whispered, "Avalanche."

Jack jumped to his feet and grabbed Abe's arm. "Run!" Plumes of snow whipped through the air, and a dozen little birds scattered out of the trees, flying to the safety of the sky like shrapnel. Abe groaned as Jack yanked him forward.

The two men plunged and bucked through the snow. Their boots broke through the thin crust of ice only to sink deep into the soft snow beneath. Ollie was far ahead; he reached the next ridge, then disappeared over it.

The rush of snow above and behind them sounded like bowling balls rolling down the gutter, but a million times louder. The mountain shook. As he ran, Jack glanced back at what looked like fluffy white clouds on a warm summer's day floating down the slope. But as those fluffy clouds reached the tree line, the trees shattered, snapped, and disappeared in the white wash.

Jack pushed harder. "Faster!"

The wave of snow fanned out as it bore down on them. With every step Jack took, the beast grew in size, reaching out for them. Abe tripped and pitched forward. He landed on his chest, his lanky legs arching over his back. The wall of snow billowed like a massive wave cresting over the rocks on a beach. The roar was deafening.

Jack grabbed Abe, pulled him to his feet, and shoved him toward the ridge where they'd last seen Ollie. Moving sideways, away from the center of the force, was their only choice. Chunks of snow and ice pelted them. The ground beneath their feet shifted as they ran. Jack slammed into the rocks. With one hand, he grabbed stone, and with the other, he caught Abe's jacket.

"Climb!" he shouted, pushing Abe higher.

Abe pulled himself on top of the rock and clung there.

Snow slammed into Jack's legs and pulled at him like an angry sea trying to drag him to its depths. The bright sun was blotted out as the wave of snow smashed into the rock and shot high into the air. His hands slipped on the rocks, and the snow sucked him down into it, up to his waist. Jack frantically kicked his legs and reached up for the rocky outcropping in an effort to free himself. Abe grabbed Jack's jacket, and the two of them pulled with all their might. Their combined effort was enough to lift Jack up and out of danger.

Beneath them, snow flowed like a river, but it was slowing.

Gradually, the cloud of snow dissipated. It settled to the ground, and the sun gleamed off it once again. The white flash flared across the field, but this time Jack didn't freeze. This time he threw his head back and roared.

12

AN UNLIKELY ASSISTANT

Seated across from Alice at the kitchen table, Mrs. Stevens held the *Planet Survival* pen in her hand and studied the NDA in front of her. "Why do I need to sign this again?"

"I told you, Mrs. Stevens. I'm not allowed to tell you about the case unless you sign this nondisclosure agreement."

"But I won't tell anyone. I swear." She gave Alice the Girl Scout salute.

"And that's good enough for me," Alice said. "But the client needs that oath to be legally binding."

Mrs. Stevens sighed, but she signed and initialed the NDA. "Done," she announced. She tapped the pen against the table. "Now. What is this all about?"

Alice smiled. "Jack and I got a new insurance case. I'm running background checks and reviewing footage. I set up the bedroom as an office. I'll show you."

She walked over and opened the bedroom door. Mrs. Stevens stopped in the doorway, her eyes wide.

Alice had shoved the bed into the corner to get more workable space, and the wall was covered floor to ceiling with pictures, printouts, and notes.

"It looks like a serial killer lives here," Mrs. Stevens said.

"It's easier to see the whole picture if I can see the whole picture."

Mrs. Stevens walked closer to the wall and suddenly clapped her hands like a little girl getting candy. "You're investigating the avalanche on *Planet Survival!*"

"Remember, this is totally hush-hush. No one can know about this."

"I won't say a word." She gave the Girl Scout salute again. The landlady's broadening smile made Alice's stomach tighten.

Alice grimaced. "I know you won't, because you signed a document that legally stipulates you can't say *one word.*"

"I understand. You explained the nonexposure agreement, and I promise—no exposure."

"Disclosure."

"What?"

"Non*disclosure* agreement. It means you could get sued for saying *anything.*"

Mrs. Stevens clicked the pen several times and studied the wall. "Got it. My lips are sealed. Mum's the word. I won't repeat a single word, nothing, not one."

Alice sighed. *Yikes, fifty words to tell me she isn't going to use one. Not a good sign. This better not get me in the doghouse with Jack.* "Okay, just making sure we're clear here."

"I wouldn't do anything to jeopardize *Planet Survival*. It's my very favorite show."

"I know, you're a superfan. That's why I hired you."

"I don't care about the money. You can give me a dollar just for record-keeping. I'm *glad* to help."

"When do you want to start?"

"Right this minute!" Mrs. Stevens moved along the wall, studying everything. "I can't tell you anything about the crew, though. They only showed them on the special broadcast, and I didn't meet them on the tour."

"Tour?"

"The *Planet Survival* tour. It was right before the start of last season, and Mount Minuit is so close, I just had to go."

"You've been up on the mountain? That's great!"

"Oh, yes. I took a ton of pictures I can show you later. I don't know the crew, but I can tell you everything about the cast. Let's see. We already talked about Frida. These two"—she pointed the pen at a fiery redhead and a middle-aged man with a square jaw and buzz cut—"I don't care for The redhead, Vicky Hill, is aptly named for a mountain because she lets everyone climb her, if you know what I mean. First, she shacked up with George. He was an extreme skier from Colorado who got booted off in episode two. Three episodes later, she sneaks into Mr. Military's tent." She tapped the man with the buzz cut. "Eric Sanders. He tries to bully *everyone*. Yells, kicks snow, swears like a sailor. They're the villains right now, and I think they both relish that role."

Alice had pulled out her notebook and was scribbling as quickly as Mrs. Stevens spoke. "You said earlier that they should have listened to Frida. Can you tell me more?"

"Well, I don't know for sure, but on the TV special they featured the attempted rescue. The poor crewman that was killed, Charlie, it turned out that his GPS locator thingy came off him in the accident. It was so sad. They didn't know where he was under all that snow." She shook her head and her eyes welled up with tears. "Poor man was buried alive." Alice took her hand in hers.

Mrs. Stevens took a deep breath. "Anyway, they didn't know where to look for him, but Eric, the big bully, ran up yelling and told the crew to dig at this one spot, like he knew. Everyone but Ollie helped. Ollie's one of the cameramen, but he had a broken arm. He broke it in the 'Over the Hill and Through the Dale' challenge. He was using one of those long poles to poke the snow, but he couldn't dig with one arm."

Alice was nodding to keep Mrs. Stevens talking, but she could hardly keep up with the flow, and she had no idea whether any of it would be useful.

"Like I was saying, they should have listened to Frida. She's done avalanche search and rescue before, and *she* thought Charlie was trapped farther down the slope. But Chiri was the only one who listened to her, and they dug together. And of course, they were the ones who found poor Charlie. But by then it was too late. He was already dead." Mrs. Stevens' chin quivered.

"That's awful. I'm surprised they showed video of all this." *For the ratings, I'm sure.* "Who's Chiri?"

"His name fits his personality perfectly. Cheery. A small man, just adorable, happy-go-lucky. Always smiling. He's a great climber, a Sherpa, but he speaks perfect English because he's lived in the States for a long time—in LA, if you can believe it!"

Alice smiled at Mrs. Stevens' enthusiasm and thoroughness. "So all the contestants were on the scene?" Alice asked, still taking notes.

"All except Cornelius." Mrs. Stevens pointed to a picture of a man who looked like a homeless Grizzly Adams. His skin was dark and leathery, and his gray hair and beard shot out in all directions. "Nutty old mountain man plucked straight out of Appalachia. He said he was on the other side of the mountain and didn't hear a thing."

Mrs. Stevens' phone beeped, and she jumped. "Another pie!" She headed for the door. "I only have one more pie shift. I promise I'll come right back up. Maybe I can help look at some videos. If you tell me what to keep an eye out for, I'll spot it." She winked and hurried out.

Alice turned back to the wall of photos and notes. Mrs. Stevens was incredibly observant and in a short time had brought personalities and stories to life, saving Alice valuable time. But there were hours of video footage to go through. Even with Mrs. Stevens' help, every minute that went by made Alice imagine all the risks and dangers Jack was exposed to on the mountain.

Nonexposure agreement. If only there were such a thing.

What she needed was the cheer of work and Mrs. Stevens' bright chatter and a warm cup of tea, but instead, almost against her own will, she walked to the living room and looked out the window toward the massive peak hidden in the overcast sky. She touched the window's glass, trying to feel the reflections of the snowflakes whirling and drifting by. She wasn't fooled by those sweet little flakes.

The thick gray clouds and everything in that space between her and Jack brought a foreboding sense that a snowstorm wasn't the worst danger Jack faced on Mount Minuit.

13

WEATHER JACKPOT

Leah charged out of the lodge like a rodeo bull from its gate and headed straight for Jack, Ollie, and Abe.

"What kind of idiotic stunt did you pull this time, Oliver?"

"It wasn't my fault," Ollie snapped.

Leah stepped in front of him and stood in a power pose, hands on hips and feet planted wide. The Australian had four inches on her, but her fierce warrior glare made him stop in his tracks. "I put you in charge, so if something goes wrong, it *is* your fault. And something definitely went wrong up there—the whole mountain shook! What happened?"

"He almost blew me up and then ran away, *that's* what happened!" Abe said with a mix of anger and disbelief.

"What was I supposed to do?" Ollie snapped. "Hug you so we could die together?"

"Both of you shut up." Leah turned to Jack. "*You*. What happened?"

"What are you asking the greenie for?" Ollie said. "The equipment malfunctioned, that's all."

"Shut up now or I'm docking your pay." Leah's voice had dropped to a normal level, but her eyes still blazed. She pointed at Abe and Ollie. "You two. Inside."

Still bickering and shoving each other, the two men trudged into the lodge.

"Talk," Leah said.

Jack was used to giving reports, and almost unconsciously stood at parade rest: chest up, feet shoulder-width apart, his hands clasped behind his back. "We reached the ridge where we were supposed to set the charges. Ollie set the first charge and tossed it onto the snow field. We were walking to place the other charges when suddenly the ones that were still in Abe's pack started beeping. They were all armed, and Ollie couldn't disarm the charges using the remote. I had to cut Abe's backpack off him and throw it. The resulting explosion caused an avalanche." He had to distance himself from it now; he'd deal with the flashbacks later.

Leah studied Jack's face. He was used to this method of extracting information: waiting. Everyone from drill sergeants to therapists and police chiefs used it, but Jack could wait anyone out. The hardest part about it was trying not to smile. Besides, he wasn't here to answer Leah's questions. He was here to see if there was a threat to the cast or crew, and clearly there was. Right now, he wanted Leah to do the talking.

"Did Ollie run away?"

"When he was unable to shut off the charges, yes, he ran."

Leah folded her arms. "Then he's fired."

"You can't fire a guy for running away from a bomb."

"His coworker was *wearing* the bomb."

The words hit Jack hard, and he struggled to hold his memories at bay. "Ollie did try to shut them off first. Then he panicked."

Leah's fathomless brown eyes narrowed. "Every person who works on this crew knows that the first requirement is to have each other's back. If he ran away, that makes him a coward."

"In my opinion, it makes him human. But it's your crew. Anyway, the question you should be asking is, how could all of those charges get set to go off at once?"

Leah shook her head. "They can't. You have to enter the code for each charge. I was told it was impossible for them all to go off at the same time. That's one of the reasons we use that product."

"Who on the crew is the most knowledgeable about the charges and that remote?"

"Ollie."

"Well, then, you definitely can't fire him yet. We need to keep an eye on him while we get to the bottom of this explosion. I'll need to send that remote down to Alice so she can have it analyzed."

She shook her head. "Ollie stays, but that's needed equipment."

"You really plan on using it again after what just happened?"

Leah scowled. "Fine, I'll send Harvey to get another one." Almost as an afterthought, she asked, "Are you all right?"

Jack drew in a halting breath without truly assessing his feelings. He was sore from falling and running and climbing, and there were a few scrapes from ice, but nothing she'd be interested in. "I'm fine. But Abe's pretty shaken up."

"Well, not to sound callous, but I need you both to set up for the contest."

"You're going ahead with production? Three members of your crew almost got blown up." He was almost at his wits' end trying to figure out how to deal with this woman.

"For all we know it was a mechanical glitch. They happen. No one got hurt. It's not the end of the world."

"Me getting blown up would be the end of the world for *me*."

"Don't take it personally. This is business. It's my job to watch out for this show, and the studio will cancel us if we shut down taping again."

"You're taking a big risk."

"This *show* is a big risk. Always has been." Leah ran her hand over her face. "And you don't know if this is anything more than that remote going haywire or Ollie screwing up. Either way, there were no reported injuries. Technically, accident reports don't even have to be filled out on this. Read the policy."

"Hey!" A shout from up the trail.

They both turned to see a very tall man hurrying toward them, nearly running, and waving his fist.

"Oh, please, not now," Leah muttered under her breath. Then she plastered a polite smile on her face and said cheerily, "Hi, Wally. What brings you by?"

"Have you seen what your flying monkeys have done to Emmett's Field?" The man jabbed a long, thin arm back the way he came. "Explosives! They used explosives and displaced half the field! Do you have any idea how many plant species were just decimated?"

"It was a controlled—"

"Controlled? You can't *control* this mountain, and you shouldn't even try!" He shook his head so hard that his thick glasses slid down his hooked nose. "If there are avalanche conditions, you should avoid the area. Would you build a house on a floodplain? No! Would you put a hospital on a fault line? No!" He stuck a finger in Jack's face. "Would you hang-glide in a hurricane?"

Jack smirked.

Leah held up her hands in surrender. "I get it. Look, we're here for another three weeks, tops. Then you can have the mountain back, okay?"

Wally ran his hands over his long, greasy hair in frustration. "Who knows what permanent damage you'll do in the meantime, you and your lot." He glared at Jack. "It's on you, too, you know."

"What is?" Jack asked.

"Don't think you'll get away with pissing all over this mountain. And just saying you work for her is no excuse. The Nazis tried it at Nuremberg, and they were hanged."

Jack stepped forward. "Are you threatening me, Wally?"

Wally's long neck stretched till he stood eye to eye with Jack. "Me? No. I'll let Mother Nature do it." He turned to sneer at Leah. "I'll let the blizzards do it!"

"The weather report said the storms will miss us."

Wally chuckled bitterly. "No, both those storms changed course, and in two days they're going to converge right here. Congratulations, you just hit the weather jackpot. It's going to be a monster storm."

Jack glanced at Leah's satellite phone. He half expected it to ring and for Alice to be on the other end, freaking out about him facing such a blizzard and letting him know that Mrs. Sawyer's hip was right. He'd have to wait for the call tomorrow to calm her down.

Wally pointed at the gondola. "Take my advice. Get off this mountain before that storm hits. And don't *ever* come back." He marched ten feet away, spun around, and yelled, "And if you stay, I hope this blizzard blows you and your whole damn crew right off this mountain!"

14

LYING EYES

Leah clapped her hands. "Attention, everyone!"

Jack and the rest of the crew were gathered in the lodge's main room. Jack rubbed his eyes and took another sip of coffee. Good and strong, which he desperately needed this morning. Last night, after setting up the gates for the contest and anchoring flags into the side of a cliff, they'd had to set up a dozen remote cameras. He hadn't gotten to bed until almost one, and four and a half hours of sleep hadn't helped much.

"I've handed out the taping schedule. The five remaining contestants will be at the site in three hours. Before that, we need to tape Gavin's intro. Ollie, you're the only one not involved with the intro, so you'll cover the contestants preparing for the slalom climb. Then we all head over to the challenge course. Any questions?"

Abe raised his hand. "That weather geek came over while I was checking on camera forty-three. He said a monster blizzard's coming. Do you have an updated weather report?"

Harvey answered. "We just got it in from the National Weather Service." He walked to the front of the room. He pulled his belt up over his potbelly, but then his hands didn't seem to know where to land. He crossed and uncrossed them and finally stuffed them into his pockets. "NWS still thinks the main storm will continue up the coast and miss us, but the storm up north is now tracking in our direction. The forecast is for snow flurries tonight, with increasing winds as the hours pass. It's going to get down to about minus ten degrees, and that's *without* the wind chill factor."

"You just described winter," Ollie said. He laughed at his own joke, then took a swig of coffee. "But it don't really matter if there's a blizzard or not; the show must go on and all that hoopla, right?"

"Ollie's right, folks," said Leah. "This is reality TV, so we're shooting, rain or shine. Bundle up and get ready. Ryan, Harvey, and I will be in the booth. Let's do this."

* * *

Jack handed Bree some tape from her audio kit. She seemed very distracted as she shoved the tape into a pocket. She picked up two microphone covers from the hinged black box on the snowy ground and held them palm up, like her hands were a set of scales. One cover was black, the other was blue, and both were thick and furry, like puffy, long-haired cats.

"I'd go with the blue," Abe said. "The stronger the wind, the longer the hair."

Bree's lip trembled as she put the black one away.

"Sorry to remind you."

"Don't be sorry." Bree slipped the cover over the microphone and attached the mic to a long pole. "Charlie must have told me that at least a hundred times. I should've known which cover to pick."

"You know what to do. You'll be fine," Abe said. "Just don't let Gavin get you flustered. I have to go make the trail."

"What trail?" Jack asked. "Do you need a hand?"

"Nope. I'm the only man who can do it." Abe puffed out his chest and made a silly face. "The opening shot is supposed to look like Gavin walked up the mountain or something. We need footprints in the snow, so I have to circle around and walk up to make them. Then Gavin will stand at the end of my trail and we'll take the shot."

Bree rolled her eyes. "You'd think Mr. Big Shot Action Hero could handle his own *walking*. I'm surprised he didn't tell you to give him a piggyback ride."

Abe laughed, then handed Jack a photo; a still shot of where they were standing. "Harvey shot the drone B-roll yesterday. The shot finishes with the drone rising over that ridge and then sweeping over here, where I set up my tripod. This picture is the final frame. My prints will lead up to here, then they'll drop in a tree digitally, overlay the logo, and blend the shots together. The audience will never know it wasn't taped at the same time."

"It's so ridiculous. Like Gavin's some great adventurer," Bree grumbled.

Abe chuckled again, but Jack picked up on the sideways glance he gave Bree and the slight shake of his head. "All right, well, gotta go make the footprints. All in a day's work." He began trotting through the snow.

"I take it you're not a Gavin Maddox fan?" Jack said once Abe was out of earshot.

"Have you ever worked on a TV show before?"

Jack shook his head.

"Well, Gavin doesn't use a teleprompter like most TV stars. Instead, he has Ryan hold a mirror so he can look at himself." Bree laughed. "It's funny, but I'm serious. That says it all. I think Gavin's middle name is Ego."

Jack chuckled. "How long have you been with the show?"

"Since season three. Do you remember Abe saying how someone in the Alps made them a wind muff? That was me. I was hiking across the Alps with my boyfriend, who developed a sudden fear of heights—and commitment. He dumped me and flew home. I continued on alone and ran into Abe and Charlie. I made them a stupid-looking muff, and they got Leah to hire me as a gofer. They convinced her I was a female MacGyver."

"I'm sorry about what happened to Charlie." Jack suddenly realized that the woman who dropped to her knees on the videotape of the accident was Bree.

"Yeah. He was a great guy."

Bree looked out across the snow for what seemed like minutes. They stood silently; the only sounds were the wind and the settling snow.

"Have you ever seen anyone die?" Bree asked quietly.

Dozens of images flashed through Jack's mind like a macabre flip-book of death. "I was a soldier," he said simply. He clenched his teeth and tried to focus on a pine tree, anything to force the pictures from his head.

Bree reached out and touched his arm, encased in his thick winter coat. Even though he couldn't feel her fingers, the compassionate gesture made his skin tingle and took the edge off his pain.

They worked in silence for the next half hour, each lost in thought. When Abe returned, they could hear him coming from a hundred yards away, singing "The Sound of Music" at the top of his lungs, way off-key. He climbed onto the rock where Gavin was going to stand for the shot, threw his arms out, and began spinning around. He finished his ballad with an air guitar solo that made both Jack and Bree burst out laughing.

"Thank you. Thank you." Abe bowed. "Feel free to supplement my meager pay with generous tips."

"Here's a tip for you," Bree said. "Knock it off and look busy, because here they come." She pointed back down the trail at two men striding up to them.

"You ever met a real-life diva before?" Bree asked Jack with a smile.

"Just a few."

"Well, you're in for a real treat. Here come *two.*"

Gavin Maddox looked more like a newscaster than an action hero. He was six feet even and looked fit, but there was something soft about him that chafed Jack as soon as he heard the man's voice.

"I'm still not... *comfortable* with the opening." Gavin sighed, stretching out the sound to a whine. "I should be doing something *more* than just standing there. What are my fans going to think?"

"You know what they'll think?" Ryan put a hand on Gavin's chest. "They'll see your heart. They'll *feel* you, Gavin. Trust me."

Gavin smoothed his meticulously groomed blond hair. "Yeah. That'll work. A soft sell. We'll push my sensitive side. The chicks will love it! Okay, let's do this."

"All right, people," Ryan bellowed, even though there were only three of them and they were right there. "Places. You heard Gavin, let's do this. Headsets on, everyone."

Jack flicked the power switch on the box at his waist. The over-ear microphone was so comfortable he'd forgotten he had it on. He made a mental note to look into getting one if he ever got back into police work. He'd at least pass the thought on to Undersheriff Morrison. A microphone system that was always on would be perfect for fieldwork and a good addition to body cameras.

Bree raised a hand. "I need a mic check on Gavin, please."

"You already ran me through one when you put the mic on, sweetie." Gavin winked. "Where's my spot?"

"I still need a check because of the wind," Bree said.

Ryan waved her off and said, "Stand right on top of that rock, Gavin." As Gavin took his position, Ryan moved behind Abe. "Okay, on three. Hey!" He snapped his fingers at Jack. "Where's the slate?"

"The what?" Jack said.

"The slate. The slate board. You're the new gofer, right?"

"It's my fault," Bree said. "I didn't give it to him." She pulled a slate board out of her bag and a dry erase marker from her pocket. She wrote something on the board, then handed both marker and board to Jack. "For each take, add one to the number. Hold it up in front of Gavin, and when Ryan says 'Action,' click the bar. They use it for editing, so—"

"Ding-ding." Gavin mimed ringing a bell. "Film school's over. Can we get this show moving?"

"Of course, Gavin." Ryan glared at Jack. "You, over there."

Jack walked over and held the slate board in front of Gavin's face.

"Don't block my face," Gavin snapped.

He grabbed Jack's outstretched arm and tried to yank it down, but Jack's arm stiffened and didn't budge. Jack just looked calmly at Gavin's hands. Gavin let go, and Jack lowered the slate so it was no longer blocking Gavin's face.

Prima donna much?

"We need a sound check," Bree said insistently.

Gavin puffed a sigh into the cold air. "Fine. Testing one, two, three. Testing one, two, three. She sells seashells by the seashore. Are we ready now?"

"Got it." Bree smiled. "Thank you."

"Before my cheeks start to pink." Gavin shook out his hands and opened and closed his mouth several times. Some sort of acting warm-up, Jack figured, but it looked ridiculous.

"All right." Ryan held up a hand and started counting down with his fingers. "Action in five, four, three…"

Jack clicked the slate on "Action" and hurried out of the shot.

As soon as the camera started rolling, Gavin's presence completely changed. He was smooth and articulate, and if Jack hadn't heard him speak before, he would have thought Gavin was in fact an action hero. *The creep is really good.*

"Welcome to *Planet Survival*. I'm your host, Gavin Maddox. As you at home are only too aware, during each and every show, myself, the contestants, and the crew are in constant danger. This planet we live on can be a beautiful but treacherous place. And while I do my personal best to ensure that everyone is safe, despite perilous hazards, accidents happen. Last year, we lost one of our *Planet Survival* family. And yes, we are a family. That's how much my crew means to me. I lost more than a coworker—I lost a friend… and a brother." Gavin wiped a tear from his eye. "Chucky Parker was family."

Bree's hands balled into fists.

"Charlie!" Abe snapped. "His name was *Charlie* Parker." Judging by the dark scowl on his face, he was about ready to kill Gavin.

Ryan shouted, "Cut!"

Gavin shrugged. "Wasn't Chucky a nickname or something?"

"No." Bree glared.

"Right." Gavin flashed a broad grin. "Charlie. Got it."

"Okay, take two." Ryan pointed at Jack. "Change the slate sometime today, gofer?"

Gavin repeated his entire speech. Again, he made the gesture of wiping tears from his eyes. This time he got Charlie's name right.

"But," he continued, "as we say in this business of entertainment, 'the show must go on.' Our contestants have waited a year to resume their competition here on Mount Minuit, and Charlie would want nothing less than for us to see this season through to its thrilling conclusion—for the sake of our contestants, our crew, and most importantly, our fans. So it's in memory of my dear friend Charlie Parker that I say…" Here, Gavin shifted from Mr. Sensitive to Mr. Showtime as he flashed a broad smile and held his hand out to the cliff looming behind him. "Welcome back! This winter's going to be white-hot. Tonight, I give you the 'Jack and Jill Solemn Challenge.'"

Jack cringed when Gavin mangled the word *slalom*, but no one else seemed to notice.

"Each contestant must traverse a different route up this sheer tower of icy rock. The individual routes are marked by seven gates anchored into the cliff face that each contestant must pass through." The camera panned up the face of the cliff. Red, white, blue, yellow, and green gates dotted five race paths that zigzagged upward. "Risking death, today's contenders will battle it out to conquer the 'Jack and Jill Solemn.' The first contestant to retrieve their pail from the top and make it back down to the start, wins. Let me show you how it's done."

Gavin walked over to the blue course and pulled himself up about a foot off the ground. Jack thought Gavin was going to climb the course, but after hanging there a moment, Gavin looked back, rolled his eyes, and yelled, "I'm waiting!"

"Gofer!" Ryan shouted.

Bree pointed to the equipment bag. "Get the blue pail."

Jack raced over to the equipment bag, found a small tin pail painted bright blue, and held it up.

"Don't just stand there," Ryan snapped, "give it to Gavin." Jack rushed over to Gavin and handed him the pail.

"Now get out of the shot!" Ryan yelled. Jack ran back toward Bree.

Who said TV work was glamorous?

Gavin dropped down to the snow. He turned around and exhaled loudly, his shoulders rising and falling like he'd actually climbed the cliff. *"Veni, vidi, vici!"* He panted dramatically, lifted the pail high, and smoothed his hair. "Each path is fraught with jagged rocks, ice, and deceptive handholds, but I made it. Now it's their turn— and the players will have the added pressure of racing each other to the finish line. But one thing is for sure: the last climber to finish will be eliminated."

Jack wouldn't have thought it was possible, but Gavin's grin actually got bigger.

"Cut!" Gavin yelled. "Perfect. I nailed it."

"Mr. Humble he's not," Abe whispered.

"Should I tell him he mispronounced *slalom*?" Bree asked, her eyes sparkling mischievously.

"Why?" Jack shrugged. "He was *perfect*, right?" He winked, and all three chuckled.

Gavin walked over and tossed the blue pail at Jack's feet. "Going forward, you'd better get on the ball, gofer. We don't need your lack of professionalism delaying production."

Jack was about to retort, but out of the corner of his eye he glimpsed Abe shaking his head.

"All right, let's keep it moving!" Ryan called out. "Leah, we're waiting on Ollie."

"He should be almost there." Leah's voice came over the microphone. "I needed him to get more B-roll."

Abe pointed down the trail at the approaching snowmobile. "Here he comes now."

Ollie parked next to the equipment and Ryan waved him over. "Gavin needs to get ready for the next shot, so you'll have to fill in for him and climb."

"No rest for the wicked," Ollie muttered as he got off the snowmobile. He unzipped his jacket and switched it out with another from an equipment bag. He also swapped out his goggles for another pair. When he had the new gear on, he looked just like Gavin—at a distance, anyway.

As Ollie trotted over to the base of the cliff, Ryan and Gavin walked over to Abe, Jack, and Bree.

"We need a wide shot of Ollie making the climb," Ryan said to Abe. "Stay on the ground and just follow him up and down. Then get a few close-ups of hands and feet that we can cut to." He turned back and shouted, "Ollie, climb fast! We need Gavin to look great."

"I could make that climb in my sleep," Gavin muttered.

"I know," Ryan said soothingly, "but we need to get you back to the lodge to warm up. When the contestants get here, you're going to be doing interviews with lots of close-ups, and you're looking a little splotchy."

Gavin's hand went to his cheeks like Ryan had slapped him. "I need a trailer. Or a remote tent. *Something.*" He pulled his scarf up around his face, and the two launched into an animated conversation as they strode away.

Jack glared after them. "No one told me they needed a pail. They didn't have it on the prop sheet."

"Didn't anyone tell you that 'scapegoat' is part of the gofer's job description?" Abe was smiling, but already concentrating on filming Ollie's climb.

"Don't worry about it, Jack," Bree said. "*They* can't make any mistakes, so it must be your fault."

But Jack fumed in frustration. His *job* was to check the prop sheet before the shoot—and he'd done that. There wasn't any mention of a blue pail.

"Forget the pail," said Abe. "You know what we *really* needed during Gavin's little speech about 'family'? A barf bag."

"Just swallow it back down," Bree said. "That's what I did."

Abe made a gagging face.

"Wait a sec," Jack said. "They're going to edit the footage and make it look like Gavin made Ollie's climb?"

"It's 'television magic'!" Abe said, shaking his head.

"The deception of a digital age." Bree crossed her arms. "It's scary. You can't trust anything anymore. Not even your own lying eyes."

15

BUSINESS IS BOOMING

"What's wrong, dear?" Mrs. Stevens asked as she brought Lady in from her walk.

Alice leaned back in her chair and pointed at the computer screen. "Charlie's camera was never recovered after the avalanche." That fact bothered Alice to no end; yet another detail bothered her even more. "*And* no one from *Planet Survival* filed an insurance claim for the missing camera."

"I'm sure they must have lots of other cameras." Mrs. Stevens unfastened Lady's leash, and the dog trotted over to her bowl.

"The cameras they use for video start at fifty thousand dollars."

Mrs. Stevens whistled. "I'd file a claim for that."

"You'd think anyone would." Alice drummed her fingers. "But they didn't. And I can't find a missing camera in their inventory reconciliation."

"That's odd. Maybe it was extra?"

Alice glanced over her shoulder at Mrs. Stevens, who shrugged.

"That's not even the inventory discrepancy that's bugging me the most." Alice clicked another window, and a scanned document appeared.

"An invoice?" Mrs. Stevens asked, squinting over Alice's shoulder.

Alice shook her head. "It's a manifest for a delivery received by *Planet Survival* from ATD Control. I found it in a file marked 'Miscellaneous.' ATD Control is a relatively new avalanche mitigation business. This slip shows they provided a large sample shipment of their avalanche control products to *Planet Survival* at the beginning of last season. It's signed by the producer, Leah Coleman."

"That makes sense. The show does a lot of product placement. In season four, Gavin started each show by driving up in a different SUV."

"This wasn't product placement. This was to entice *Planet Survival* to buy their goods. They're very costly. But the weird thing is, none of the products that ATD provided are listed on any of the current inventory sheets. They're completely off the books. Where did it all go?"

"Hopefully not *boom!*" Mrs. Stevens said, half joking.

Alice put her hand on the mouse. "Maybe."

Mrs. Stevens let out a long, slow whistle.

"The accident investigation concluded that propeller wash from the helicopter caused the avalanche. Primarily because there was no evidence to the contrary. The investigation notes the *Planet Survival* crew insisted that they didn't deliberately set off an avalanche and that all of the avalanche charges were accounted for."

Mrs. Stevens' eyes widened. "But they *did* have these additional avalanche charges. And they *aren't* accounted for."

Alice nodded. "So, the million-dollar question is: Did someone use them to deliberately start that avalanche?"

16

SEEING RED

Jack waited with a clipboard at the base of the cliff. He'd been told to ask each contestant four questions. Were they in poor health? Did they need food or water? Did they require any medical attention? Was there any reason they should withdraw from the competition?

A short man wearing a multicolored hat bounded out of the woods and headed straight toward him, the three bright pompoms bouncing on the top of his knit cap as he made his way across the field. He thrust out a hand and grinned up at Jack with a bright smile. "I'm Chiri. You're new."

"Name's Jack." At the man's introduction, for a moment he thought the man was speaking about his temperament and had said "cheery," but then Jack realized this was Chiri Gombu.

Jack ran through the four questions, and Chiri answered no to all of them. Then Chiri leaned in close like he was about to share a secret. He seemed to have no trouble with English, though he had a heavy accent. "I can save you some time, friend. Everyone will give the right answers to these questions, even if they aren't true. If they don't, they're kissing five million dollars bye-bye."

Jack had figured as much; this was strictly for the lawyers. "I still need to ask."

"Hey, Chiri." Bree walked over and held out a battery. "How's the headset holding up?"

"Great." Chiri took the battery and removed a cigarette-sized box from his pocket. "But I still think you need to put a mute button on these things. No one wants to hear me eat." He grinned.

"People forget to turn them back on." Bree pointed to the tree line. "Looks like your competition is lagging behind you."

Three more contestants, two women and a man, emerged from the trees. The man broke into a jog.

"I hope it stays that way." Chiri's pompoms bounced as he laughed. "Me first, and everyone else following far, far behind."

Bree made a locking motion in front of her mouth.

"I know you can't *say* you hope I win, but I see it in your eyes." Chiri laughed again and walked over to the cliff while Bree returned to her sound equipment.

"Don't forget, Jack." Leah's voice in his ear made Jack jump. He had forgotten about his own microphone and earpiece. "Keep your interaction with the contestants to a minimum. Especially the redhead coming your way."

The man reached Jack first. He was a little shorter than Jack but built like a linebacker. He stood ramrod straight, glanced at the clipboard, then stared ahead. From the way he refused to turn his head, Jack had the impression the guy was upset with one of the two female contestants behind him.

"Eric Sanders." The man's voice was gruff.

Jack asked the questions and received a crisp response to each. The minute the questions were done, Eric marched over to Chiri.

A flaming redhead stepped in front of the blond contestant and offered her hand. "Why, *hello*. You're new." Her voice was as sultry as her bombshell good looks.

Jack shook her hand. She had taken off her glove, and her skin was warm in the cold air. "Jack Stratton."

"Vicky Hill. Welcome to my show." She laughed. "I'm kidding."

"I need to ask you the standard questions."

"Go right ahead, *Jack*." Vicky said his name slowly, with an emphasis on the *k*. She looked at him over long lashes as she pulled on her glove. "I like the sound of your voice. Are you an actor? You're hot enough to be one."

The sound of metal on rock made everyone look at the cliff. Eric had his climbing ax in his hand. He stared at Jack, then drove the spike down against the rock again. *The alpha male has revealed himself. That didn't take long.*

"Don't mind him," Vicky said, rolling her eyes. "He just pretends to be the bad boy. He's got the 'boy' part right. All talk, no action."

Jack asked her the questions, and Vicky answered. Then she stepped a little closer. "And what's your position? Not your favorite one"—she winked—"but your job on the show."

Her approach was so overt that Jack wondered if this was the real Vicky or part of her show persona. Either way, Jack had no intention of responding to her lewd advances, with or without Leah listening in. "Gofer."

Vicky's smile flickered and faded in disappointment. "Oh." She walked over to the cliff. She stopped several yards away from Chiri and Eric.

"Good morning," said the second woman. Her German accent was as thick as her blond hair, which she wore pulled back in a ponytail. "I am Frida Becher. Nice to meet you."

Jack introduced himself and asked the questions again. Frida listened closely, as if hearing them for the first time, and answered just as carefully.

She lifted her face to the gray sky. "Looks like snow." She grinned.

"That makes you happy? And you're up here in a tent?"

"The winter here is… what's the word I look for? Mild? Where I am from, we call this weather *Frühling*."

"What is that in English?"

"Spring!" Frida teased. She was very pretty, but when she smiled she was downright stunning. "I love snow. The more snow, the happier Frida is. Snow keeps the plants safe and warm. It's going to get very cold. The grass and trees need more snow." With that, she made her way over to gaze up at the course.

"Hold on, just hold on. I'm coming." The final contestant, an older man dressed in camouflage from head to toe, came stomping through the snow toward Jack. He spat out a nasty stream of chewing tobacco that left a long line of dark brown on the snow. "Cornelius Green. Now, I don't lose nothing being last checking in, right? I forgets some of y'all's rules. You've got a million of 'em."

"You're fine. The contest hasn't started yet. I just have to ask you four questions."

"Yeah, I know 'em. Kinda stupid questions, but go ahead."

"Are you in poor health?"

"Fit as a fiddle."

"Do you need food or water?"

"I've got plenty. Y'all should know that. You seen me eatin' with that red-eyed spooky spy camera. Watching me all night and day like I'm in Germany or something."

At the mention of Germany, Frida looked back at them over her shoulder.

"*East* Germany!" Cornelius yelled over to her. "They used to do that stuff back when you were commies. Hey, we're good now." He gave her a thumbs-up.

Frida's face twisted in confusion, but she nodded and waved.

"Personally, I was against putting that country back together," Cornelius whispered. "I mean, how many world wars have we had? Two. And who started both of 'em?"

"Actually, Serbia started World War One," Jack said.

Cornelius spat more tobacco. "That's just what the history books say."

Jack decided against arguing. "Do you require any medical attention?"

"Depends on who's doing the checkup." Cornelius chuckled. "You? No. But if that cute producer lady is playing doctor again, then I think I'm dying."

"Just ask him the question again, Jack," Leah said in his earpiece.

"Leah was playing doctor? When was this, Cornelius?" Jack said, a mischievous smile crossing his face.

"That tall, lanky fella cut his hand last year. Leah patched him up real good. Not too many gals that don't turn all squeamish when they see that much blood."

"Repeat the question, Stratton." Leah's voice was all business.

"Do you require any medical attention?"

"Nope." Cornelius spat again, adding to the patchwork of dark brown at his feet.

"Is there any reason you should withdraw from the competition?"

"Hell, no. I'm gonna win. You can write that down, too." Cornelius tapped Jack's paper with a worn glove.

"Well, thanks for answering my questions."

"Anytime. Much obliged."

"Jack?" Leah's voice came over his earpiece again. "In the equipment bag is the lot basket. You need to give it to Gavin."

Jack jogged over to the same bag that Ollie had gotten the jacket and goggles from, a big blue gym bag emblazoned with the *Planet Survival* logo. He unzipped it and looked around inside.

"The covered brown basket," Leah said.

Jack took out a battered wicker basket the size of a basketball. It had a removable top attached by a cord. Inside were tiles in different colors.

"Make sure there are five tiles in there. Red, white, green, yellow, and blue."

"Yep, got 'em," Jack said.

"Good. Give the basket to Ryan," Leah instructed.

As Jack stood, he saw Eric and Vicky standing toe to toe. Eric's ax was in his climbing belt, but Vicky's was now in her hands.

"Where were you?" Eric asked, his voice raised.

"Sleeping. In my tent," Vicky said.

"That's bull. I went there. You weren't there."

"Maybe I was using the bathroom."

"I waited there for a long time."

Vicky shrugged. "Are you sure you got the right tent?"

Abe circled around them with his camera. When Eric saw the cameraman, he huffed and waved his hands dismissively. "Like I care," he fumed. "You want to get cozy with one of these losers, go right ahead. You'll be going home tonight anyway."

"All right, everyone!" Ryan called out as he strode up with Gavin at his side. "Abe and Ollie, places, please. Gofer! Where's the lot basket?"

Jack jogged over to Ryan, gave him the basket, and backed out of the shot.

"Can you move a little faster next time?" Ryan said, snapping his fingers repeatedly while making a snide face. He opened the basket and reached inside. He made a big deal of counting the tiles, even reaching inside and moving them around. "At least you can count to five." He handed the basket to Gavin, and they both laughed.

Taking a deep breath, Jack counted all the way to ten, fighting the urge to knock their heads together.

Bree waved Jack over to her. "There shouldn't be anything for you to do, but you can stand here."

The contestants formed a half circle in front of Gavin, who stood with his back toward the cliff-side course. He lifted the basket up and shook it. "In this basket are five colored tiles. Each color matches a marked route on the cliff-side. Survivalists, pick your fate." He stepped toward Cornelius and held the basket above his head.

Cornelius reached in and pulled out a white tile. Eric got red, Frida green.

When Gavin came to Chiri, he held the basket well above the shorter man's reach. Chiri went along with the joke and jumped up a few times.

"Come on, Chiri." Gavin laughed. "Or should we get you some climbing gear?"

Chiri made a motion like he was going to punch Gavin in the stomach. When Gavin brought his arms down to cover his midsection, Chiri's hand shot into the basket and pulled out a yellow tile.

"Smile, Gavin." Leah's voice sounded in Jack's earpiece. "It's part of your joke, right?"

Gavin smiled and laughed, but he didn't look too happy.

"That was priceless," Bree whispered.

Vicky reached into the basket and pulled out the last tile.

"Looks like I'm blue." She flashed a dazzling smile at Gavin.

"In your places." Gavin tossed the basket aside and lifted his hands dramatically into the air. "Climbers, are you ready?"

Everyone shouted yes.

"On three, two, one, GO!"

The contestants raced toward the rock wall. Chiri moved effortlessly up the face of the cliff, while Frida and Eric vied for second place. Vicky was next, and Cornelius brought up the rear. But all of them were remarkably fast, considering the conditions. Jack was impressed.

As the contestants got closer to the top, the route Eric was on forced him to climb out over a rocky outcropping. His legs dangled in the air as he pulled himself up, but it caused him to fall behind the others.

Chiri reached the top first and grabbed his pail. He was followed by Vicky, Frida, and then Cornelius.

Bree made a face. "There's no way we're going to be able to use any of Eric's audio. He's totally freaking out up there."

Eric finally made it to the top, seized his pail, and started his descent. But by now the other contestants had a huge lead; there was no way he was going to recover the lost time. Chiri won, Vicky came in second, and Cornelius came in a surprising third. He had rappelled down the cliff, dropping like a stone. In fact, he'd come down so fast that Jack had to resist the urge to rush forward, thinking Cornelius was falling instead of in a controlled descent.

When Frida's boots touched the ground, Eric started screaming above. He swore at the top of his lungs and smashed his climbing ax off the rocks. "That was bull! My route went straight-out vertical! I was hanging for half my climb!"

"Eric, please keep your voice down." Gavin cast a sideways glance toward Ollie and motioned him over. "In every contest you have winners, but you also get—"

"Screw you!" Eric shouted. "I'm saying straight up that this contest was fixed!"

"Remind him about the random tiles, Gavin," Leah said.

"You yourself chose that route," Gavin said. "Each contestant had the same chance you did of pulling the red tile and getting that route. It's just bad luck."

Eric finally dropped to the ground. He spun away from the cliff and walked straight up to Gavin. "Luck? What are the chances that in *every* contest Vicky's got good luck and I draw the short straw?" He pulled out his red tile and held it up. "Red is the hardest route, blue's the easiest. It's not luck, it's crap." He dropped his tile to the frozen ground.

"You're getting ahead of yourself, Eric. We haven't asked if anyone wants to use their rescue flare and save you from elimination. There are still two flares remaining in the game. Cornelius and Vicky each have one."

Eric glared at Vicky and Cornelius. "Well?"

"Sorry, Crew Cut, but I'm saving mine," Cornelius said. "Can I go back to my tent now?"

Gavin scowled. "We're almost done. Well, Vicky? Will you use your rescue flare to save Eric?"

Vicky did her best to look like she was struggling with the decision. Overacting, she rubbed her temples and then shook her head slowly, her red hair swinging.

"I don't think so."

Eric erupted. "This is what I think of the lot of you!" He swore and held up both middle fingers toward the camera.

"Cut him off, Abe," Leah said.

"Don't you dare," Ryan snapped. "This is gold."

Eric stomped toward Vicky, and Jack moved to cut him off. "You need to back off," Jack warned him.

"Get out of my way," Eric snarled.

"Move the hell out of the shot, Jack!" Leah ordered.

"Let this go, Leah," Ryan said. "Keep rolling, guys. Jack, why don't you step toward Eric? Get in his face a little?"

Jack held his ground. "It's just a show, Eric. Just walk away. It's not worth it."

"Not worth it? You're kidding. It's worth five million dollars!" Eric stared down everyone who dared meet his menacing glare. "This isn't over. I'm not forgetting this." He pointed at Vicky. "Or you."

He snarled at Gavin, who stepped behind Jack, then he stormed off.

"Keep it moving, Gavin. Congratulate them," Leah said.

Gavin stood before the group. "To the remaining contestants," he said, "I salute you. The next challenge will take place in three days' time. For those who manage to survive that long," he added ominously.

"Abe, get close-ups," Ryan directed. "Ollie, get me some long shots. If you can still see Eric, try to get a shot of him moping away."

"Get the colored tiles from the contestants before they leave, Jack," Leah said.

Jack picked up the wicker basket and the red tile Eric had dropped. He had to jog over to Cornelius to get his, as the old mountain man was already walking away.

"That was dramatic," Chiri said as he gave his yellow tile to Jack.

"Congratulations on finishing first," Jack said.

"I actually slowed down to make it look good," Chiri whispered. "I want everyone to underestimate me. They think Chiri is just a happy little man. Hey—you don't think Eric's mad at *me*, do you?"

"I think he's mad at the world."

Frida came up and handed her green tile to Jack. "I think what you did was... plucky."

Jack cracked a crooked smile at the word choice. "Thanks."

He walked over to Vicky, who was talking to Ryan. "Eric's gone now, right?" Vicky was asking.

"Oh yeah, very gone. He has to clear out his tent and head directly to the gondola."

"You need to make absolutely *sure* of that, Ryan. Did you see how he was looking at me? I mean, if looks could kill, I'd be dead." Vicky put her hands on her hips. "Do I need to talk to Leah?"

"No." Ryan's lips pressed together. "Once Ollie gets a couple more shots, I'll send him over to make sure that Eric vacates." Ryan went off to talk to Gavin.

"Vicky, I need your blue tile," Jack said.

Vicky zipped up her jacket. "You'll have to frisk me for it."

Yikes. "Please drop the tile in the basket."

"I must have lost it in the climb." She pointed up the cliff. "You're welcome to go up and look for it. Sorry." She gave a little wave over her shoulder as she walked away.

Jack clamped his mouth shut.

"Aren't you glad you stood up for her now?" Bree said as she strode up.

"I didn't do it for *her*," Jack muttered. He walked with Bree over to the equipment bag.

"Then who'd you do it for?"

Jack shrugged. "It was the right thing to do."

"Well, right or wrong, I'd stay away from Eric. He's got a bad, bad temper and he's ex-military. He should be on the gondola heading down soon. Until then, steer clear."

"That's good advice," Leah said in Jack's earpiece.

"You jumping into random conversations is a little creepy, Leah," Jack said. "Are you always listening?"

"And watching." The nearest remote camera wiggled back and forth on the pole it was mounted to.

"Super creepy." Jack cleared his throat. "I'm sorry if I messed up the shot. I said I wouldn't interfere, but that situation was escalating rapidly."

"Don't do it again, but I get it. You're a regular Boy Scout."

"You say that like it's a bad thing."

"Touché. But I didn't mean it that way. I guess I should have said it was… plucky." She laughed.

"I can see I'm not going to live that down." If she'd been standing in front of him, Jack would have thrown a snowball at her.

"See you back at the ranch," Leah said, seemingly happier now that taping had resumed.

Shaking his head, Jack unzipped the equipment bag to put the lot basket inside. When he straightened up, he had just enough time to curse under his breath—Gavin was marching his way.

"Hey, Gavin, I'm sorry if I overstepped," Jack said, trying to head off a temper tantrum. "I'm sure you could have dealt with Eric, but you know how fights go, right? Someone gets a lucky punch in, you end up with a broken nose, then what happens to production?"

The host had been primed for another fight when he walked up, but now his eyes widened in alarm, and Jack was certain that Gavin would have nightmares about rhinoplasty tonight.

Gavin straightened up like a frightened mouse, scanning the field for signs of danger. "No. You were right to get involved." He cleared his throat. "For the sake of the production."

Jack nodded.

"But I *am* going to make sure Ryan gets that hothead off this mountain." He reached down, lifted the top off the lot basket, dropped something inside, and stomped off. Jack smiled as he watched Gavin hurrying to catch up to Ryan. Turned out the diva host was quite easy to manage. *Stoke his fears, stroke his ego.*

Crisis averted. Nothing left to do for now but fetch Vicky's tile, pack up, and head back to the lodge for lunch and the next production meeting. *Joy of joys.*

Gavin had left the top of the lot basket ajar. *Gofer. More like Do-everything-fer.* His eyes narrowed. There were now five colored tiles inside the basket.

Including Vicky's missing blue one.

17

COOKIES HELP

"Here you go, sweetie. Cookies help." Mrs. Stevens set a cup of tea and a cookie next to Alice's mouse pad.

"Yes, they sure do." Alice smiled. "How are you doing?"

"Great." Mrs. Stevens scooted over to the counter and picked up her own cup of tea and a plate with five or six cookies on it. "I just came out to get a little snack. It's so much fun going through all this behind-the-scenes footage… Anyway, I'll let you know if I find something." She grinned and disappeared back into the bedroom.

Alice turned back to her computer. So far, she'd pored over the work history, financial statements, and criminal charges against the contestants and crew. Both cameramen had arrests for minor offenses; Ollie had been arrested for public intoxication twice, and Abe had an arrest in Texas for marijuana possession. Gavin had been sued several times, and his credit rating was in the toilet. Divorced twice and taken to the cleaners both times, he was struggling.

And then there was Eric Sanders, the bad boy on the show—and apparently in real life, too. He'd been dishonorably discharged from the Army and had subsequently been arrested for assault twice, including once against his neighbor. The neighbor had confronted Eric about loud music, and Eric had responded by breaking the man's jaw.

Still, so what if these people had issues? Nothing here suggested any connection to Charlie Parker, and there was certainly no indication that any of these people would be likely to commit a premeditated murder.

Alice sighed. Brian had wanted her to look at Charlie's death first, so she had. But she had a hunch she might have more luck looking into another accident—the death of *Planet Survival's* helicopter pilot, Mack Carson.

Maybe it was time to listen to her hunch.

Brian hadn't included much about Carson in the materials he sent, but a quick internet search brought up a news article about the incident. She clicked the link and began to read:

> *An expert American climber was killed Thursday in an avalanche while approaching the summit of the Zugspitze. The victim, 36-year-old Mack Carson of Los Angeles, California, was ascending the south face when the avalanche occurred. The avalanche danger was rated as "low" at the time of the slide.*

Initial witness statements indicate that the victim impacted with the rocky terrain on his way down. Mr. Carson is believed to have been killed instantly.

Search and rescue personnel reported one casualty. The American's climbing partner was not injured in the slide. The death marks the...

Alice read the last line again. *Climbing partner?* She clicked on the link for the article's author, a reporter named Joel Fischer, then typed a quick email.

Dear Mr. Fischer,

I read your article about the fatal avalanche last month on the south face of the Zugspitze with great interest. I am researching an unrelated avalanche death here in the United States and believe that additional information on the accident you covered would help me in my efforts. I would greatly appreciate it if you would please provide me with the following: (1) a contact name and email for the leader of the search and rescue crew that responded to the accident, and (2) the identity of Mack Carson's climbing partner that day. Thank you in advance for your kind assistance.

Sincerely,
Alice Campbell

She hit send and pushed back in her chair, musing about the person who was with Mack and somehow escaped the avalanche, and probably saw Mack get swallowed under. Alice had been through enough in her life to know that surviving something so tragic changes a person. Forever.

18

MISSING MADMAN

"Is Ollie back yet?" Leah called out as she walked into the lodge's drab dining room.

"I haven't seen him," Jack said. He was seated between Abe and Bree around the wobbly dining table.

Harvey sat across from him, shoveling food into his mouth. "You want me to go put eyes on him?" he asked through a mouthful of microwaved mac and cheese.

"When you're done," Leah said.

A piece of macaroni dropped from the side of Harvey's mouth onto his plate.

"Harvey," Bree whispered, "maybe a little less caveman?"

Harvey wiped the back of his mouth with his sleeve. "Sorry."

Leah pretended she didn't notice. Harvey's table manners weren't on her agenda. "I have a meeting with Ryan. We'll reconvene in the great room in twenty minutes."

Harvey nodded and finished off his can of soda.

"'Caveman,'" Abe said after Leah left. "I like that nickname. It suits you."

"Shut up," was Harvey's witty retort, topped off with a burp.

"Well, you didn't like 'Doc,'" Abe said.

What kind of doctor? Vet?

"After the cutbacks, you're the closest thing to a medical professional we've got!" Abe laughed.

"I never should have told them I used to be an EMT," Harvey grumbled. "It didn't get me a raise, just more responsibility." His hands flew as he spoke. "Besides, this show is high risk for serious injuries. Season one, we had a doctor and two nurses on staff. The next season, just the nurses, and now it is just me. It doesn't make any sense that the higher the ratings go, the more they slash the budget."

Abe waggled his eyebrows. "Look on the bright side. Maybe you can practice CPR on Vicky!"

"Come on, guys." Bree shook her head. "Can you *try* to keep things the tiniest bit civilized around here? You do need to reenter society when this show is done."

"And I'm looking forward to that," said Abe. He pulled out his wallet and flashed a picture at Jack like a badge.

Harvey groaned. "Here it comes."

"What?" The image was of Abe hugging a little girl missing three teeth, but with a grin so wide her eyes were reduced to slits. "This is my little Annabelle."

"She's beautiful," Jack said.

"Isn't she? She stays with my parents while I'm on location. Her mother—" Abe cleared his throat. "Sorry, still kills me. On drugs, she was no mother at all." Abe shook his head, looking both sad and embarrassed.

Abe's words hit Jack like physical blows. The same was true of his birth mother, a prostitute. "She's blessed to have such great grandparents and a hardworking dad."

Abe smiled. "Her birthday's next month, and she really wants one of those kid-sized Jeeps. I've got a bunch more pictures." An accordion of photos tumbled down. "Lemme show you."

Bree leaned behind Abe's back and waved her hands at Jack in warning, but Abe saw her and frowned.

Bree laughed. "I'm just kidding. But you're going to have to wait to tell Jack all about Princess Annabelle. Leah asked me to check the remote pics, and I need your help."

"You can show me those photos later," Jack said.

Abe grinned. "I was planning to."

As they pushed away from the table, Harvey said to Jack, "We've got a few minutes before the meeting. You want to see the control center?"

"Sure."

Abe pushed Harvey's keys across the table. "Don't forget your keys, Caveman. You might need to feed the beast."

"What's the beast?"

"That's what we call the generator," Harvey said, leading the way up the stairs. "It's one of those new propane ones. It's gigantic. Total overkill for a lodge this size. They must have plans for expanding."

On the second floor, orange electric cables ran down the hallway from both directions and into a room on the right.

"The monitors draw a lot of power," Harvey said. "That's usually the hardest part of these remote shoots." He stepped over the cables and into the control room. "The equipment puts out a lot of heat. This is the warmest room in the whole place."

The old meeting room had no windows and there were no lights on, but it was as bright as day from the glow of giant computer monitors along the back wall. Jack counted twelve, in three separate banks. In front of the monitors was a long desk with a multitude of switches, keyboards, and other equipment.

Harvey slid into a high-backed chair that looked like it belonged on the bridge of the starship *Enterprise*. "Welcome to the control center." He fanned his hands out to the monitors. "From here, I can display a single image..." He pressed two buttons, and a blue-and-red tent filled all twelve screens, making it look like they were one giant TV. "Or, if I don't mind a bug's-eye view..." He pressed more buttons, and the monitors all switched to split-screen views, a dozen shots on each TV, for a total of one hundred and forty-four different shots—though some of them were black. "I could show up to two hundred and eighty-eight different shots at once, but we only have a hundred and twenty-four functional units."

"You have that many cameras?"

Harvey grinned. "Well, some are no better than nanny cams, but we've got some cams that are really sweet."

"Was it the same setup last season?"

"No, we had more cameras then." Harvey frowned. "They cut us back *again*. It's stupid. I mean, this year is going to be a ratings bonanza. At least, I hope. Who knows? If something else goes wrong..."

He let the thought trail off, so Jack finished it. "Your ratings would tank?"

"Tank?" Harvey laughed. "If something else goes wrong, we'd probably go back to being the number one show on television! It's human nature to want to watch scary things play out in front of you. Think of drivers passing an accident scene, folks rubbernecking just to get a glimpse of the damage. And for TV, that rubbernecking means dollars. Excitement is entertainment—even if it's chaos for those of us behind the scenes." He raised a hand defensively. "Don't get me wrong, I'm not wishing anything bad to happen to anyone. But boring is bad for viewership, and I need this job. I just bought a condo in Florida." He gave a wheezy chuckle, assuming Jack—and everyone else in the world—understood and shared his jaded, money-grubbing worldview.

Jack tried not to scowl. Harvey was no better than a sleazy ambulance-chasing lawyer, taking advantage of misery just to make a buck. Jack didn't know what he disliked more, that kind of attitude or the fact that there were so many people in the world who regarded other people's real-life tragedies as thrilling entertainment.

Make some more popcorn, honey; he's really up the creek now!

"Let me show you what else I can do," Harvey said.

Jack was tempted to say he'd seen quite enough already, but instead cultivated his best poker face while Harvey pressed buttons and bustled about between a few keyboards. The TV in front of him switched to a single shot inside a large tent.

"The contestants' tents are special," Harvey explained. "They're much bigger than your standard mountaineering tent so we can get shots like this."

Harvey pressed more buttons and the camera panned down to a shot of Frida lying on top of her sleeping bag. She was reading a book and absentmindedly twirling her hair.

Harvey laughed. "Is this job great or what? They actually pay me to be a peeping Tom." Harvey wiped the corners of his mouth with his index finger and thumb.

Great, the guy's a perv, too.

Harvey switched the camera again, this time to Vicky's tent. The redhead was writing something in a book. Harvey rotated the camera, and it must have made a noise, because Vicky looked straight into the lens and waved. Harvey waggled the camera back and forth, and Vicky stuck her tongue out.

"I keep asking Leah to get two-way microphones, but for now we can only hear them. They can't hear us." He pressed a button and Vicky's voice came over the speakers in the control room.

"Hey, Harvey. Miss me?" She pouted her full lips toward the camera.

"Do you have any idea how badly I want to reply right now?" Harvey leaned back in the chair.

"Do you need some more shots of me 'getting over' Eric losing?" Vicky started dancing around the tent, a huge grin on her face. "It couldn't have happened to a bigger jerk. Now I've got a one-in-four shot at five million big ones." She held up her hand with all five fingers splayed out. "The money's as good as mine, baby!" As she pranced for the camera, she took off her bulky sweater. When she pulled it over her head, it lifted her shirt high enough to reveal her toned stomach.

"She's such a flirt for the camera," Harvey said. "Ryan eats up these shots."

And so do you, apparently, Jack thought. He was anxious to curb Harvey's enthusiasm, and besides, seeing Vicky reminded him of something a lot more interesting to him. "So, from here can you check that Eric left the mountain?"

"Yeah, sure," Harvey said absently, his eyes fixed on the screen. Vicky was now spinning the sweater over her head, and she tossed it into the corner. She strutted toward the camera, running both hands through her hair and swaying her hips like an eighties' music-video vixen.

"Switch it to Eric's tent now, please," Jack said.

"Are you crazy? She just got started!"

"I'd listen to him, Harvey," Leah snapped.

With the speakers so loud, they hadn't heard her come in. Beside her was Ollie, his jacket still wet with snow.

"I-I was just about to," Harvey stammered, fumbling with the buttons. "I was just, uh… showing Jack the setup. What's this all about?" The shot on-screen changed to another tent, completely empty. "That's Eric's tent," Harvey said.

Ollie leaned toward Leah and poked his chest with his thumb. "I waited for that idiot at the gondola for an hour and he never showed. So I went to his tent. It was empty, and his gear was gone. I hiked all the way back to the gondola again thinking I missed him, and still never saw him."

"Switch to the motion-activated camera," Leah snapped.

"Okay, boss."

As Harvey worked the control panel, Leah explained to Jack, "There are several cameras at each site. Some are always on, some only turn on when they're activated by motion. We can go right to when the action starts, which reduces editing time—"

Jack liked where this was going and couldn't resist finishing for her. "By reviewing the footage on the motion camera in Eric's tent, we can see him coming and going, and the times."

"I've got Ollie," Harvey said.

The monitor showed Ollie opening Eric's tent flap, looking around the empty tent, and leaving.

"Yeah, that was about an hour ago," Ollie said.

"How far back can you rewind?" Jack asked.

Harvey pointed to a computer rack that contained dozens of hard drives. "I can go back to the first snowflake that fell when we resumed the season."

"Just roll it back to the previous motion," Leah said impatiently.

"All right, here's Eric. About two hours ago."

They watched Eric rip open his tent flap and kick a box. He swore nonstop while he stuffed several items into his backpack and stormed back out.

"Well, he packed up. That's a good sign—it shows he intended to leave. Pull up the gondola camera," Leah said.

Harvey shook his head. "What gondola camera? You had me use it to replace the one we lost outside Chiri's tent."

Leah sighed. "I forgot about that. Do we have any camera between Eric's camp and the gondola that might have picked up Eric?"

Harvey shrugged. "Sorry. Nothing between his tent and the gondola."

Leah turned to Ollie. "How long did you wait for Eric at the gondola the second time?"

"I didn't. I wasn't gonna wait again. It's getting dark."

Leah turned to Jack. "Get your jacket. We're taking a walk."

* * *

The snow was coming down steadily by the time Jack and Leah reached the gondola, and Ollie's boot prints were already disappearing. They'd been calling Eric's name as they went along, and Jack yelled again now. Leah stuck two fingers in her mouth and whistled loudly.

They both stopped and listened. The gondola cables creaked in the wind, but other than that, the mountain was quiet.

Leah opened the gondola door and checked the console.

Jack followed her inside. "Who has the key?"

"Ollie has one. I have the spare." She tapped her ring against the metal bar. "What a jerk."

"We can organize a search and rescue," Jack offered.

Leah shook her head. "He's a survivalist. A night on this mountain is nothing to him. He has gear; he may have headed to one of the unused tents. He knows where they all are. When we resumed filming, we had to set up all the past contestants' tents too. The rules state that any equipment utilized in any given season must remain in use for the remainder of the season." She paused to think for a minute and came to the only logical conclusion. "In the morning I'll have Harvey start looking for him with the drone."

"You need to let Vicky know that Eric is still up here."

"Believe me, I know." Leah crossed her arms. "This is just great. On top of everything else, now I've got her latest crazy ex-boyfriend running around."

"Can she stay in the lodge?"

"No. Not unless I pull in all the other contestants, too. It would give her an unfair advantage."

"You can't just leave her out there by herself. Eric made specific threats against her."

"What the hell am I supposed to do?" Leah kicked the side of the gondola. "Post a guard outside her tent?" She paused, then looked at Jack. A smile slowly spread across her face.

"No way. Are you serious?"

"Look, we have a tent back at the lodge. I'll give you a portable GPS and you can put your tent right outside hers."

"Me?"

"As long as you don't give her any assistance, you're not violating any rules."

"From a security standpoint she'd be safer in the lodge."

"That's not happening. My other option is to do nothing. Eric is a bigmouth and likes to talk tough, but I don't think he'd actually *do* anything. He's probably sulking in his sleeping bag somewhere."

"You can't be certain of that." Jack shook his head and looked toward the mountain. "Were Eric and Vicky a serious item?"

"They had a fling, that's all. Ryan played it up for ratings."

"Clearly it was more than a fling to Eric," Jack said. "This morning, before the contest, he was furious that Vicky wasn't in her tent last night."

Leah's brow creased. "Do you mean… You think she was fooling around with another contestant?"

"No. Harvey would have caught it on camera if she had. I think she was fooling around with a crew member."

Leah chuckled, then laughed. "No one on my crew is stupid enough—" Her laugh trailed off, and she closed her eyes and pressed her lips together. "Gavin."

Jack nodded. "I was going to share my suspicions with you at our next meeting. And there's something more. After the 'Jack and Jill' contest, when I went around to collect the colored tiles, Vicky didn't have hers. She said she lost it on the course during the climb. Five minutes later, Gavin dropped that same tile into the lot basket."

"What are you suggesting?"

"Vicky drew her tile last, right? And when she drew her tile, she didn't hold it up, didn't show it to the camera—and we didn't question that, because everyone already knew it was the blue tile. But I think her hand was empty. I think Gavin removed the blue tile from the basket before offering it to the contestants—to make sure no one else could pull it. Gavin and Vicky worked together to ensure that Vicky would get the easiest course."

Leah let fly with a stream of swears. "Eric was right! Gavin, that stupid idiot! And you didn't bring this to my attention right away?"

"I wanted to watch them first to gather more evidence. Right now, we've got nothing concrete. Gavin can always say he found the tile lying in the snow."

"So why are you telling me now?"

Jack crossed his arms. "Look, I don't know about all the drama on this show. Before this, I'd never even heard of *Planet Survival*. I'm looking at this like a cop, and from that point of view, what happened back at the cliff was basically a domestic violence incident." She showed increasing disbelief, but he had to barrel over her skepticism. "And knowing what I do about situations like this, with Eric as mad as he was, and now missing? I'd tell both Vicky and Gavin that they need extra security. You need someone watching Gavin. But don't mention the tile. Eric threatened him—that's enough to make him cautious."

Leah groaned. "What a mess. Fine. I'll have Ollie stay in Gavin's room tonight. I'm sure they'll both love that. And I take it you'll keep an eye on Vicky?"

Jack nodded. "I just hope we find Eric sooner rather than later." He looked down the gondola cables that disappeared into the darkness. "There's no other way off the mountain?"

"Not unless he can fly."

19

TENT TROUBLE

"Hello?" Jack called outside the tent. "Vicky?"

The ditzy diva peeled back the flap and popped her head out. "Seriously? Are you trying to make me wet my pants? People don't exactly drop by to visit out here. You scared the crap out of me."

"Sorry. I just wanted to let you know I'm setting up a tent out here. Eric never showed up at the gondola. Ollie looked for him for over an hour, and Leah wants to continue the search in the morning." Jack gave her a moment to process that.

"Wait. What? You're saying he's running around loose up here?"

"Yes. He's probably just blowing off steam someplace. But to be on the safe side, I'll be right outside your tent."

"I want to talk to Leah. This show has a responsibility to keep me safe."

"That's why I'm here."

"Great. Now I have nothing to worry about." Vicky scowled and yanked her tent flap closed.

It took Jack a few minutes to set up the tent and drive a few stakes partially into the frozen ground to secure it. He put it close enough to Vicky's door that if Eric decided to show up, he'd have to push past Jack's tent to get to her. He didn't blame Vicky for being upset. She had a lot to worry about. The cold alone, not to mention an angry jilted survivalist armed with ice-climbing tools, was enough to worry Jack, too. He threw in his sleeping bag and pack.

But he was hesitant to go inside. The cold, wind, and danger were fanning his testosterone into a slow burn, and he liked it. Surrounded by darkness, he listened to the howling wind and wanted to howl back. He felt like nature was throwing down a gauntlet—and he wanted to pick it up and run with it.

A big gust of wind smacked him in the face with a swirl of icy snow, and he finally decided he could contemplate the majesty of nature just as well from the tent, cocooned in his high-tech featherweight sleeping bag. But in this weather, you're either in or you're out, though he'd sleep in his clothes in case he did need to go outside again. He wasn't concerned about falling asleep; he was used to pulling double shifts.

Now the cold-weather drill: he got down on hands and knees to crawl in—his tent was much smaller than Vicky's, too low for him to stand.

He'd just gotten comfortable when he heard the zipper on Vicky's tent.

"Hi, there," said a sultry voice from outside.

Jack sat up as she pulled back his tent flap. "Are you okay?" he asked.

"I wanted to apologize." Vicky slid into his tent, pressing her body against his as she did.

"Don't worry about it. You had a right to be upset." Jack scooted over to the side. The tent was barely large enough for the both of them. "But I don't know if you can come in here. Doesn't that break the rules?"

Vicky smiled. "There are no cameras in here. No one will know."

"I will."

"You're not going to tattle on me, I hope." She tipped her head down and gave a doe-eyed, pleading gaze, then pouted her full lips, adding a sultry smolder.

"You're safe in your tent. I'll be right here."

Vicky stretched out on Jack's sleeping bag. She lay on her side and placed her head on her hand, her red hair draping down her arm. "But I'm still scared." Her finger softly traced an outline on the fabric. "You did come here to protect me, right?"

"No one can come into your tent without my knowing."

Vicky laid her head down on her arm. "But I don't want to be alone tonight."

"Look, there's no camera in here, but there's one in your tent, and I guarantee Leah's watching. If you're gone too long, she's going to get worried, and then she'll have to send someone else out here, in the middle of a snowstorm, to check on you."

Vicky's expression darkened. "What gives? You really want me to leave?" Judging by her shocked look, she didn't get turned away often.

"I just don't want to see you jeopardize your chance of winning five million dollars…" He stared her down until he could tell from her eyes that she knew she didn't have a snowball's chance in hell with him.

"Fine. Stay out here in the cold, but once I leave, I know who you'll be thinking about *all night long*." She yanked the tent flap open and left in a huff.

Jack listened to be sure Vicky entered her tent and zipped herself in, then snuggled into the sleeping bag she'd so thoughtfully warmed up for him. She'd been right about one thing: he *would* be thinking about someone all night long. He closed his eyes and pictured Alice, her green eyes with dancing gold flecks and the dimples that melted him every time she smiled.

She'd be furious with him for missing tonight's scheduled call. What with Eric's and then Vicky's shenanigans, he'd forgotten about the call until now, but hopefully Leah would fill in the general outlines so Alice wouldn't be too worried.

Jack wondered if she was as lonely without him as he was without her. Probably not. She was warm and safe; she had Lady and Mrs. Stevens and—

Kiku.

"Kiku and Alice together? What could go wrong?" he muttered.

20

COMPLICATED COLLEAGUES

In the passenger seat, watching the wipers struggle to clear the heavy snowflakes from the windshield, Alice let her mind go where her heart was. After Jack left, all she'd wanted was to be up on the mountain, helping him with the case, but now she desperately wanted Jack down here with her, helping her with the case of her lifetime. She closed her eyes to speak to the deep ache somewhere, everywhere inside her. Could you love someone so much it hurt?

I miss you, Jack. Can you hear me? She hadn't heard from Brian or Leah yesterday, but both Mrs. Stevens and Kiku had tried to allay her fears, citing the many things that could temporarily go wrong with communication up on the mountain, even without a storm brewing.

"Your landlady seems to enjoy the task you've given her," Kiku said, snapping Alice out of her fog. They were driving through the section of town that wasn't featured in the glossy Chamber of Commerce welcome packages—the no-tell motels, used-car lots, and pawnshops.

"Mrs. Stevens is awesome and really great company. She takes my mind off Jack being gone. I'd be climbing the walls without her." Alice felt guilty leaving her to watch film footage, but she couldn't pass up a chance to meet with the detective who'd worked her family's car accident. "I still can't believe that I didn't get to go on assignment with Jack. It's hard not seeing him, but not talking to him is killing me. I just can't help wondering what's going on up there. I worry… " Alice fidgeted in her seat. Kiku had heard it all before.

"Jack has military training, and even if he is no longer on the force, he is still a police officer inside. He can more than hold his own."

"It's hard not to worry about him. If Jack's comfort zone had a name, it would be In Harm's Way. It seems to be where he thrives." Alice pulled a pair of gloves from her coat pocket and began to put them on.

Kiku chuckled, her brown eyes sparkling from the street lights.

"What?"

"You and Jack are like-minded. Right now, I imagine his thoughts mirror yours and he is lying awake worried for you. It would seem you are already married. You think as one."

Alice resisted the urge to squeeze Kiku's hand. There was something about Kiku that put up an invisible barrier. It would be like petting a tiger. But she knew Kiku was trying to comfort her.

Kiku pulled up outside a small bar set between a diesel gas station and a used car lot filled with vehicles already blanketed by a fresh inch of snow.

Zipping up her winter coat, Alice glanced at Kiku's leather jacket. Fawn-brown and waist-length, it complemented her figure and went well with her jeans and boots—but it was awfully thin. "Is that jacket warm enough?"

"I do not wear the jacket for warmth," Kiku said with a smile.

I suppose if I had a body like hers, I wouldn't cover it up that much either. "Are you nervous?" Alice asked.

Kiku laughed. "I have to thank you, Alice—I *do* enjoy your sense of humor. But I am afraid you are projecting. Something like this does not make me nervous." Kiku tipped her chin toward the bar. "Meeting two detectives in a seedy bar elicits quite different emotions."

Alice studied Kiku. She was only in her mid-twenties, and no wrinkles lined her face, but there was something about her that seemed ancient. As Alice looked into Kiku's brown eyes, she wondered what they might have seen.

"You aren't nervous at all? I'm ready to leap out of my skin."

"I am not concerned. It is true that Detective Clark knows something about me. But he trusts Jack. And I trust myself."

Alice exhaled. "I guess I was just worried that you were a wanted criminal or something."

"Did I say I wasn't?"

Alice sat there waiting for some sign that Kiku was joking, but it became clear she wasn't. *Oh, great...*

Alice jumped at the knock on her window. Detective Clark stood outside the car. After they had exchanged greetings, Clark briefed them.

"Ladies, I thought it was best if I meet you out here, then go in with you and make introductions. I asked him to review the file, but he didn't know I'd be bringing you. Joe was a good detective—had a memory like a steel trap—but he's had a hard time leaving it behind. Maybe he remembers too much. Jittery, you know?"

"Thank you for reaching out to him on my behalf," Alice said.

"Happy to help. But I might have picked a bad time to stop carrying my gun." He gestured to the bar. "This used to be a pretty rough place back in the day."

"I am sure we will be fine," Kiku said. "Shall we, Detective?"

A man exited the bar, fumbling with his keys. When he saw Kiku, his eyes traveled up and down her body. He stumbled down the stairs and managed not to fall only by grabbing the railing with both hands.

Kiku winked at Alice.

Clark's laugh drifted off as they entered the bar. It didn't feel like the kind of place where good cheer or laughter were welcome. From the worn wood floor to the ebony bar, all of the furnishings were dark. The oak paneling on the walls seemed to soak up the few dim lights.

To Alice, the men appeared just as unwelcoming. A group of five big guys in matching blue-and-white shirts surrounded a table on the right near the fire exit, and two more sat at the bar. None were the kind of man she'd want to run into in a well-lit public place, much less a dark and seedy bar. She wished she'd taken the Taser out of her purse and put it in her pocket so it was more accessible—like Jack had taught her.

"There's Joe." Clark headed for a table in the corner.

An older man leaned heavily on his elbows, staring at the beer bottle and empty shot glass in front of him.

"Joe." Clark held out his hand.

Bloodshot blue eyes searched Clark's face and slowly softened in recognition.

"Derrick. Good to see you. Have a seat." Joe didn't stand or extend his hand but just nodded to the chair across from his and ran a trembling hand over his stubbly chin. His drawn complexion and the whites of his eyes had a yellowish hue, and Alice didn't think it was just because of the dim lighting.

Clark introduced Alice and Kiku as friends, and they settled around the table.

Alice tried not to make a face as she noticed the contrast in the way she and Kiku sat down. Alice had just flopped into the chair, while Kiku had displayed a consummate grace of movement. Always elegant, even in the simple act of sitting.

"Kiku?" Joe asked. "Like the flower?"

Kiku nodded.

"My ex-wife loved them. I couldn't stand them. They stink; made my nose itch."

Alice felt her lip curl slightly at the man's brusque manner, but once again she noted the difference between her reaction and Kiku's. Kiku was the one who'd been insulted, but you'd never know it. Her face was a mask, while Alice's every emotion was written on her face.

Clark gently defused the tension. "Have you had a chance to look at the police file on the fatal car accident in Westford?" Clark asked.

"Yeah, and besides, I remember. That's not something you could see and ever forget." Joe shook his head like he was trying to erase a picture from an Etch A Sketch screen. "What are you drinking?" He held up his hand and a bored-looking bartender strode over.

"Draft beer for me," Clark said to the bartender.

"For me as well, please," Kiku said.

Alice shook her head. "I'm all set, thanks." She and alcohol didn't mix well, and the last thing she wanted was to blow a chance to get information about her family's accident.

"Draft with a whiskey chaser," said Joe.

The bartender walked off, and Joe put his hands flat on the table and looked at Clark. "I've been off the job a long time. Why are you asking me about this now?"

"This is Alice Campbell," Clark replied.

Joe blinked a few times as he studied Alice's face. "The little girl who lived?"

Alice's throat tightened, but she nodded. A wave of fear washed over her. She'd spent years trying to forget about that night, and now the thought of stirring up those sleeping memories was making her stomach flip.

"I need to know what happened," she said quietly, again wishing that Jack was with her.

Joe picked up the empty beer bottle and held it to his lips. Like a parched man in the desert, he let the last drop trickle down the glass and fall on his tongue. "Hold on a second."

They waited until the bartender came back with three beer mugs in one hand and a whiskey shot in the other. He set the shot down first, and Joe threw it back before the beers even touched the table.

"I'll cover his tab," Clark said.

The bartender nodded and left.

"Are you trying to force me to help you, Derrick?" Joe asked.

Clark's jaw flexed. "No. I thought if I picked up your tab, you wouldn't be as offended when I say that beer should be your last tonight."

Joe rubbed his chin and wobbled in his seat. "It is. My ride's on the way. Lost my license again."

"Then the clock is ticking," Kiku said. "Will you assist us?"

Joe's yellow eyes tried to focus on Alice's. He leaned closer, and the reek of whiskey, stale cigarettes, and beer wafted across the table. "Finding out what happened won't bring your family back or give you any peace." He leaned back and looked at Clark. "You know that. I know that."

"This isn't the same thing at all, Joe," Clark said.

Alice opened her mouth to speak, but Kiku's boot pressing against her sneaker cut her off. With a subtle narrowing of her eyes, Kiku signaled her to be quiet.

They waited for Clark to elaborate, but he and Joe just stared at one another. Joe looked away first and reached for his beer.

"Derrick's talking about old cases," Joe said after a long swallow. "My first homicide and my last." His bloodshot, yellowed eyes seemed to stare past Alice. She'd seen the look before. He was living in a constant nightmare, unable to shake the ghosts of his past. "The first murder case I was assigned, I solved. I had the guy dead to rights, but it got pleaded down to manslaughter. Man. Slaughter." He tapped his glass against the table as he said each word. "You ever been to a slaughterhouse? Tell me how *slaughtering* a *man* should be a lesser sentence?"

He downed half the beer in three long gulps. "The victim was a nurse and a mother. Her boyfriend killed her, but he let their daughter live. The guy served twenty years, and when he got out, the little girl tracked him down. She needed answers. She thought it would bring her some peace, give her some closure. She just wanted to ask him one question. *Why?*"

"What did he tell her?" Alice asked, hanging on Joe's every word.

"Nothing. He slit her throat. He blamed her for testifying against him. Putting him away again was my last case. Bookends that sum up the meaning of all I did in my career. Much ado about nothing."

Kiku looked at Alice, urging her on.

"I need to know," Alice said, bracing herself for the information to come.

Joe shook his head. "Leave it alone. You might as well ask the tornado why."

"Unlike Job and that little girl you spoke of," Kiku said, "Alice does not want to know why. *Who?* is the question to which she needs an answer. And you may be able to help."

Joe eyed Kiku. "You know your Bible. Job was sitting there after he lost everything and God showed up as the whirlwind." He pointed a trembling finger at Alice. "What do you think that story means?"

Alice felt the prickle of tears and looked down so the men wouldn't see—it was impossible to hide anything from Kiku. "Bad things happen to good people."

"Yes." Joe dropped his hand onto the table with a loud thump. "And bad men are usually the cause."

"And they must be stopped," Kiku added imperiously. "That is how you and

Detective Clark lived. You are detectives. You stop bad men."

"Please, I need your help," Alice said, at last having to resort to drying her eyes with a cocktail napkin.

"It was over fourteen years ago," Joe said. "There's no way a DA will touch the case without a confession. Even if you did find the guy, there's nothing you can do to him now."

"I am not bound by the same limits as you, Detective." Kiku's lips pulled back in a slow smile. Her long canines and sharp features produced a grin that made Alice shiver. "When I find the man, I will deal with him in my own way."

Joe glanced at Clark and then studied Kiku. He leaned closer, his sickly eyes searching hers. He didn't stare for long. He took another sip of beer and nodded. "I don't know how much help I can even be. I didn't really work the case. I only had it for a day before it got bumped up."

"Can you run through what you remember?" Clark asked.

"I think you're opening Pandora's box, but…" Joe held his beer with both hands and spoke directly to Alice. "How much do you remember about the accident?"

"Nothing." Alice twisted the cocktail napkin in her hands and her knee began to bounce under the table. Kiku shot her a glance that intimidated and strengthened her at the same time. "I woke up in the hospital. I think… we were happy, tired from the sun. I fell asleep in the backseat."

"I got on the scene after you were taken away in the ambulance. The responding officer said you were in shock when he got there. When he reached the car, he didn't think anyone had survived. The car was crushed and the truck, a dump truck, was stuck on top of it. The driver of the truck was long gone."

Alice looked up, waiting to hear her lost story, but almost crying out, *"Stop! Don't tell me!"*

"The officer heard a soft voice coming from the backseat area. You were pinned to the floor in the wreckage."

Singing a lullaby. I thought everybody was asleep.

She dug her fingernails into her palms and fought the tears. For the first time, that memory came to her, as if it had been lurking there all along. The thinnest sliver of a memory… and it pierced her soul like a dagger. She was singing and stroking her brother Andrew's blond curls. They were wet, as if her mother had just taken him out of the bath.

"I interviewed you later that night at the hospital," Joe was saying, but Alice barely heard him. He sounded far away. Her chest felt heavy, like someone was pushing down on it. Each breath felt like a struggle.

"You didn't remember anything then, either. The doctors said you might later, but if you haven't by now…" Joe shrugged. "Your parents were heading home on a back road. There's nothing out there but a trailer park and a convenience store that closed down."

"Why was a detective called to a car accident?" Kiku asked, giving Alice a minute to regroup.

"Multiple fatalities, and the other driver had fled the scene. We didn't know the truck was stolen until the next morning, when A.R. Construction reported it missing. It was a dump truck loaded with rocks, from their site a mile down the road. It completely crushed the car."

Alice's mind reeled, like she'd been hit in the head. Her heart hurt and her temples throbbed. *Focus on what's in front of you.* Aunt Haddie, the foster mother who raised her, had taught her that trick, and she used it now, staring at a stain on the table and forcing herself to focus on the words being spoken.

"Were there any witnesses?" Clark asked.

"None we can check now. An old guy lived in a little trailer down the road. He's dead now. He heard the crash, went outside, and saw a motorcycle rider checking on the car. Then he went back inside and called it in."

"He didn't get any description of the man or the motorcycle?"

"He saw the rider on foot; he didn't see the bike."

Clark looked like he'd smelled something bad. "How did he know the man checking on the car was a motorcycle rider if he didn't see a motorcycle?"

"Because the guy was wearing a motorcycle helmet." Joe finished his beer.

"No other witnesses?" Clark asked.

"None that came forward. And we didn't have cameras all around back then. An earlier patrolman noted a dark four-door sedan parked to the side of the closed convenience store. He was going to check it out when he swung back on his loop. The sedan was gone when the responding officer got on scene. I figured whoever crashed the truck might have stolen the car, too, to make their escape."

Clark's index finger tapped the table like he was sending Morse code. "Anyone ever report a stolen car matching that description?"

"Not that I heard. So you gotta figure it isn't connected to the crash."

"Did you find anything in the cab of the truck?" Alice asked.

"Nope. Clean."

"Hey, Joe!" the bartender called out. "Your taxi's here."

Wait! I have a lot more questions!

Joe reached toward the back of his chair and fumbled for his coat. "You're getting my tab, right?"

"I've got it. I'll give you a lift home, too," Clark said.

"I have more questions," Alice heard herself say.

Joe shook his head, planted one hand on the table to stabilize his swaying, and picked up his beer with the other. He gazed forlornly at the empty glass but still tipped it to his lips. "I told you everything I know. Why keep rehashing it?" He looked at Alice. "If you want my opinion, I'd leave it alone. Why torture yourself?"

Alice's fist crushed the napkin in her hand. *I'm tortured by this every single day and can't even escape it in my sleep. I can't leave it alone.*

Joe set the glass down, misjudging the height of the table by an inch. The glass bounced once and started to fall to the floor, but Kiku's arm shot out. She caught it by the handle and set it down.

"One last question, if I may," she said. "Who was the case reassigned to?"

Joe grabbed the seat back for support. "Feds took it. Organized crime unit. Probably 'cause the truck was stolen from A.R. Construction. There were always whispers they were mobbed up."

He gave them all a loose wave and staggered for the door. "Thanks for the drink, Detective." He left without looking back.

A gloomy silence settled around the table, which Clark finally broke, muttering, "There but for the grace of God go I."

"Yours is a hard profession, Detective," Kiku said. "You cannot unsee what you have seen."

Clark pushed his unfinished beer away. "I've got a friend in the Bureau. I'll reach out to him. If the FBI was investigating A.R. Construction, it doesn't make much sense they'd tip their hand over a stolen truck."

Kiku nodded in agreement.

Alice stared at Joe's empty shot glasses. She wasn't a drinker, but for a moment, the thought of getting blind drunk flashed through her head. If it offered an alternative to reality, she was all for it. Her temples throbbed with every heartbeat. What she really needed was aspirin and the comfort of Jack Stratton, not Daniel's.

The bartender came over. "Total is fifty-seven dollars."

"Keep the change." Kiku handed him four twenties and made a discreet signal to Clark to let her have her way.

"I would have gotten that," Clark said.

"I know." Kiku crossed her legs.

"Hey!" A beefy man in jeans and a blue-and-white shirt approached their table. "That old drunk called you 'Detective.' I thought I recognized you. You Detective Clark?"

Four other men in similar blue-and-white shirts came to stand behind the first.

Alice cast a nervous glance at Kiku, who sat calmly and sipped her beer.

Clark stood. "I am."

The man leaned closer to Clark and snarled, "You sent my father to prison for life, you stinkin' pig."

Alice held her purse under the table and quietly unzipped it.

Clark faced the men as calmly as if he were ordering a sandwich. A lifetime of dealing with criminals showed in his demeanor; his voice and hands remained steady. "Technically, your father's crimes landed him in prison. I only shined a light on them."

The guy's beefy face was pinched as he played back what Clark had said and got to the punch line. Then he shook his head and jerked his thumb toward the door. "Outside, old man."

"Five-on-one is very unfair odds." Kiku picked up one of Joe's empty shot glasses. "I am assuming your friends will back you up?"

"He arrested Frank and Tim's old man, too."

"And my mom," a shorter guy in the back added.

"You guys aren't stupid enough to beat up an old cop." Clark looked at Kiku and Alice and tilted his head, trying to signal to them to move to safety. The women exchanged a look and remained where they were, watching and waiting.

The designated spokesperson pointed at Clark and called over to the bartender. "Hey, Victor! This guy drank a lot of beers then started picking fights, right?"

"He sure did." The bartender's bored expression had changed to a creepy grin that reminded Alice of a brat burning insects with a magnifying glass. "He started it."

Alice wrapped her fingers around her little Taser. She'd only used it once. Jack had promised to give her another lesson, but hadn't had a chance. Judging from the way the drunk vigilantes were looking at Clark, she was about to learn real fast.

Kiku smiled and stepped forward, holding a shot glass in her left hand and her beer with her right. "Would you be so kind as to hold this, please?" She handed the beer to a guy with a big nose. "This is for you"—to the beefy guy. "Catch."

Kiku tossed the shot glass into the air, high over his head. When he looked up, tipping his head back and stretching out his throat, Kiku slammed the side of her hand into his vulnerable windpipe.

The odds turned out to be quite a bit better than five-to-one. While the first guy was gagging and dropping to his knees, Kiku caught the shot glass and slammed it on the bridge of the second man's nose, the one holding her beer. As he tumbled backward, Kiku's leg snapped out, catching the third man solidly in the groin and lifting him an inch off the ground.

The fourth man stepped forward with his fist pulled back, met Clark's solid right cross with the base of his jaw, and dropped to the floor in a heap.

As the fifth guy reached for his knife, Alice ripped out her Taser and fired. The man shrieked and arched his back, dropping the knife.

While Clark was kicking his assailant's weapon across the room, Kiku leapt over the bar. She snagged a hunk of the bartender's greasy hair and slammed his face against the beer taps. The baseball bat fell from his limp hands and rattled on the floor, followed by a couple of teeth pinging down the wood bar as she bounced his head against it.

Kiku exhaled slowly. "I expected a shotgun." She dragged the man off the bar and let him fall to the floor, then walked back around to the front of the bar, where the beefy guy was making an effort to get to his knees, and knocked him out with a punch to the base of his skull.

"Are you okay, Detective?" she asked.

Clark gazed around the room and flexed his right hand. "Now I know why Stratton thinks so highly of your abilities."

Kiku smiled. "I am sure you were more than capable of handling the situation without my intrusion, but I thought I should defuse it before it escalated."

Clark arched his eyebrow, looking at the men groaning on the floor among the Taser confetti. "So that's... defusing."

"What do we do now?" Alice asked as she stuffed the Taser back in her purse.

"I should call it in," Clark said. "It will dissuade them from retribution in the future."

Kiku said, "You'll need to wait with him, Alice."

Alice grimaced, but Kiku was right; she needed to stay—and Kiku couldn't be found here.

"What do I say about you?" Clark asked.

"The truth. You don't know me. You offered to buy me a drink, and we were having a lovely time when these men came up and tried to assault me." Kiku picked up her purse. "I would recommend not pressing charges and only having the incident noted." Kiku walked to the door. "I trust you will give Alice a lift home?"

"Of course. And thanks." Clark nodded and proceeded to call the police.

"Wait," Alice called, stepping over one of the men, but Kiku shook her head.

"There is no time. We can discuss what we have learned back at your apartment. I will stop by later." Kiku hurried outside.

Alice stood in the doorway and watched her go. Kiku reached the car as sirens wailed in the distance, coming closer, and pulled out of the rear exit of the parking lot just as the police cruiser zoomed in at the front, lights flashing.

How Alice wished it were Jack coming to get her, so handsome in his uniform, and she saw herself running out and throwing her arms around him, nuzzling her head into his strong, hard chest...

Detective Clark put a hand on her shoulder and gave her a wink. "I think it might be best if you let me do most of the talking."

21

WALKIE-TALKIE TROUBLE

Jack unzipped the flap a bit and peered out of the tent. The night had paled, revealing a morning sky dotted with dark clouds.

He covered his earpiece with a gloved hand and cupped the other hand in front of his mouth. "Leah, come in. Can you hear me?" Jack had no idea if the earpieces were constantly monitoring or not, but he was hoping Leah was listening now. She had checked in with him a little after midnight, but the conversation had dissolved into static. Jack had tried a few times that morning to reach her but had gotten no response.

The earpiece buzzed in his ear, and Leah's voice broke through the static. "Jack. Come in. Jack, can you hear me?"

"This is Jack."

"Still no"—static cut her off—"you two should head back... the lodge. We'll—" The speaker buzzed and crackled, followed by silence as the line went dead.

Jack flipped his tent flap open, knocking a small pile of snow off the tent in the process. Large flakes swirled around both tents. A blast of frigid air shot down the slope and whipped the icy snow against his cheeks.

"Sun's up. Leah wants us to head back. How long do you need to get ready?" Jack called out.

Vicky's mumbling voice came from inside her tent. "Fifteen minutes."

Jack gathered his gear and rolled up his pack, then waited outside for Vicky. He was eager to get back to the lodge and was glad when Vicky's tent flap unzipped after only a few minutes had passed.

She stepped out, tilted her head back, and squinted, her eyes traveling back and forth across the sky as if she were reading. "I'm going to go talk with Leah." She reached back into the tent and grabbed her pack. "I've got a feeling it's going to get really windy."

Jack pulled out the GPS Leah had given him.

"You don't need that," Vicky said. "I know the way back. And the trail's marked well enough."

Jack thought, not for the first time, that Vicky was a rare bird. A glamorous knockout with stellar survival skills—and a fierce competitor, too. Jack had learned a long time ago that people are not always as they appeared. Kiku came to mind.

Jack stuffed the GPS in his jacket. "How'd you sleep?"

"Like a baby. Did you toss and turn thinking about me all night?" She smiled as she shouldered her backpack.

"No, I spent my night guarding your tent."

Vicky's snarky smirk vanished. "You didn't need to do that."

"You're welcome."

"I didn't say thank you."

"I know. But I figured that was the closest you'd come."

Jack started walking, and Vicky hurried to catch up. They hiked for several minutes before Vicky muttered a "Thank you" that was almost lost in the wind.

Jack nodded.

The sheer rocky slope back to the lodge was now covered in fresh snow. The going was slippery and slow. Jack had to feel his footing with each step.

"I think you must be more of a runner or a swimmer than a climber," Vicky said as she followed after him.

"Why do you say that?"

"Your butt. Most guys who climb have thick calves and thighs, and big, wide butts. You've got a tight little butt."

Jack opened and closed his mouth a couple of times before finally saying, "I jog."

"I knew it. I bet you have a six-pack, too?"

Jack cleared his throat. "I think one of those storms decided to switch direction. The temperature's really dropping."

"Funny, I thought the temperature was rising. Are you not comfortable with your body?"

"I'm comfortable with it. I'm just not comfortable discussing my abs or the shape of my butt with you." They had reached a short, steep slope they needed to climb, and Jack found a handhold and pulled himself up.

"I'd prefer not to *talk* about it either." She put her hand on his butt and squeezed. "I'm more hands-on."

"Keep your hands to yourself," Jack said, hoisting himself out of her reach.

"If a man did that, he'd be called assertive."

"What world are you living in? If a guy grabs your butt, he's called a creep. It's not just uncool, it's illegal. And, for the record, I'm engaged."

Vicky climbed up and stood, staring at Jack. "Okay, but also for the record, I know it's awful to be touched when you don't want to be. I'm sorry."

He hadn't expected a mea culpa. She wasn't just unusual, she was unpredictable. Maybe a good quality in her line of work, but not so much in his.

Leah's voice crackled over his earpiece. "This must not be working right. I thought I just heard *Vicky* apologize."

Jack sheltered his mic from the wind with his glove. "Can you hear me?"

"Yes. We've been trying to reach you. I need you both to come back to the lodge. There's a… here. I'm hav—" Static filled his earpiece.

"Big Brother is always watching," Vicky said, pointing at the red glow of a camera mounted to a post. "Now, *that's* creepy."

22

THE TWO-HEADED BEAST

Jack and Vicky crested the ridge that sloped down to the lodge. Four tents, in the four contest colors, had been set up directly in front of the building.

"What are those for?" Vicky asked.

Jack shrugged. "Don't know. They weren't there when I left."

They crunched through the last few yards of deep snow and were met by Leah walking out of the lodge, snow swirling around her.

Vicky's demeanor instantly changed. Gone was the flirty survivalist, and back was the fierce woman you wouldn't want to cross. "Ryan promised me that Eric would be *gone*," she snapped at Leah. "I'm not putting up with that psycho lurking around on this mountain. Have you found him yet?"

"He hasn't shown up, but he will," Leah said. "Either way, it doesn't matter, because we're keeping you close. We've set up tents for the contestants right next to the lodge. All of you will ride out the blizzard here. She turned to Vicky. "You're in the green tent. No contestants are allowed in the lodge."

"Blizzard?" Vicky said. "I thought the storms were supposed to miss us."

"The forecasters were dead wrong. Both storms changed direction, and they're both heading our way. They're calling it the two-headed beast. Two storms slamming together and making the mother of all blizzards." Leah leveled her gaze at Jack. "And guess where the epicenter is?" She pointed at her feet.

"But what about all my gear?" Vicky asked.

"You know the rules: you carry everything you need to survive at all times. I assume that's why you brought your pack. The other contestants are being told no more than you were: that I want them to come back here."

"But they don't have to worry about some psycho roaming the mountain, looking for them," Vicky grumbled.

"We're doing everything we can to locate Eric, and to keep things going. I'm sorry that you actually have to do some *work* like everybody else here, but I'm going to ask you to go over to the green tent or leave the contest."

Jack held his breath, waiting to hear—or see—what Vicky's reaction might be, but she just spun on her heel and stomped over to the green tent.

"Any sign of Eric last night?" Jack asked.

Leah looked haggard, putting her back to the wind. "No. The camera feed inside his tent cut out at nine."

"Did Harvey see anything before he lost the video?" Jack asked.

Leah shook her head. "No, something hit the camera from behind. It's possible his tent collapsed in the wind, or maybe he cooled down, returned to his tent, and took his frustration out on the camera."

"Do you want me to go check it out?" Jack asked.

She shook her head wearily. "No, Abe is getting Chiri; I've already asked him to check on it on the way back."

"I didn't see anyone last night. What about your idea of using the drone to look for him?"

"Grounded because of the wind."

"I still think you're taking a risk leaving her outside with Eric roaming around."

"Well, I can't do better for Vicky's safety than having them camp on our doorstep. Personally, I think Eric's just trying to extend his fifteen minutes of fame. Once the cameras start rolling, he'll show up, make a big scene, and then leave for good."

Jack searched Leah's brown eyes. As a policeman, he had gotten used to people lying to his face, and something didn't ring true. "Are you saying you *think* Eric will do that, or you're *sure* he will?"

Leah's eyebrows rose, and her voice dropped. "Are you accusing me of staging Eric's disappearance?"

"I've seen some collusion on your show, so yes, I'm asking. Are you or is anyone else on your staff working with Eric to pull off a dramatic scene? Is this whole thing— his disappearance and moving the contestants closer—a big setup?"

Leah gave him a look that said it was beneath her dignity even to answer such a question. Instead she said, "I spoke with Gavin. He said he 'found' the blue tile."

"Shocking." Jack gritted his teeth. "I told you to wait to confront him about that."

Leah bristled. "*You* work for *me*." She jabbed a finger at Jack's chest.

He backed away, in a way that made it clear he was not backing down but digging his heels in. "I work for McAlister Insurance. And let me remind you of the situation. I make one call and inform Brian that in my opinion this production is unsafe, and he pulls the policy." He called on the stone-munching voice and pit-bull stance of Tom Ricketts, a drill sergeant he and Chandler had learned to imitate perfectly— during their many hours of punishment runs and push-ups for him. It usually got good results, and this was no exception.

Leah clenched her fists. "You'd really shut us down? You—"

"All I'm doing is asking, for the third time, is the whole thing with Eric staged?"

Leah paused, then loosened her fists and let out a slow, controlled breath. "No. This is all Eric's doing."

Still, he had the impression that she wasn't exactly upset about the idea of filming some sort of dramatic showdown between contestants.

She changed the subject again. "Is there a possibility that Gavin's telling the truth about finding the tile? He swore up and down that's what happened. He was convincing."

"Of course there's a possibility. That's why I wanted you to wait."

Leah snapped an icicle off the railing and tapped it against the metal, breaking it into a hundred little chunks.

He tried to establish eye contact again. "I think Gavin is sleeping with Vicky. I also think Gavin took the blue tile so Vicky would get the easiest route. But I can't be a hundred percent sure, and I can't prove it. The blue tile was in the basket when I gave it to Ryan. Ryan handed the basket to Gavin."

"Now you're accusing my *director* of fixing the contest?"

"What I'm saying is, *if* anyone fixed the contest, it can only be Ryan or Gavin. They both knew Vicky was drawing last, and both of them had an opportunity to take the blue tile out."

Leah pinched the bridge of her nose, as if easing a migraine. "All right, let's back-burner this for now. The radio is barely working with the storm coming in, and it's getting worse, so I've sent Ollie out to make sure Frida comes in, and Abe is getting Chiri. That leaves you to go bring in Cornelius. His camp is on the south side, the green trail. The coordinates are in your GPS."

"I'll go right now."

"You need to hurry. The storm to the south is coming closer than expected. Things are going to start to get really bad."

* * *

Jack opened the tent flap, and a pungent mix of odors hit him. Cornelius sat cross-legged in the back of the tent, a bowl in front of him. Plants and grasses hung from the ceiling, but whatever the mountain man was eating seemed to be the source of the stench.

"I didn't expect company. It's almost gone, but you're welcome to some fresh stew." Cornelius held out the bowl.

Jack declined, while trying to breathe through his mouth. "Leah needs to speak with all the contestants."

"About the blizzard?"

"You know about that?"

Cornelius chuckled. "The barometric pressure's dropping like a rock and the temperature has come up a bit. Plus, my nose is runnin'. Sure signs precipitation's moving in. You can feel it. The storm's heading this way. It's gonna get sloppy bad." He tipped the bowl to his lips, poured the remainder of the contents into his mouth, and gulped. "How 'bout I miss this little meetin'. I'm fine right here."

Jack shook his head. "Not an option. She ordered everyone to come to the lodge."

Cornelius leveled his spoon at Jack, his bushy eyebrows knitting together. "This isn't some kind of trick, is it?"

"No, sir."

"What about the others? Are they going?"

"Yes. Vicky's already there, and the others should be on their way. If you don't go, it could get you kicked out of the contest."

"Oh, hang on just a minute, I'm comin'." Cornelius wiped his bowl out with a rag and set it down. "I bet those yuppie babies are tuckin' us under their wing 'cause they're worried about a few flakes. Some survivalist show," he muttered. "Buncha pampered city folk pretendin' at livin' off the land." He grabbed his backpack and a walking stick. "But I ain't gonna get accused of breaking no rules. That money's mine."

23

A DELIBERATE ACT

Alice anxiously paced the floor, listening to the wind howl and shake the apartment's old windows. The weather stations were all reporting the same thing—they were calling it the two-headed beast. The storms had changed direction and were expected to converge in a monster blizzard. One channel had gone so far as to call it a thousand-year storm.

And the beast was heading straight toward Mount Minuit… and Jack.

Brian hadn't been able to get ahold of Leah since morning. He said the last thing he'd heard was that she'd ordered everyone back to the lodge, and they would all ride out the storm there. Lady raised her head when Alice's fist came down on the arm of the couch.

What kind of plan is that? She needed a better plan; one that got Jack safely off the mountain and down on the ground, riding out the storm with her.

She couldn't wait to tell him what she'd learned from Joe. And with this storm, who knew when she'd get through to him again. Alice thought about the threats against anyone on the mountain and wrapped her arms around herself.

I just want Jack home.

Lady raised her head and scrambled to her feet. A moment later, someone knocked on the door.

"Sit," Alice begged, trying to pull Lady away from the door. Lady whined and held her ground.

"Sit, Lady," Kiku commanded from the other side of the door.

Lady immediately stepped back and sat down.

"How do you do that?" Alice asked as she let Kiku in.

Kiku patted Lady's head. "One, Lady respects me. And two…" Kiku held up an enormous rope chew toy. "She likes me."

Lady grabbed the toy in her jaws, turned, and raced over to lie next to the couch.

Alice crossed her arms. "She *loves* me."

Kiku slipped off her jacket and held it out to Alice. "It's the respect part you need to work on. You're gentle with Lady, but you need to be firm also. That way, she'll love *and* respect you. The same method will work on Jack."

Kiku's thin smile made Alice blush.

Alice hung Kiku's damp jacket on a hook. "Has the snow picked up?"

"Not yet, but it is supposed to increase in intensity very soon. Are we alone?"

Alice nodded. "Mrs. Stevens took a break. She's coming back in half an hour."

Kiku walked over to the recliner and sat down. Lady got up, trotted over, and lay at Kiku's feet. "This will be brief. I need to speak with you regarding the meeting with Joe. Some things he said do not make sense."

Alice felt like the floor shifted a little. She grabbed the edge of the couch and nodded. "Go on."

Kiku rubbed Lady's broad back. "Why was the man wearing a motorcycle helmet?"

Alice's stomach felt like she had been on the Tilt-a-Whirl too long. She tasted acid in her mouth, but forced herself to picture the scene as Joe had described it. "I keep thinking... if it were me, and I witnessed an accident, I'd take my helmet off when I checked on the family. Why didn't he?"

"Right. And the police received only the one emergency call—from the old man. No call came in from this helmeted man."

"Do you think the motorcycle rider was involved?"

"I think the man *wearing the motorcycle helmet* was involved."

"Isn't that the same thing? Wait—" Alice's stomach went from churning to falling.

"No one reported actually seeing a motorcycle. It was assumed that there was one because of the man wearing the motorcycle helmet. And the witness didn't see anyone running away from the stolen truck. Only one man was seen. What if the man who stole the truck was the same man, wearing the motorcycle helmet?"

"Why? Instead of a mask? Unless..." Alice sank to the couch. Kiku's words hammered against her temples. "Are you saying..." She felt like she was going to throw up. "You're saying someone stole the truck and put on a motorcycle helmet because... because they *knew* they were going to hit my family's car... *on purpose!*"

Kiku nodded slowly. "And the sedan parked at the convenience store was the getaway car."

Alice shook her head. "No. That doesn't make any sense. Why would anyone want to hurt my family?" Alice hopped to her feet, wanting to scream. "This is crazy. How could anyone do such a thing?"

Kiku crossed her legs. Alice thought Kiku was rubbing her thumb and forefinger together, but between Kiku's fingers an old coin appeared and delicately traveled across her knuckles. It disappeared into her palm, then reappeared and made another pass over her hand before she spoke. "I think it was a professional hit."

A strange chuckle caught in Alice's throat. "That's ridiculous, Kiku. My father was a florist!"

"And your mother?"

"She helped him with the flowers. Just because an old friend said my mother traveled overseas doesn't make her a target for assassination." Alice scowled and just about spat the words from her mouth in anger.

"True. But the facts are pointing to a deliberate act," Kiku said calmly.

Alice wanted to deny that, but she couldn't. With all the facts laid out in her mind, she had to agree that someone intentionally hitting her family's car was a very real possibility. "Maybe it was a sicko. Are there other reasons why you think it was a hit?"

The coin in Kiku's hand stopped moving, and her gaze locked on Alice's. Her eyes were so dark they looked black. "Yes. Because it is a method of killing someone I would use."

All the cables on the Tilt-a-Whirl abruptly let loose, and Alice's stomach seemed to plunge down a hundred feet in a second.

Kiku's coin began moving again. "At the moment, what I am most interested to find out is what Detective Clark's friend at the FBI will give as the reason they took over the case from the local police department."

24

ON THE FRITZ

The snow was accumulating fast. Then there were the blasts of bitter wind that pelted Jack and Cornelius with icy pellets as they trudged along. To give credit where credit was due, the Appalachian mountain man was as spry as an Alpine billy goat and never seemed in doubt about the direction of the green trail, though there were no signs visible to Jack until they came right up on them. Visibility in general was so poor, they almost tripped on one of the tents in front of the lodge.

Cornelius punched Jack in the arm and crowed over the howling wind, "I knew it! Four little cribs! Like campin' in your folks' backyard. Disgustin'."

The front door opened, and Ollie peered out. "About time. You two take the scenic route?"

"That rented mule needs a whuppin'," Cornelius muttered.

"Did you see Abe or Chiri?" Ollie asked. "They're not back yet, and Harvey can't put eyes on them. Sun sets in a couple hours."

"We didn't see anyone," Jack said.

"So when's this talk?" Cornelius asked.

"Leah's going to address everyone in a little bit," Ollie said. "You're in the blue tent."

"Why, they all look white to me." *He's enjoying himself!* Jack thought enviously.

"The one on the end there." Ollie pointed.

The mountain man eyed Jack. "You coulda told me to bring some more grub. I knew they was gonna make us move." He stomped off, but he didn't really seem that upset. If anything, the old man's cheerful grousing seemed to energize him.

Jack and Ollie exchanged a *Whatcha gonna do* look and clomped the last few yards over the snow to the lodge. Inside, Bree was stretched out on one of the couches, reading a magazine, and Ollie sat down at the table as Jack went through the rituals of knocking the snow off his boots, hanging up his parka, and stowing his backpack.

"Hey, Ollie." Jack pointed. "There's Abe's backpack. You sure he's not back?"

Ollie shrugged. "I must've taken it by mistake when I went out."

"That's crap," Bree called over. "You took Abe's backpack and gear so that you wouldn't have to prep your own stuff. Abe knows exactly what you did. He had to prep your gear instead, and he's ticked. He's telling Leah."

"It was a joke." Ollie waved his hand dismissively.

"You took it by mistake, and it was a joke?" Sarcasm dripped from her voice. "Which story are you going with again?"

Ollie scowled.

Jack was glowering. "And by the way, if that was a joke… not funny at all."

"Is that Abe and Chiri?" Leah shouted from the top of the stairs.

"No, it's Jack. He came down with Cornelius," Ollie called up.

Leah appeared on the landing. "Jack, did you see Abe and Chiri?"

"No, sorry."

Leah kicked a baluster, causing the whole banister to shake. "They should have been back two hours ago." She locked eyes with Jack.

Jack shared the concern he saw in Leah's dark eyes. "I'll go out," Jack said, without hesitation.

"No, you won't." Leah shook her head. "Harvey's searching with the cameras."

"Visibility is awful—the cameras are useless in this," Ollie said. To Jack's intense annoyance, he added, "Let Jack go. It's not a hard climb. He can be back in an hour."

Gavin and Ryan strolled into the main hall in the midst of a conversation, interrupting Jack's fantasy of strangling Ollie. "That was in Dubai," Gavin was saying. "The shopkeeper had no idea how much it was *really* worth. I turned around and sold the piece for more money than that rube sees in a year!"

Ryan laughed loudly. But his smile faded when he looked up at Leah. "You look like something's wrong. Is there a problem with the cameras in the new tents?"

"We have a bigger issue. Abe's not back with Chiri. They're long overdue."

Gavin pointed at Jack. "You there. Don't just stand around. Go get the little fellow and the cameraman so we can get this show moving again."

"*You there?* My name's one syllable, Jack. Use it," Jack said, sounding a bit like Clint Eastwood.

Gavin took a step behind Ryan. Leah exhaled loudly. "We don't need to send anyone out there yet. For now, Ollie and Harvey can shoot a bunch of B-roll. Ryan, why don't you have Gavin record the audio and we'll lay it over footage of the temporary setup?"

Gavin looked horrified. "And not show my face?"

Ryan snapped his fingers. "Picture-in-picture. We'll do a close-up of your face and superimpose it in the corner of the screen."

"That's why you're the director." Gavin shot Leah a smug look and marched toward the kitchen. "I'll need some avocado first. An avocado a day keeps the wrinkles away."

Ryan, like a trained seal, laughed and clapped his hands at Gavin's attempt at wit.

Leah gestured Jack over, and said in a low voice, "I need to speak with you."

Jack followed her up the staircase and into an empty room—no furniture; bare walls. She shut the door, took a deep breath, and pulled a folded sheet of paper from her jacket. Her fingers trembled as she handed it to Jack. "I got another note."

"When?"

"This morning, when I woke up. At the foot of my bed. It factored into my decision to pull everyone close to the lodge."

First thing this morning? If she held that fact back, what else was she not telling him? Jack wasn't on the force anymore, but his internal police radar never turned off. "Why didn't you tell me when I came back with Vicky?"

"You were threatening to shut us down. But now…" Fear was evident in her voice. "I'm worried something may have happened to Abe and Chiri."

Jack unfolded the paper. The dark-red block letters were smeared but easy to read: *TOO LATE.* His throat clenched and his stomach tightened, but he forced his expression to remain neutral. Leah had never wanted to hear the truth before; why start now?

"Is that blood?" Leah's voice warbled, and she wrapped her arms around her own chest.

He remembered seeing something similar during a domestic violence case he'd worked. The husband had violated a restraining order, punching out the glass in the front door, and when he discovered his wife wasn't home, he wrote SEE YOU SOON in his own blood on the wall.

"Leah!" Ollie bellowed from downstairs. "You'd better get down here!"

Leah snatched the note and shoved it in her pocket, and she and Jack rushed out of the room and down the stairs. Harvey and Bree stood in the main hall, with Ollie holding open the front door as Chiri trudged in with Abe slung across his shoulders in a fireman's carry. The tall man's head and legs nearly touched the ground.

"His legs are broken," Chiri panted.

"Set him here," Ollie said. He swept everything from the table onto the floor with a crash.

Harvey and Ollie helped turn Abe over and lay him down gently on the table. His face was pale and splotchy. Suddenly, Abe screamed, his back arching and his white-knuckled hands grasping the table's edges. Then his scream abruptly stopped, like someone flicked a switch, and he passed out.

The sight of so much blood and the familiar sounds of the injured began to trigger Jack's PTSD. His heart began to race and his mouth went dry. *Focus. It's not Iraq. You're in charge.* He had to let the hot panic blast through him before he could embrace cold logic and focus on the emergency. "Bree! Get the med kit!" he ordered.

She ran off past Ryan and Gavin, who emerged from the kitchen.

"What exactly happened out there?" Jack asked Chiri.

"I was in my tent and heard someone scream. I went as far as the cliff but didn't see anyone. Then I heard it again. I found him lying in the snow halfway down the side of the cliff."

"We're going to need more than a med kit," Harvey said. "The right leg is a compound break. He's bleeding profusely."

Gavin stood in place, frozen, as green as the piece of avocado in his hand.

Leah pulled out her satellite phone. "Ryan, help Harvey stop the bleeding. Ollie, get the backboard. Chiri, I need you to keep an eye on the contestants. Don't let any of them in."

Ollie ran down the hallway. Harvey sent Ryan to get some scissors and dishcloths from the kitchen, and when he returned, began cutting Abe's pants off. Chiri went outside, looking utterly exhausted, and through the window Jack saw Frida meet him and the two speaking and gesturing.

Leah shook the sat phone and glared at it. "The phone isn't working," she hissed.

"Where's the backup?" Jack asked.

Leah shook her head. "With all the cutbacks—" Her hand balled into a fist. "We don't have a backup."

Abe's sudden scream cut her off. "Don't pull it! Don't pull it!" He shouted the words like his life depended on it.

Harvey was bent over Abe's mangled right leg, trying to remove his bloody boot, when Bree ran in with the med kit. Jack's last encounter with Harvey had revealed an unpleasant side to the man, but Harvey was at his best now—competent, caring, and completely on task. He began giving directives like the captain of a sinking ship.

"We need snow," Harvey said. "A lot of it. We need to pack his legs." He yanked some bandages from the med kit. Ollie had come in with the backboard, and Harvey told him, "Get a trash can or something from the kitchen. Anything that will hold snow. Load it up."

"I'm on it."

Harvey moved to the middle of the table. "Jack, get over here and hold Abe's shoulders. Ryan, make sure his legs don't move."

They worked furiously for the next fifteen minutes, making a splint and a tourniquet, handing Harvey the things he needed, and packing the right leg in ice. Finally, Harvey lifted his head and said, "There's no more we can do for now." He turned to Leah. "Both legs are badly broken, but his right leg is completely mangled. I hope I stopped the bleeding. He needs to get to a hospital."

"The sat phone's not working," Leah said.

"Do we have *any* equipment that's not on the fritz?" Ollie snapped.

Jack stared down at the blood on his hands and tightened them into fists to stop the tremor that was slowly building. "We need to take him down in the gondola. *Now.*"

"Ollie and Jack, get Abe on the backboard." Leah handed Harvey the phone. "You've done all you can for Abe. See if you can get this phone working."

"I'll try."

Jack grabbed the foot of the backboard while Ollie and Leah each grasped a handle at the head.

"Ryan, you're in charge until I get back."

Ryan, his eyes wide, the front of his shirt bloody from holding Abe's legs still, just nodded.

"I'm going with you," Bree said, and held Abe's hand while they walked outside.

The sting of snow only fueled Jack's resolve. He wondered again if he was cross-wired, somehow. Most people struggled to keep it together in a crisis, but for Jack, the more pressure he was under, the clearer he thought; the calmer he became. Once he navigated beyond the initial stage and stared down any potential PTSD, that is.

The worst part was poor Abe, awake again and moaning on the stretcher. They trudged to the gondola as quickly and smoothly as they could and set Abe down on the floor, then Leah sent Ollie back to the control house to operate the lift.

Bree knelt down beside Abe and squeezed his hand. His eyes fluttered open. "No. No. I can't leave. I can't. Leah?"

Leah leaned close to Abe's face. "We're taking you down to see a doctor, Abe."

"Please. I'll be all right. I need this job." Abe tried to sit up, but the straps held him in place. "Bring me back to the lodge." He seemed to know where he was but had no idea how badly he was hurt.

Bree stroked Abe's brow. "Sure thing, right after we get you checked out by a doctor."

"I'm fine..." Abe's voice was getting softer. "My carabiner broke."

Leah stiffened. "That's impossible. We use only steel carabiners."

"Broke in two," Abe mumbled. He closed his eyes. "I watched the pieces fall as I fell..."

Bree looked toward the control booth. "What's taking Ollie so long?"

"Jack, go check on him," Leah said.

Jack pulled back the door of the gondola and raced uphill to the cement shed that housed the controls. "Ollie, why aren't we moving?" He peered out the window that looked down the length of the cables, where they swooped into icy invisibility.

Ollie twisted the key in the control panel. "Something's wrong. It's not even clicking. There's no power."

"But the lights are working."

"The control panel is on a separate circuit." Ollie yanked open a panel on the wall, and his shoulders relaxed. "All right, it's just a blown fuse. I'll have you guys going in a minute."

He pulled out the old fuse and set it on a cabinet, next to an identical fuse covered in dust. Then he unlocked a nearby cabinet.

"Bloody hell! You've got to be kidding me." He pulled out two empty fuse boxes and tossed them at Jack's feet. "Out of fuses! Cheap bastards. *Now* what do we do?"

25

SOMETHING SPECIAL

Alice! I think I found something!"

Alice hurried into the bedroom with Lady prancing behind her.

Mrs. Stevens sat in front of the monitor, pointing a cookie at the screen. "What do you think about that?"

Alice looked at the paused video, a behind-the-scenes shot of the crew. Gavin was speaking to Ryan, while Ollie and Charlie were pulling equipment out of a bag.

"Look at Ollie's jacket." Mrs. Stevens waved her cookie back and forth, sending crumbs everywhere. Lady nosed around to lick up each tiny morsel like a furry vacuum cleaner.

Alice examined Ollie's crew jacket. It was blue, with two thick green stripes down the arm and a large gold *Planet Survival* logo on the front. "Is there something special about it?" she asked.

Mrs. Stevens' voice rose to an unusually high pitch. "That's not a *crew* jacket. It's *Gavin's* jacket!"

Alice grabbed the mouse and made the image zoom in. Gavin's blue jacket also had two green stripes and the gold logo.

Mrs. Stevens gave the remainder of her cookie to Lady, who snatched it and hurried out of the room.

"Cookies aren't good for her," Alice chided.

"*These* are. They have peanut butter for extra protein!" Mrs. Stevens innocently folded her empty hands in her lap. "Besides, it was just a *little* cookie."

Kiku wants me to be more firm; Mrs. Stevens wants me to be more lenient. Everyone seemed to have an opinion about Lady's upbringing. *Jack would side with Kiku and Lady would definitely side with Mrs. Stevens.* Alice smiled, realizing how very well loved their adopted Lady had become.

"Gavin's jacket does look the same as Ollie's. But they're both working on the show..."

"You don't understand, honey." Mrs. Stevens tapped the monitor. "Do you see the gold logo? It's a *host* jacket. The crew's logo is silver. Only the host has a gold one. Gavin made a big deal about there being only one host jacket. I didn't think two existed. Now look at this."

Mrs. Stevens rewound the footage until another shot of Ollie appeared. She paused it. "See?" She wiggled the mouse pointer up and down Ollie's arm. "*One* green stripe, and a silver logo."

Alice tapped her pen against her thigh as she thought. "So Ollie was wearing a regular crew jacket earlier in the day. Why would he change into a host jacket?"

26

LEAP OF FAITH

Outside the room where Abe was resting, Jack leaned against the wall, also trying to get some rest, in spite of the steadily growing pain signals looping between his brain and his heart. During his tour in Iraq, on many occasions he'd had to try to block out the screams of the wounded as fellow soldiers waited to be medevacked out, and now Abe's cries were added to the echoes of all those other men.

Jack and Ollie had carried Abe back to the lodge and set him up in his room at the end of the hall, at the opposite end of the building from Jack's room. The trip back had been hard on the injured man, and now Leah and Bree were trying to make him as comfortable as possible.

The door opened, and Leah slipped out.

"How is he?" Jack asked.

Leah shook her head. "Not good. He needs a doctor—badly. The only pain reliever we have up here is aspirin, and Harvey told us we can't give him that because it'll make him bleed more."

"Well, I hate to give you more bad news, but Harvey opened up your satellite phone and found the problem. The SIM card is cracked."

"Cracked? How does that happen?" Leah said in disbelief.

Jack looked away. He was wondering the same thing, among so many other questions that he hadn't even had time to ponder…

Abe's pack… the carabiner…

"Do you think someone broke it on purpose?" Leah's voice was halfway between a whisper and a sob. She was clearly freaked out.

In an effort to keep them calm and focused, Jack replied, "Whether someone tampered with it or not isn't our biggest concern. We need to get Abe off this mountain."

"Without those fuses or the satellite phone, we're out of options, Jack."

"I have a Plan B. The weather station. Wally must have a radio or satellite phone we can use. I'm going there now."

"That's a *good* plan. Let's go. I'll get a GPS and lights. It's pitch-black outside."

"I already got them from Ollie. I wasn't asking permission or extending an invitation. I was just letting you know."

Leah frowned. "And I'm not asking permission either. But I am going with you."

"No." Jack tipped his head toward the door. "You need to watch out for Abe."

They stood with eyes locked for a moment, each holding their ground.

"You may not work for me, but I still run things up here. Bree can take care of Abe. Besides, Wally may not like me, but he knows me."

* * *

The steel tower disappeared high into the darkness. Below it, the boxy cement building was surrounded by a chain-link fence. A light shone from a window beside the front door. As they trudged up the path next to the fence, they could hear the hum of the generator.

"Wally's not running out of power anytime soon." Leah jerked her thumb at the enormous propane tank.

"Let's just hope he has a radio." Jack shined his light up the tower, but the beam didn't come close to reaching the top. "If he does, you figure with a tower that big, we could reach Pluto."

Leah pounded on the metal door while icy snow plinked off Jack's goggles and gleamed in the beams of their flashlights. After a minute with no response, Jack reached out and tried the door handle—it was unlocked.

The main room looked more like a teenage boy's bedroom than the top-notch weather station Jack had envisioned. Workbenches covered with electronic equipment lined two walls. A couch piled with blankets had been shoved into a corner at an angle; a desk sat right in the middle, stacked with papers. A door on the left wall was open to a messy bathroom. Two mesh-covered windows bracketed a door on the back wall that revealed a metal balcony. The sole window, on the right-hand wall, was blocked by the propane tank outside.

"Wally?" Leah called again.

Jack poked his head into the small bathroom. "He's not here."

"But his radio is." Leah walked to the equipment beside the back door.

"Can you operate it?"

"I produce a survival show that goes to the most remote places on the planet. I've had to use string and tin cans to communicate. If we can get a signal, I can get through."

While Leah tried to get the radio working, Jack rifled through the equipment on the workbenches. "Wally may have a spare fuse for the gondola," Jack said.

"All the fuses are kept in the control booth at the platform," she answered absentmindedly while fiddling with dials and jiggled wires.

Jack moved aside some kind of barometer covered with dust. "In my dorm at college, the spare toilet paper was kept in the janitor's closet. But I still took a roll and kept it in my bedroom, just in case. If I was working on a mountain, I'd want to have a backup fuse, just in case."

"Good thinking." Leah adjusted a knob and spoke into the microphone. "Break. Break. Break."

Jack lifted a stack of papers and set them to the side. Underneath sat an old VCR with a tape sticking out.

"Break. Break. Break. Come in."

There was a picture on the wall of Mount Minuit, blanketed in snow. Jack paused, his eye caught by the brass plaque at the bottom of the frame: KANIEHTIIO.

Kaniehtiio. The name used in the first threatening letter. Snow Mountain.

He looked outside, trying somehow to comprehend the foe he was up against. Jack couldn't see much out the window besides the propane tank, falling snow, and the blinking yellow and green lights of the radio dials behind him, reflected in the glass.

"Break. Break. Break. Come in," Leah repeated. "Stupid radio! I'm not getting anything."

"Try another frequency?"

Leah shot him a look that let him know that was exactly what she'd been doing. She grabbed a three-ring binder and opened it up. Her finger traced down the page. "I've tried all these emergency frequencies. The storm must be"—she gasped—"oh, no way."

Jack heard hope, not despair. "What?"

She held up the binder. "This emergency manual has instructions for a PLB."

"What's a PLB?"

"A Personal Locator Beacon. It gives you a one-way connection to an emergency satellite. You press a button, and search and rescue shows up like the cavalry."

"This is a remote, *manned* weather station." A flash of hope surged through him. "If there are instructions here for a PLB—"

"Then there has to be one here!" A broad grin spread across Leah's face, and the blinking yellow lights from the radio sparkled in her eyes. "We need to find that PLB." She began frantically searching the desk.

In the window, the radio lights were blinking, yellow and green.

Green?

He peered out the window through the misty whiteness once more. The blinking green light wasn't a reflection in the glass—it was coming from *outside*. Strapped to the bottom of the enormous propane tank was an avalanche charge.

Its green light blinking on, off; on, off.

No, no, no...

Armed.

The breath caught in Jack's throat. He stepped away from the window, and the green light turned solid red.

"OUT!"

Jack ripped the back door open, grabbed Leah by the waist, lifted her right off her feet, and raced out onto the balcony.

"What are you doing?" Leah shrieked, struggling in his arms.

A ten-foot drop to a field below sloped gently down into darkness.

"Bomb!" Jack shouted. "Jump!"

He swung Leah over the railing. She shrieked again and grabbed for the railing but missed. Jack leapt over after her.

Leah swore as she hit the ground. Jack tucked and rolled and the snow absorbed most of the impact. He reached back, grabbed Leah by the hood of her jacket, and yanked her to her feet.

"Run! Avalanche charge!"

Leah finally understood. She lowered her head and they both dashed across the field. Fifty yards beyond, the slope ended at a line of rocks that dropped off steeply into the darkness below.

Leah's face contorted in fear. "Is this far enough?" she panted, looking back at the weather station.

Jack saw the angry red flash blink just before the roar of the explosion slammed into his chest. The impact knocked them both off their feet and sent a fireball a hundred yards into the air. Jack landed on his side, Leah on her back, her wide, blank eyes reflecting the glow of the fire. Jack reached over her, grabbed her shoulder, and jerked her onto her stomach.

There's more to come.

"Cover!" He tried to protect the back of her head with one hand, while covering his own head with his other hand. The echo of the explosion rumbled through the mountains, followed by another sound—soft thumps falling all around them as the debris blown into the night air dropped back to earth. Shards of metal and chunks of debris rained down on them like meteorites.

Then a whole section of the chain-link fence landed practically on top of them. Leah screamed and started kicking her feet. "I'm on fire!" she shrieked. Flames raced across the back of her jacket and Jack felt the heat on his arm.

Jack rolled her onto her back as she tugged wildly on the zipper.

The flames hissed and went out as they hit the snow. Leah scrambled to her feet, ripping the smoldering jacket off.

"Are you burned?"

Leah's mouth opened and closed. Her brown eyes searched Jack's face, but she didn't answer.

Jack examined her back, but her sweater was unmarked.

"What's that noise?" she yelled.

His ears were still ringing from the explosion, but he began to distinguish a different sound. He cocked his head. It sounded like the hinges of a giant metal door creaking open. Jack's eyes followed the flames as they leapt high into the night sky, where the enormous weather tower's metal beams glowed a hellish red. And something else was wrong.

The tower was leaning toward them.

Closer every second.

Jack grabbed Leah's wrist, turned back toward the cliff, and jumped, pulling her with him into the darkness below.

27

STUNTS, LIES, AND VIDEOTAPE

Each time the wind buffeted the window, Alice jumped in her chair and her heart sank through the floor. All she could think about was her Jack atop the mountain while the worst blizzard in a hundred years pounded the peak. Alice had known it would be a dangerous assignment but never dreamed it would be *this* dangerous.

Lady growled at the windows and moved protectively closer to Alice. The computer monitor displayed several different windows simultaneously. After each attack of wind, Alice began work again, her hands a blur as they fluttered between the keyboard and the mouse.

"Look at you go," Mrs. Stevens said as she came out of the bedroom, rubbing her tired eyes. "What are you up to?"

"I'm trying to get into the crew forum."

Mrs. Stevens stepped up behind Alice's chair. "The crew has its own forum?" Her eyes widened with excitement and she pressed her hands together like a child about to open a present.

"They used it to communicate in the off season. Ideas for contests, upcoming locations, things like that. And to keep each other updated about where they were. I want to see if Mack said anything about who he was climbing with in Germany."

Joel, the man who wrote the article about the accident had emailed Alice back, but he didn't have a name; his notes only said "climbing partner."

"Joel gave me the contact information of the search and rescue leader, but that guy is on vacation in the Bahamas. I even called the hotel where Mack was staying, in Garmisch-Partenkirchen. They said Mack had his own room and they had no information about an additional guest."

"Well, I don't mean to interrupt you, but I think I found something you should see."

Alice rubbed her bloodshot eyes, stood up, and stretched. She'd been at the computer for hours and was starting to feel the strain. It didn't comfort her the way it had before; cookies and insurance work were no longer enough to push aside her other worries. There'd been no word from Jack or Leah. Or from Brian, for that matter. She'd called several times, leaving voicemails, and finally, when she spoke to someone at the answering service, they told her the office was closed due to the weather emergency.

"Sure. Let's see what you've got."

Mrs. Stevens hurried into the other room and sat in front of the video monitor. "I was going through the footage looking for Ollie in the host jacket, and… well, there's something odd about Ollie's broken arm. The thing is, I just went through all the video of the challenge, and I just couldn't find any footage of him getting hurt."

"But he filed workplace accident paperwork on it," Alice said. "It was a fracture. He injured it during—I think it was the 'Over the Hill and Through the Dale' challenge."

Mrs. Stevens nodded excitedly.

"Did you check the footage a little before the challenge and after it? Maybe a couple of hours either way? He could have broken it taking down those gates."

Mrs. Stevens' red hair swayed up and down. "I did check. I even went through the next day. Besides Gavin taking a nasty tumble, nothing went wrong."

"What's this about Gavin?" Alice asked, pulling up a chair and sitting down beside her assistant researcher.

"I'll show you." Mrs. Stevens double-clicked to open a clip. "They were taping the show opening for the following day."

The video opened with Gavin sitting in a helicopter, yelling over the whirl of the blades. "Today's challenge is going to be unlike anything we've ever done before! Last week you watched our contestants going 'Over the Hill and Through the Dale,' and today it's 'Off to Grandma's House We Go'!"

The camera panned down a slope to the painted plywood façade of a German cottage at the end of the field. "The contestants must not only get down the slope, but they'll have to cross the open stretch of field to reach Grandma's. Looks easy, right? Not so fast. We've brought in a pack of Saint Bernards. Normally, these gentle giants play the role of rescue dogs, but today they're filling in for the wolves. If one of the dogs reaches a contestant before he or she reaches the cottage, that player is instantly eliminated. And you know the rules—if more than one contestant is eliminated in a challenge, it goes to a rescue vote. Who knows? Tonight may be the night that *no one* makes it!" Gavin pulled his goggles down over his eyes.

The view cut to a wide shot of the helicopter hovering over the ski slope, while Gavin scooted to the open door and dangled his skis over the side. Then he gave a thumbs-up to the pilot and jumped off.

"He's fearless!" Mrs. Stevens gushed.

Gavin kicked up a plume of snow as he landed and raced down the slope, the camera following him for about a minute. Then the tips of his skis caught on something as he slid over to avoid a clump of trees; he lurched forward and tumbled end over end, his legs gracelessly splayed, until his bindings popped, sending his skis flying.

Someone yelled "Cut!" and the view began jerking all around as the cameraman, along with everyone else, rushed over to Gavin. Gavin was sitting in the snow, cradling one arm, the pole strap still wrapped around his wrist. As the camera got closer, he made a slashing motion across his throat with his good arm and the video cut out.

Alice's foot bounced up and down in time with her pen, which she gently tapped on the desk. "Pull up the raw footage," she said.

"Well, that's another thing. There *is* no raw footage of this."

"Are you sure? The camera in the helicopter is a fixed camera. It would have kept rolling after Gavin put his goggles on. Legally, they had to provide the insurance company with *all* the footage."

"It cuts right there. There's no video after he puts his goggles on."

Alice stopped tapping the pen. "Rewind the video to right before Gavin wipes out, please."

Again they watched Gavin ski down the slope, tumble, land hard, and start a freefall slide. Someone off-camera called "Cut!" and the view started bouncing around.

"Pause there! Back up, okay, slowly… Stop there!"

Mrs. Stevens had stopped on a frame where the jerking camera had captured the crew running to Gavin—Charlie, Bree, Ollie, and Ryan.

Alice shook her head. "Zoom in on Ollie."

Mrs. Stevens' mouth dropped open. "Oh my goodness. That's not Ollie. It's *Gavin!*"

Alice nodded. Mrs. Stevens looked at Alice with raised eyebrows. "But how can he be in two places at once? He's…" Her voice trailed off as she realized the truth.

"That's right," said Alice. "So the person we just saw tumbling down the slope? That wasn't Gavin. It was Ollie."

28

SHELTER OR BUST

J ack and Leah dropped a dozen feet before they hit the ground below. Jack tucked, but he hit with such force that his jaw clacked against his bent knees. The icy snow had formed a slick crust, and he slid down the steep slope into the darkness at breakneck speed. He tried to stay on his back like he was riding a waterslide, but his boot caught soft snow and he started rolling.

Behind him, the weather tower toppling to the ground sounded like a fifty-car pileup, with metal shrieking as it smashed against rocks.

"*Leah!*" Jack shouted as he finally slid to a stop. He couldn't see much, but a huge cloud of snow puffed high into the air where the tower landed.

"Over here." Leah's voice sounded from above him on the slope.

Jack did a quick self-check. His ankle throbbed and his side burned, but it felt more like a scrape from the ice than something internal. His hat, gloves, and goggles were gone. He reached for his flashlight, but his pocket was empty. His radio was gone, too; the GPS remained. He powered it on, and the screen cast a faint glow.

If you're breathing, you'd better get back on your feet. Jack could picture his old drill sergeant standing over him and yelling at him to get up.

Jack forced himself to his feet. "Are you hurt? I'm coming to you!"

Leah limped down the slope. "I've got road rash on my back, but otherwise I'm fine." She wrapped her arms around her chest and shivered.

Jack unzipped his jacket. With the tower coming down on top of them, neither had given a thought to grabbing her burned jacket.

Leah shook her head. "Save the macho stuff. You need it."

"I'm wearing a thick sweater over another shirt. I'm not being macho, I'm being nice-o." He held the jacket out, still sweating profusely from the sheer adrenaline of the last few minutes. His body could take being unprotected, but his ears and face couldn't. They needed to get out of the cold—fast.

Leah took his parka and thanked him. The glow of the flames on top of the ridge revealed the fear in her eyes. "Wally wasn't there, right? Do you think he's okay?"

"I think Wally may be the one who tried to kill us."

"*Wally?* Why?" Leah stammered in disbelief.

"He had a picture of the mountain. The little brass plaque said 'Kaniehtiio.' Just like the first note you found."

"But why would Wally…" Her voice trailed off, then she answered her own question. "He's such a tree-hugging environmentalist. Wally hates us being on *his* mountain."

Jack nodded. "Maybe the charge on the propane tank was just a booby trap. Maybe there was something inside the weather station he didn't want us to find."

"What if he goes back to the lodge?"

Jack's fists tightened. "They're already on guard because of Eric—"

Leah grabbed Jack's arm. "You don't think Wally hurt Eric, do you? Or maybe Eric tried to get Wally and then came after us!"

"We could drive ourselves crazy with what-ifs. Right now, we need to get out of this wind. I lost my radio."

Leah swore. "Mine was in my jacket." She glared up at the fire. "There's no way we can climb back up."

"Going around would be a long hike, and crazy to even try in the dark." Jack scowled. "My flashlight's gone. I don't suppose you kept hold of yours?"

"*Everything* was in my jacket."

"Well, we can't stay here." Jack looked down at his GPS and pressed a couple of buttons. "But…" He smiled. "I think I just found us a hotel for the evening."

29

A BIG DEAL

He was regretting loaning Leah his parka, but it probably saved her life. The harsh wind gusting was brutally cold, chilling him to the bone. His hands shook uncontrollably as he tried to open the flap of the tent. Leah reached past him, shook the snow off the top, and pulled the flap aside.

"Get into the sleeping bag," she said.

Jack didn't argue. His upper body felt like it was on fire, and his teeth clacked like a wind-up toy. He took off his boots, handed Leah the GPS, and climbed into the bag.

She zipped up the flap behind them and shined the GPS's faint light around the tent. She found a small LED lamp and clicked it on. Its glow was dim, but it was better than using up the GPS's juice.

"I'm glad you programmed every tent's coordinates into the GPS." Jack's teeth chattered.

"I debated against re-setting up the tents of contestants who'd already been kicked off. This is the first time I've ever been glad I listened to the lawyers."

Jack nodded at the camera perched off to one side. "Do you think the others will see us with that thing?"

Leah shook her head. "Harvey has no reason to even be checking this view. And for all we know, the camera signals have gotten as bad as the radios."

"What will they do when they figure out we haven't made it back?"

"I left Ryan in charge, so probably nothing." She leaned back on her elbows and grimaced.

"You're hurt," Jack said. "Take off your coat."

"*Your* coat," Leah corrected him. "I don't think anything's broken." But she lifted up the back of her shirt, revealing a nasty scrape.

Jack reached out and gently felt the area around the wound. Her skin was burning against his trembling hands. He pressed, and Leah pulled away.

"Did it hurt that bad?" Jack asked. "I hardly put any pressure—"

"Your hands are freezing." Leah pulled her shirt back down. "You're like Jack Frost."

"Sorry. You're sure you're okay?"

Leah drew her knees up to her chest and rested her chin there, looking a bit pale. "Am I okay? Let's just say I've never had someone try to kill me before."

Jack felt his eyebrow arch and smiled as if to say, *Are you sure about that?*

"Ha ha. Some people might think I run things like a dictator, but no one's actually tried to *murder* me."

"I wasn't making a face because of that." Jack rubbed his hands along his forearms, trying to get feeling back into his fingers. "I was actually thinking of how many people have tried to kill *me*."

"In the Army?"

"That's some of it, but it's a given in war—the other side wants to kill you. Since then… the list has gotten kind of long."

"It doesn't seem to bother you that much."

Jack shrugged. "I don't take it personally."

Leah looked at him like he had four heads. "Seriously, what could be more personal than someone trying to kill you?" She burst out laughing.

"I don't think any of them were doing it because they hated *me*." Jack's face was pinched. "Well, maybe one or two. But for most of them, killing me was a means to an end. And that includes right now. Wally wants to protect and preserve *his* mountain, and he's willing to kill to make that happen."

"Do you think he killed Charlie, too?"

"It's possible. The investigation into the avalanche was focused on the crew. I don't even know if they considered ecoterrorism."

"Ecoterrorism?"

"Like when you scare people so they stay off a mountain."

Leah looked shocked. "I knew Wally was out there, but I never thought he'd take it this far." She rubbed her arms and shivered.

"Let's trade places," Jack said, flexing his fingers and toes. "I'm starting to warm up. You take the sleeping bag and give me my jacket back."

Leah started to unzip the coat, then stopped. "Wait a second. You're not thinking about trying to go back to the lodge and leave me here?"

"If I use the GPS and go real slow…"

"That's insane," Leah snapped. "We have to wait till first light. It's too dangerous trying to—"

The red light on the camera blinked on, and Leah gasped.

"Harvey!" they shouted and waved at the camera.

"Listen, Harvey," Jack said. "The weatherman, Wally, tried to blow us up."

"He tried to kill us!" Leah said. "He destroyed the entire weather station. We barely got out alive!"

"Can you hear us, Harvey?" Jack asked. "Wiggle the camera if you can."

The camera moved back and forth, and Leah clapped.

Jack explained everything that had happened, then said, "Is Ollie there with you? Wiggle the camera for yes."

The camera wiggled.

"Ollie, you're in charge of security. I want you to get everyone together in one room. The contestants, too. Everyone inside and lock the doors. The competition doesn't matter at this point. You'll be safer if you're all together."

"What about Abe?" Leah asked. "They can't move him, and everyone can't fit in his room."

"I'd prefer everyone squeeze in, but if you can't do that, have Harvey stay with Bree and Abe, and get everyone else together in the great room. Do you understand?"

The camera wiggled.

"Leah and I will come back at first light."

"Tell Ryan that I'm holding *him* responsible," Leah said.

The camera wiggled.

Leah exhaled. "Thank God. Do you think Wally will try anything?"

"He seems like the type who would avoid direct confrontation, but you can't ever be sure. At least now they know to be on the lookout for him."

The wind howled outside, shaking the tent.

"We should get some sleep." Jack unzipped the sleeping bag and pointed to one side. "It'll be snug, but we're gonna have to share the sleeping bag."

"I suppose that idea is mildly more appealing than freezing to death," Leah said with a smirk.

"Be grateful we both can fit. This thing is huge."

"This tent was for Bob Turner, an eliminated contestant. He wasn't just a mountain man; he was a mountain of a man. I complained about having to get him a custom extra-extra-large cold-weather sleeping bag, too. Now it's saving my life." She climbed in and—squished like a couple of sardines—they managed to zip the bag closed.

Jack lay his head down, and his eyes immediately started drooping.

"Thank you for saving my life," Leah whispered.

"Okay. It's not a big deal."

Leah stiffened against him. "Saving my life isn't a big deal?"

Jack exhaled. "I didn't mean that. I meant, I didn't know if we'd make it; I just took a risk. What was I going to do? Leave you behind?"

"Some people might have."

Jack thought of the times his life had been in danger. He thought of the policemen and soldiers who hadn't hesitated to risk sacrificing their own lives for his. "Maybe you hang around with the wrong people."

Leah was silent for a while before replying. "Where did you serve?"

"Iraq."

"So you're used to explosions?"

Jack chuckled. "You don't really get used to stuff blowing up. Especially if you're not the one who set it off."

"You looked so calm. On the balcony. You screamed 'bomb,' but when I looked at your eyes... you weren't scared."

"I should have been."

Leah shook her head. "No. Don't say that. I've worked my whole life to drive fear out of me."

"No offense, but that's a dumb thing to do. Fear keeps you alive. A little fear is a good thing. Staying alive is a good thing."

Leah wiggled lower in the sleeping bag. "This morning, I would have done anything to stop you from shutting us down. Now that I know someone is trying to kill my crew, I can't wait to get everyone off this mountain."

"Once we catch Wally, you should still have time to finish shooting."

Leah shook her head. "No. After this, the network will pull the plug. If not for the show, definitely for me. They don't like failures. Though you'd better believe they'll profit from this. I can see the special now: *Murder on Mount Minuit.*" She sighed.

"I'm sure you'll get another show."

"Don't count on that. In this business you're only as good as your last gig. Today a peacock, tomorrow a feather duster."

They fell quiet for a while, and Jack was almost asleep when Leah spoke next. Though she was right next to him, her voice was barely audible. "I should have been here that day. When Charlie…"

"I read your deposition. You had a doctor's appointment." Jack rubbed his eyes.

Leah shrugged. "I should have waited until filming wrapped. But I panicked. I got scared. Did the report say why I went to the doctor?"

"No, it didn't."

"I had my physical right before the show started taping. And out of the blue I got a call that they'd found an abnormality in my mammogram. My mother died of breast cancer when I was twelve. She was a doctor. I thought she was Wonder Woman, but I stood by and watched that disease eat her alive. Here was a woman who had put herself through college and made this amazing life out of nothing. She was so strong. But when it came to cancer…"

"What happened?" Jack asked. "With the mammogram? Was everything okay?"

"Benign calcifications; I'm fine. But I remember how mad I was that day. Cancer had already gotten me once by killing my mother. I wasn't going to let cancer get me again. I was only thirty-nine. Do you know how few women producers are in TV? And black women? I'm no Rosa Parks, but I'm not gonna roll over. I fought too damn hard to get where I am."

She laid her head down and took a jagged breath. "You know that saying 'blind ambition'? It's true, you know. I eat, sleep, breathe *Planet Survival*. But do you know what I didn't do? I never called my dad. Not once. I don't even know the last time I thought about him or my little sister—until tonight, when that propane tank blew up. At that moment, all I could think was, I'm going to die and my family thinks I don't care about them."

"You care."

Leah shook her head. "Not enough. Not enough to call. Not enough to visit. I *say* I care. I even convinced myself that I do. But the truth is, I've always cared more about adding another line on my résumé."

"Then be grateful." Jack closed his eyes. "You got a second chance. Don't blow it."

"Well, *that's* sympathetic." Leah's shoulders slumped.

"I didn't think you're the type who needs to be coddled. I just meant that not everyone gets a second chance. When we get down off this mountain, call them."

Jack listened to Leah's breathing. It was getting shallow, and his own started to synch with hers.

"Is Alice more than your business partner?" Leah asked.

"She's my fiancée."

"I knew it." Leah sighed.

"How?"

"She was so insistent on coming up here with you. Protective. You can see she loves you. I didn't know if it was reciprocal."

"It is."

Jack closed his eyes.

Alice loves me. Now that's *a big deal.*

30

WIND WALKER

Jack used duct tape and Leah's knife to fashion a jacket and hood of sorts out of the sleeping bag. "Not bad, Michelin Man," Leah teased. He felt ridiculous, but it would keep him warm enough on the walk back to the lodge.

"Are you ready for this?"

Leah nodded.

Jack glanced back at the camera. The remote light had gone out sometime during the night, and now there was no response when they called to Harvey. Jack pulled the flap back, and freezing wind blasted swirling snow into the tent. Somewhere out there the sun had risen, but with all the clouds and snow, the sky had lightened only to a depressing gray.

"Stay close to me," Jack said. "It's clear as mud out there."

He set a fast pace, but the going was rough. The wind had created waist-high snowdrifts in some places, and in others exposed slick, icy rocks. He kept his head down; without goggles, icy snow blinded him every time he looked up. Even so, his eyelashes were crusty with icy bits, and the exposed flesh on his face burned. Jack's hands balled into fists and retreated as far up his makeshift jacket as they could. Grateful he'd worn two pair of socks, he'd wrapped one pair on his hands, but this was the type of cold that sucked all the warmth right out of you.

After a while, they paused to take a break in the shelter of some rocks, and Jack asked Leah how she was holding up.

"Me? How about *you*? I bet you're wishing you took your jacket and made *me* wear the sleeping bag."

"Are you kidding?" Jack yelled over the wind. "When we get out of here, I'm patenting this jacket. I'll be a billionaire. It's got warmth *and* style." Jack tapped the duct tape with his sock-covered hand and tried to smile, but his chattering teeth made it impossible.

Leah grabbed his arm. "Let me take point. It'll block some of the wind."

"I'm fine."

"That's one hundred percent macho talking. It's my turn." Leah held up the GPS. "And I've got this."

Jack held out a hand. "Lead the way, wind walker."

For another half hour or so, with Leah in the lead, the snow shrieked in a steady, blinding onslaught. Visibility dropped to less than ten feet. They had to fight against the wind every step of the way. Finally, the lodge appeared, like a ghost taking form.

Jack knew the contestants' tents were only a few feet away, but he still couldn't see them. Leah grabbed his arm and pulled him into the lodge.

The two of them surveyed the main room, snow dripping off them and pooling on the floor. The place looked like a fraternity house after a party. Empty food wrappers, cups, and bottles of whiskey and vodka lay on the table in front of the couch, where Ollie was currently passed out. Harvey was snoring loudly in a chair, his feet propped up on the table.

Leah stomped over and kicked the table aside. Harvey awoke with a start, and Ollie sat up and rubbed his eyes.

"There's a psycho on the loose, two of your fellow crew members are out in a blizzard, Abe is injured, and you two bozos throw a *party*?" Leah shouted.

Ollie stood up, swaying a bit. "It's not like that—"

"Don't," Leah snapped.

"What the hell is wrong with you?" Jack said. "I told you both to get everyone together and post a guard."

"What the hell are you talking about?" Ollie asked.

"When we talked to you last night, you agreed to get everyone inside."

Harvey and Ollie shared a confused look.

"You weren't even here last night." Harvey wiped the back of his mouth with his hand. "Didn't you sleep at the weather station? We figured you took shelter there."

"I was all for going after you," Ollie said, "but Ryan said no."

Harvey nodded rapidly. "He did. Ollie wanted to go, but Ryan said no."

"Both of you shut up," Jack snapped. "We talked to you last night."

"We were in Bob Turner's old tent," Leah said.

Now Ollie and Harvey looked even more confused. "The radio's not working," Ollie said. "How could you talk to us?"

"On the camera." Leah grabbed Harvey's shoulder and gave him a shake. "The camera came on, we told you what happened at the weather station, and you wiggled the camera back and forth."

"I didn't even check the camera in Bob's tent," Harvey said. "Why would you go there?"

"Was it you?" Jack asked Ollie.

Ollie shook his head. "First I'm hearing about it."

Leah's mouth was tight and thin. "Where is Ryan?"

"Sleeping it off," Ollie said. He motioned upstairs.

Jack struggled out of his makeshift jacket and tossed it aside. "Ollie, just go get the contestants and bring them into the lodge. Then lock the doors."

"*Now,*" Leah added, jogging up the stairs.

Jack followed her. He expected her to head to Ryan's room to blast him, but she went to Abe's instead and knocked softly on the door.

Bree slipped out and into the hallway. "Did you get a mayday call through?" Her eyes were red-rimmed, and her face was pinched with worry.

"No. How's Abe?"

"Bad. Harvey thinks he may have internal bleeding. His leg is burning up. I keep icing it, but… we have to get him to a doctor." She twisted a washcloth in her hands.

"We will. Once the storm clears, we'll set off so many flares, people will think we're having a fireworks show."

"We'll figure something out," Jack said. "For right now, do me a favor and go inside, lock the door, and don't answer it unless it's me or Leah."

Bree's face paled. She looked to Leah, who nodded and marched down the hallway to Ryan's room. Bree slipped back into Abe's room and closed the door behind her.

Leah didn't bother to knock on Ryan's door; she shoved it open so hard it slammed against the wall. The room was empty.

However, just down the hall, a door opened a crack and shut quickly.

Leah stormed down the hall and flung that door wide open. It was Gavin's room, and Gavin was in bed. This room was much larger than Ryan's, and had a second door on the back wall—which slammed shut as Leah and Jack entered.

"Don't you knock?" Gavin said, irritated, pulling the sheet up over himself.

Leah raced over to the other door and threw it open. It led directly to a side staircase. Running footsteps bounced off the cement as someone raced down. A moment later, a door on the first floor shut.

Leah's brown eyes blazed. "Who was just in here?"

"No one." Gavin sat up in bed. "I don't know what—"

"You *fool.* If that was Vicky, so help me, you'll never work again. I should fire you right here and now."

"You can't prove anything. You didn't see anyone here."

"Those are yours?" Jack pointed at a pair of red panties poking out from the sheets. Gavin's lips pulled back, revealing his clenched teeth. "Yes." He squared his shoulders.

"We'll talk about this later," Leah snarled. "Where's Ryan?"

"He's in his room, I guess. But you—"

"LEAH!" Harvey screamed from downstairs, his voice filled with terror.

Jack and Leah rushed out into the hallway. Harvey came running up the stairs and stopped short in the middle of the hall. His face was pale, and he was shaking.

"What's wrong?" Jack asked.

Harvey bent over and threw up. He gagged, then threw up again.

Ollie ran up the stairs. "Ryan's dead!"

The door across the hall from Gavin's room burst open, and Wally the weatherman walked out.

31

MISSING FOOTAGE

Alice drummed her fingers as she waited for the remote computer to respond to her commands. The flash of light from her engagement ring caught her eye. *I love you, Jack Stratton.*

"I found another one," Mrs. Stevens called out from the bedroom.

Alice let out a long sigh and walked into the bedroom—their makeshift video reviewing room. Mrs. Stevens had frozen the video on a shot of a man wearing the host's jacket. His face was turned away, but the gold logo on his lapel was visible.

"That makes four times I've found background footage of Ollie wearing Gavin's jacket directly before or after a stunt," Mrs. Stevens said. "Now that I know what to look for, I can tell when it's not Gavin, even from behind. He's got a distinctive stiff posture, whereas Ollie is a sloucher."

"Clearly, this was a regular thing," Alice said.

"I was so wrong about that man…" Mrs. Stevens shook her head, setting her red hair bouncing. "At this point I seriously doubt whether Gavin ever did *any* of his own stunts."

Alice checked the time stamp at the bottom of the screen. "This video was taken on the day of the accident?" she mused. "Do you notice the time?"

"Only an hour or so beforehand."

"Let's go frame by frame," Alice said.

"Okay." While Mrs. Stevens advanced the video with taps on the right arrow key, the man turned, and his face slowly came into view, like an old-fashioned flip book.

"Oh, my word," Mrs. Stevens said, "it's not Ollie at all."

What in the world…?

"No, it's not." Alice stared into the face of the man wearing the host's jacket. "It's Charlie Parker."

32

CLOGGED TOILET

Jack grabbed Wally by the wrist, yanked him into the hallway, and slammed him against the wall. Wally shrieked as Jack grabbed his other arm and pulled both of his hands behind his back. Using one foot, Jack swept Wally's legs out from under him and swung him face-down onto the carpet.

"Help!" Wally yelled weakly through the side of his mouth.

"Shut up." Jack ripped his belt off and tied Wally's hands together behind his back. "Ollie, are you *certain* Ryan's dead?"

Ollie nodded glumly.

"You checked his pulse?"

"He's stone cold and bright blue. He's dead, mate, in the downstairs bathroom."

Leah bolted down the hall toward the stairs. Jack yelled at her to wait, but she didn't respond. With a sigh, Jack patted Wally down, removed a wallet from his back pocket, and pulled the man to his feet.

Gavin stepped into the hallway, pulling on his shirt. "What the hell is going on?"

Jack ignored him. He pushed Wally toward the stairs. "Move."

Wally trudged down the stairs with Jack holding his bound hands. Ollie and Gavin followed behind.

The contestants had been gathered in the great room, and all four of them stood up and started asking questions at once.

"Everyone needs to stay here," Jack said in his most authoritative police crowd-control voice, making eye contact with every one of them. "Gavin, you too. I'll come back and explain everything, but for now, you are all to remain in this room. Is that clear?"

There was a good deal of muttering, but nobody tried to follow as Jack and Ollie led Wally down the hallway toward the bathroom and out of earshot of the great room.

"Hold on to him," Jack ordered, pushing Wally toward Ollie. "He tried to kill Leah and me."

Ollie took hold of Wally's wrists.

"I didn't kill anyone. I'm—" Wally started.

Ollie shoved him against the wall and hissed, "Don't move, don't speak, or I'll kill *you*."

Jack found Leah standing silently in the bathroom doorway. Tears ran down her anguished face, and her hand was clasped over her mouth.

Jack squeezed her shoulder, then stepped inside to see all the doors of the toilet stalls closed except one, where Ryan's body was lying on the floor, his head against the base of the toilet. His face was blue, his eyes open and bulging, his hair wet. A puddle of water spread out beneath his head and pooled on the tiles. A hinge of the toilet seat was broken and hung at an angle. The sheet-metal toilet-paper dispenser had been torn off the wall and was lying at his feet.

Shouting sounded from the hallway, and Jack ran back to the door.

"You tried to kill Abe, too!" Leah was flying at Wally, her small fists flailing. She tried to pound him, but Jack pulled Leah back by her waistband.

"What's wrong with you people?" Wally shouted.

"Shut up." Jack glared at Wally, and the weatherman snapped his mouth closed. "Ollie, guard Wally while I go take care of Ryan. Leah, go get a camera. We need to treat the bathroom like a crime scene and get photos of everything."

Ollie crossed his arms. "Who put you in charge?"

"I just did," Leah said. "Jack isn't actually a gofer. He's private security. If he tells you to do something, do it or you're fired. Am I clear?"

Ollie nodded while Leah hurried down the hall.

"How did you find the body?" Jack asked. "Walk me through it."

"I got all the contestants into the great room." Ollie chewed the inside of his cheek. "I had to take a leak. At first, I thought Ryan was puking. His knees were on the floor and his head was in the bowl, but…" Ollie's face went pale. For all his bravado, Jack wondered if he'd ever seen a dead body before. "But Ryan's head was *in* the bowl. Like, jammed in. I pulled him out, but it was clear he was dead."

"When was the last time you saw him before that?"

"Around one o'clock, maybe two?" Ollie shrugged. "We were all drinking, and Ryan got pretty sloshed. Gavin split, then Ryan did, too."

Leah jogged back down the hallway and handed Jack the camera.

"Thanks. Keep everyone together in the great room," Jack instructed. "Don't let anyone go anywhere. Then make sure Bree is locked in with Abe."

Leah nodded.

"What about me?" Wally whined.

"*You're* going to turn around and face the wall. If Ollie says you even flinched, I'm coming back out here, and there *will* be consequences," Jack growled.

"You can't hurt me. You're a cop."

Jack stepped closer. "No, as Leah said, I'm private security. So keep your mouth shut until I'm ready to talk to you, or you'll find out exactly what I can do to the guy who tried to blow me up."

33

CONFUSED ACCUSED

Jack videotaped the entire bathroom, then took some still pictures before covering Ryan's body with a sheet and otherwise leaving the scene as intact as possible. Trapped on a mountain with a blizzard raging, it was all he could do.

When he reentered the great room, everyone immediately started lobbing questions at him, but he ignored them, marching straight to Wally, who sat in front of Ollie with his hands still tied behind his back. Jack grabbed him by the wrists and pulled him to his feet. "Let's go. Leah, come with me."

"Hold on a second, mate." Ollie stepped in front of Jack.

"Zip it, Ollie," Leah snapped. "Everyone wait here."

Ollie muttered something under his breath, but backed down and stepped aside.

"This is crazy." Wally began to turn around, but Jack tightened his grip.

"Get moving." He pushed Wally down the hallway to an empty room. "In." Jack kicked the door open all the way to a narrow dorm room furnished with just a cot and a chair. "Sit."

"Aren't you going to untie me?" Wally said.

"No." Jack spun him around, put a firm hand on his shoulder, and pressed him into the chair.

Wally sat awkwardly and looked up at Leah. "Leah, you can't really think I would hurt anyone, let alone *kill* them. You have me tied up like a criminal."

Jack didn't let Leah answer. "You killed Ryan, you tried to kill Leah and me, and you sabotaged Abe's climbing gear. I'd say that makes you a criminal."

"What are you talking about? This is absurd! Ryan was drinking a lot. They all were. Maybe he puked and passed out in the toilet bowl."

"No one drowns in a toilet by accident," Jack said. "Or breaks the toilet seat in the process. What were you even doing here in the lodge? Aren't you supposed to be manning the weather station?"

"I was trying to get off the mountain before the blizzard. I set up all the equipment to record everything, but I'm not risking my life for data. I went to the gondola, but the fuse was blown and there weren't any replacements. I was hoping you guys had one, so I came here. Ryan offered to let me stay the night. It was snowing so badly, I figured I'd ride out the storm here."

"You wrote the threatening letter about Kaniehtiio," Jack said.

Wally's eyes darted between Jack and Leah. "What letter?"

"You lying son—" Leah lunged forward, but Jack stopped her right before she got hold of Wally's hair.

"Okay, okay." Sweat beaded on Wally's forehead. "I left a scary letter on your door. Big deal. I wanted you guys to get off the mountain before you did any more damage to it, that's true. But I didn't *kill* anyone, for goodness sake!"

"You left *another* letter the other day." Leah yanked the note out of her pocket. "You left *this note* in my bedroom."

Wally looked at the note with the words "TOO LATE" written in blood. He shook his head. "I didn't write *that*. I swear!"

Jack leaned in and scowled.

"No way, I didn't write that one," Wally said, craning his neck to look more closely. "Is that *blood?* Naw, I wrote a couple of letters and spray-painted a boulder." His head tipped to the side. "It was biodegradable paint."

"What about the message on the mirror and the guy-wire you put across the snowmobile path?"

"Look, I wrote a couple of notes and sent one to the insurance company, hoping they'd shut you down before you trampled all over this fragile ecosystem again. But that's it!" Wally's voice trembled. "I tried to *scare* you off, not *kill* you off! I'm not a violent person. You've got to believe me! I didn't do any of this!"

"Did you have a PLB in the weather station?" Jack asked.

Wally shrugged. "Yeah."

"He's lying." Leah jabbed her finger in Wally's face. "If he had a PLB he would have used it."

"Why?" Wally stammered. "I didn't know the gondola wasn't working or about the hurt climber. When I found that out I said I'd get it, but we decided to wait until morning."

"Who's *we?*" Jack asked.

"Ryan."

"Where did you keep it?"

"There's a cabinet of emergency stuff up there. Flares and junk. It's in there."

"You know darn well that there *is* no more weather station. You blew it up!" Leah snapped.

"What?" Wally looked stunned. "What do you mean, blew up? You're kidding me... right?"

"No," Jack said. "And nearly killed us. We barely escaped."

Wally started to tear up. "No. No... That station is my life..."

Jack had come face-to-face with a lot of lying suspects in his time on the police force, some of whom were pretty good actors. But his gut told him that Wally was telling the truth. *He had no idea about what happened at the tower.*

Jack turned to Leah. "We have to see if that PLB survived the explosion."

Wally groaned and stared up at the ceiling. "All my work... I have to go. I need—"

"You're not going anywhere until we figure this out." Jack pulled Wally out of the chair. "Leah, go get me some more rope."

34

A VIOLENT WORLD

Kiku lifted her cell phone to her delicate ear. She was standing at the window of her hotel room. The wind screamed outside, and the icy snow pelted the glass. "Hello, Detective Clark. I trust that everything went well after your friends arrived at the bar?"

"It did. Thank you again."

"I was pleased to be of some assistance. Were you able to speak with your other friend about the matter we discussed?"

"I'm sorry, but I struck out. The FBI still has the case sealed. The only thing I learned is that the Bureau opened a separate file on Alice's mother *before* the accident. My contact either couldn't or wouldn't tell me why."

Kiku forced a smile into her voice. The elderly detective was Jack's friend, and she didn't want him to feel bad about delivering such distressing news. "Thank you for the information, Detective. You have been very helpful."

"Give Jack my best."

"Certainly."

Kiku hung up the phone and opened her laptop. She'd been over the police report a dozen times, and one detail stood out to her. The security guard at A.R. Construction, Paul Miller, was a class-A dreg of society with a long criminal record. He'd served time for arson, petty theft, larceny, and rape. Such a man should never have been hired for security, given the background checks required for such a position.

She intended to find out more.

A monstrous creak sounded from outside, and she turned to the window. A metal roofing structure swayed, bent, and buckled over the gas pumps it was meant to protect. In a flash, it was reduced to ruin by the high winds and heavy snow.

Kiku wasn't superstitious, but the ill omen reminded her that the world was an unpredictable and harsh place. Most people didn't realize how violent it could be; she did. And so did Jack Stratton.

35

A BEAST OUTSIDE

Everyone except Bree and Abe had gathered solemnly in the lodge's main room. Leah stood on the second step of the staircase, using it like a speaker's platform, and Jack stood next to her. Everyone's attention kept shifting over to Wally, who sat with his hands bound in front of him, tied to a chair that had been lashed to a column.

"Listen up," Leah boomed. As quickly as she could, over the shocked murmurs and gasps of her increasingly alarmed audience, she explained the threatening messages, the reopening of the investigation into Charlie's death, Jack's real role, their suspicions about Abe's gear being sabotaged, Eric's disappearance, the bomb at the weather station, and Ryan's death—all the information she'd been withholding, finally out in the open.

Maybe we can get somewhere now. Jack watched each face for tics and tells.

"Unbelievable!" Vicky exclaimed. "You're telling us *no one* knows we're trapped up here with a murdering psycho?" Everyone stared daggers at Wally. They seemed to have forgotten about Eric for the time being, having someone closer at hand to blame.

"That's correct," Leah said.

"Hey, here's the real problem," Ollie cut in. "Apart from the murdering psycho, of course. How are we supposed to get off this mountain, even after the storm breaks? We've got no gondola and no way of communicating with anyone down below. We're stranded up here!"

"Jack is going to search for the weather station PLB and—"

"He's not going to find it!" Gavin snapped. "The weather station has been blown to smithereens."

Jack stepped forward. "We don't actually know how badly the station was damaged. And if we don't find it, we'll cross that bridge when we come to it. In the meantime, until the blizzard passes, I'm limiting all of you to three rooms in the lodge—here, the women's bathroom, and the kitchen. The women's bathroom is now unisex. Everywhere else is off-limits. Have I made myself clear?"

Everyone seemed too shocked and numb to make any objections. Jack sought out Chiri, who sat with Frida, both looking very thoughtful. "Chiri. I need to ask you something privately." He held open the door to the kitchen and beckoned him in. Chiri exchanged a puzzled look with Frida and followed Jack into the kitchen.

Jack crossed his arms and got directly to the point. "There's a monster blizzard outside, but I have to try to make it to the weather station and see if I can find that

PLB. It's the only chance for Abe. If anyone has seen snow like this, I figure it's you. Will you come with me?"

Chiri was not smiling. "It won't be easy. It might not even be possible."

"I know."

Chiri stared at the door of the kitchen and his eyes narrowed like he was peering through the wall, giving no clue what he was thinking, for what felt like a lifetime. Finally, he looked up at Jack and smiled. "When do we leave?"

36

TWO-HEADED MONSTER

Leah had put out all her worries and warnings, and now stood silently with Jack and Chiri as they checked their packs and equipment. The two men, once committed, already had one foot on the path into the unknown future, where they had only their trust in each other and in their gear against the force of the mountain. They spoke in low tones, strapping on their gear, closing buckles and tightening straps.

Chiri pulled out a six-foot rope. He clipped one end onto his climbing belt and the other onto Jack's. "This short-roping will keep us from getting separated out there. You ready, Jack?"

Jack pulled his goggles down. "Ready." He stepped to one side. "Experience first."

"I like the sound of that." Chiri grinned and opened the door.

Chiri gave a thumbs-up, hunched over, and marched out.

As soon as Jack stepped through the doorway, the wind tried to push him sideways. He'd been through a sandstorm and a hurricane, but in both cases, he found shelter and hunkered down; he hadn't deliberately walked into the jaws of the storm.

Every couple of steps, he had to adjust his path to stay on course behind Chiri. He marveled at how easily Chiri moved in comparison, especially considering Jack outweighed him by at least sixty pounds.

And the wind by the lodge, shrieking in their ears, was only the beginning. As soon as they crossed the protection of the ridge, the wind hit with its full fury; it felt like an icy hand grabbed Jack's shoulder and tried to yank him off his feet. He leaned so low his hands touched the ground, and still the pull of the wind was relentless. The rope danced away ahead of him, disappearing into the whirl of snow and darkness beyond. Chiri was invisible, just six feet ahead.

Suddenly, like a fishing line when a bass strikes your lure, the rope shot forward and jerked to the left, pulling Jack upright, and at the same moment a hundred-mile-an-hour blast of wind knocked him off his feet and sent him tumbling across ice and rocks. Remembering one of Chiri's pieces of advice before they left the lodge, he kicked his legs out, and his boots found a foothold. Then he tightened his hands around the rope and pulled himself hand over hand until he felt Chiri.

The ever-present smile was missing from the Sherpa's face, and a spot of blood ran from his cut lip. He pressed his face close to Jack's and screamed over the wind, "It's no good! We'll never get there and back!"

Jack nodded, though he hated the thought of giving up. For a brief moment he considered sending Chiri back and pressing forward. But without the Sherpa's help, he knew he didn't stand a chance.

Jack pointed back to the lodge, and he and Chiri turned around. All around them, the two-headed monster howled in delight.

37

NIGHT WATCH

It was close to midnight, and the storm pounded against the windows. The whole building creaked and groaned as the wind pushed and pulled, striking anything that dared stand in its way.

An invisible tension filled the room, and it was getting thicker with each passing hour. Jack knew he wasn't the only one feeling the strain. Nearly everyone was still awake, staring at the ceiling and each other. Only Wally appeared to be asleep. Jack had laid out a sleeping bag for him and retied his bonds to make sure he was secure but not losing circulation. He had considered untying the man altogether. Wally had admitted to writing the first threatening note, but his shocked reaction to learning of the explosion at the weather station appeared sincere. Still, Jack was taking no chances. The list of people here he trusted completely on this mountain was short: himself and Abe. And he could probably add Chiri.

Jack thought of the photo Abe had showed him of his daughter, Annabelle, just a little girl. A little girl who loved her father. Involuntarily, his mind filled with grim possibilities. Annabelle at her next birthday, wishing her father could be there. Annabelle graduating from high school, staring at an empty seat. Annabelle dressed in white, standing alone at the back of a church, no one to give her away...

Jack prayed for the hundredth time that the weather would clear tomorrow—and that the PLB had survived the explosion. It was Abe's only chance. And maybe the only chance for all of them.

Gradually, the others drifted off to sleep, one by one, until only Jack was left awake and fatigue dragged him down as well. When his head tipped forward, he crept over to Leah and woke her up.

She shook her head groggily and glanced at her watch. "You look like hell."

"Thanks."

Jack slipped over to Ollie.

"I've got this," Leah said. "Let him sleep."

Jack shook Ollie's shoulder. "You're on watch with Leah," he said.

Leah frowned. "Both of us don't need to be up," she whispered.

Jack shook his head. "Two on watch. It makes it easier to stay awake if you have company." He didn't want to tell her the real reason he didn't want anyone on watch alone: because there was no one in this room he could trust. Including Leah.

Jack flopped into a recliner and folded his hands behind his head. He closed his eyes and tried to sleep. His thoughts drifted to Annabelle again. When he was a policeman, it had, on occasion, fallen to him to tell someone that their loved one was dead. Each time was harder than the time before. Most people cried—a wailing sound that seemed to come from the soul itself. Everyone handled the news somewhat differently, but there was one thing they all asked.

Why?

Jack cast one more gaze around the room and closed his eyes. He was so tired he knew he'd fall asleep. Even if there was a good chance he was sleeping in the same room as a killer.

38

FIRE IN THE HOLE

"So it was actually Charlie who jumped out of the helicopter that day," Mrs. Stevens was saying. "He was pretending to be Gavin—not Ollie."

"Yes, Charlie had to," Alice agreed. "With his cast, Ollie couldn't pretend to be Gavin. Charlie was the next stunt double in line. My guess is Gavin was waiting for Charlie behind the hill. It was Charlie who jumped out of the helicopter and performed the dangerous skiing part, but when he skied behind the hill and out of the shot, Gavin was supposed to take over. Gavin would ski over the hill, down a gentle slope, remove his goggles, and finish filming his hosting shot. On TV, it would look like Gavin did it all—but really he just skied down the bunny slope."

"And that put Charlie in the wrong place at the wrong time," Mrs. Stevens said. "When the helicopter set off the avalanche, the poor boy was right in the path of it."

"Actually, about that. We don't *know* that the helicopter was the cause. The insurance company came to that conclusion because they didn't have any evidence to the contrary. But we may have found it. I now think it's possible someone may have deliberately triggered that avalanche. That's where the missing avalanche charges come in."

"I followed you up to this point, Alice, but why would someone deliberately set off an avalanche?"

"Money is the motive," Alice said. "More ratings equal more money. More danger equals more ratings. Therefore, more danger equals more money."

"It's all so fake!" Mrs. Stevens exclaimed, practically bristling with indignation. "And Gavin Maddox is such a phony. It's like finding out that Elvis lip-synched."

"Oh, wait, no way…" Alice leaned over and rewound the video of the accident, then stood up triumphantly. "Mrs. Stevens, you're a genius!"

Mrs. Stevens smiled lopsidedly. "What did I say?"

"Lip-synching. An audio recording consists of different tracks. There's a track for music and another track for the vocals. Videotape has multiple audio tracks, too. *Planet Survival* records the cast audio on one track and the crew's audio on another for editing."

"But I've never heard the crew talking."

"That's because you can silence an individual track's audio. If we turn the crew audio on, then we can listen to the isolated audio of the crew." Alice had rewound the video to just before Charlie jumped out of the helicopter. She silenced the cast audio and turned on the crew audio, then pressed play.

Ryan's voice came over the computer speakers. "Okay, everyone. We've got one take on this, so make it count. Mack is in position. On three, two, one—action!"

A second later Charlie jumped out of the helicopter and started down the slope.

"On my mark," Ryan said. "Three, two, one, it's a go."

Someone else said something in the background, but Alice couldn't make it out.

Alice paused the video right at the moment the avalanche started. "Look at the snow," she said. She pointed beneath the helicopter. "It's flying *upward*."

Alice rewound the tape and cranked up the volume. They watched Charlie jump out of the helicopter once more.

"On my mark. Three, two, one, it's a go."

They listened intently several times with the volume maxed out, before they made out Ollie's reply: "Fire in the hole."

The snow shot upward, and the avalanche began.

Alice stopped the video. She stared at the screen as the realization of what happened made the bile rise in her throat. "This was no accident."

"Oh, dear Lord. They killed the poor man."

39

DERELICTION OF DUTY

Jack's deep-brown eyes fluttered but he forced them to stay closed. His aching body told him that he hadn't been asleep long, and he didn't want to wake up now.

Why would someone want to kill Abe?

The unanswered question rose from the back of his sleepy mind. That question had been driving him crazy.

Why kill Abe, unless... I was wrong.

Someone *hadn't* tried to kill Abe. Abe had just gotten in the way. And Jack had missed it. Abe wasn't the killer's target.

It was Ollie.

Jack's eyes snapped open, but everything was pitch-black; not a single light shone anywhere. For a moment the irrational thought that he'd been struck blind in his sleep grabbed at him. He dismissed it and rose from the recliner.

He fumbled for his flashlight. The click of its switch echoed loudly in the quiet room.

He turned the light's beam toward the stairs. Leah was sitting there, her head on her arm, fast asleep in a sitting position. He panned the light around the room. He spotted Ollie stretched out on another recliner, his head drooping to his chest.

No one was on watch.

Concern switched to frustration. Leah wasn't a soldier, but Ollie had been, or so he claimed, and now he'd fallen asleep at his post. And he was in danger.

He kicked Ollie's foot. "Get up."

The Australian snorted a couple of times and sat up. "I'm awake. I wasn't sleeping." He ran a hand down his face and stumbled to his feet.

Across the room, Leah's eyelids fluttered. She sat bolt upright and rubbed her eyes. "I fell asleep. Damn it."

"I think the power's out." Jack walked to the kitchen and flicked the light switch. Nothing happened.

"Must be the generator," Ollie said, pulling on his boots.

"I'll wake up Harvey," Leah said.

Harvey twitched like a frightened rabbit when she touched his shoulder. His brown hair stuck out at all angles, like he'd been electrocuted in his sleep. "What's wrong?"

"The generator's out. Get dressed. You and I are going to check it out." Jack turned to Ollie. "You're coming too. Just in case." He shined his light around until it landed on Vicky's crimson mane.

"I'm awake. Move your interrogation light, I'll talk," she groggily joked.

Jack turned to Leah. "Two on watch. You're with Vicky."

Leah's cheeks flushed as red as Vicky's hair. "I'll stand up this time."

40

POWERLESS

When Harvey opened the side door, a gust of wind ripped it from his grasp and smashed it into the wall with a bang. The three men stepped out into the punishing gale and stumbled over to the generator. A snowdrift had built up behind it, but the cement platform it sat on was clear.

"I expected more snow," Jack said.

"It's a ground blizzard," Harvey yelled.

"It's the wind that's a killer," Ollie explained. "You only get a little snow, but the wind's like a frozen Caribbean hurricane."

Jack shined his flashlight at the generator. "*That's* not a good sign."

A metal door on the side of the generator's housing banged in the wind. The control panel inside had been smashed in. Bits of plastic and metal spilled out like someone had taken a sledgehammer to it.

"Damn it!" Ollie yelled.

Harvey pointed back at the lodge, and the three hurried back inside.

"That wasn't an accident," Jack said. "Someone bashed that panel to bits." He couldn't stop thinking about his new theory. The soldier in him wanted to warn Ollie that he may have been the killer's target, but the policeman in him still wasn't completely sure Ollie wasn't the perpetrator rather than a potential victim…

"Why would they smash the generator? Are they trying to freeze us to death now?" Harvey asked.

Jack's mind came up with several reasons why the killer might want to make them powerless. Now they had no cameras, no monitors. No lights would make picking them off in the dark a lot easier, too. And the cold… yes, eventually that would become a factor, too. But seeing the panicked look on Harvey's face, Jack decided not to walk him through any of those possibilities.

"We have enough cold-weather gear; we'll be fine."

"There's no way Wally did this," Ollie said. "He's been tied up all night."

Harvey's eyes widened. "You're right. And if it wasn't Wally… that means someone else killed Ryan."

"It was Eric," Ollie said. "I'm sure of it. I bet he cut the power and then snuck back into the lodge. He can't be far ahead of us. Harvey, you and I can head up the back stairs. Jack, you check this area."

"No," Jack said. "We need to stick together and go warn the others."

"But we can catch him. The power *just* went out," Ollie said.

"You don't know that. You were asleep. The power could have gone out hours ago." Jack grabbed Harvey's jacket and pulled him down the hall.

Ollie growled as he followed. "We should still look for Eric. You were in the Army, right? I thought you Army guys didn't run from a fight."

Idiot, I'm not running. The fight's coming to us.

41

TARGET PRACTICE

Jack and Ollie stood facing each other in the kitchen. Harvey had located a couple of LED lanterns that cast a soft glow. Ollie's face was beet-red, and veins stood out in his neck like angry worms as he scowled. He put his hand on the climbing ax in his belt.

"Are you hearing me, mate? Eric killed Ryan and now he's knocked out the generator. I say we go after him."

"We don't know if it's Eric," Jack said. "All we know is that Eric is missing and someone smashed that generator. Everyone was asleep when it happened." Jack resisted pointing out that if Ollie had stayed awake on guard duty, they might not even be having this conversation.

"Who else could it be?" Ollie demanded. "It sure wasn't Wally. He didn't untie himself and tie himself back up, did he? Eric's a survivalist. He could have easily holed up in one of the tents. I'm telling you, by now he's snuck back into the lodge and has been staying in an empty room all warm and safe this whole time."

Jack still didn't know whether he could trust Ollie, but it was time to use another approach that might yield information—and find out whether Ollie trusted him.

"Or, it could be someone else in the cast or crew," Jack said. He paused. "Ollie, have you considered that knocking out the generator might have been a trap, to draw someone outside?"

Ollie scoffed. "What, you think Eric was hoping one of us would go out there alone in the dark, so he could kill us? Or maybe he thought we'd go chasing around trying to find him? Yeah, right. Who else besides me and you among this group of pansies would do that? We had to drag Harvey along with us."

"Except for the part about Eric, that's exactly what I'm saying. If any one of us would go out to check the generator, it would be you or me. More likely you, since you know the equipment. And if anyone would go looking for the killer, well… you're the only one who's eager to do that right now. Look at the facts, Ollie. You're a *target*. The killer has already tried to kill you *twice*."

Ollie looked like he'd swallowed a bug. "What?"

"I realized it this morning. Abe wasn't supposed to be carrying that bag of avalanche charges. *You* were. You made Abe lug it up the mountain, but it was *your* job to carry it. And when Leah sent you out to get Frida, you took Abe's backpack with you because you're lazy and hadn't restocked your own pack. Because of that, Abe loaded *your* pack with *your* gear and headed out to get Chiri. The carabiner that broke was *yours.*"

Ollie went a little paler. "Someone *is* trying to kill me."

"That also makes you the only person I trust to look after everyone while I go to the weather station, as soon as the weather breaks a little. Why don't you think about that before you decide to hunt this killer on your own?" Jack stared at the frightened man, hoping his words would influence him to stay put.

"So, what are we supposed to do in the meantime? Sit here and wait?"

"That's exactly what we're going to do."

42

SITTING DUCKS

Abe muttered something unintelligible in his fitful sleep. Jack leaned against the door and Leah stood with her back to him, staring out the window. Bree was sitting next to Abe's bed, her eyes staring out from the dark circles of shadow.

"Thanks for the light," Bree said, nodding toward the little lantern.

"I'm worried about you guys, alone in here," Leah said. "I don't want you and Abe to be sitting ducks."

"We can stay connected." Bree held up a walkie-talkie. "Harvey dug these out. I can lock the doors, and if someone tries to get in, I'll call you guys for help."

Jack looked at the two doors. He regretted putting Abe in this room, because now he had to worry about two points of entry: the hallway and stairwell. "The locks on these doors are flimsy," he said, frowning. "We should push the bureaus against the doors. That'll keep you safe. Leah, can you help?"

She nodded, and the two of them moved the bureaus toward the doors. Jack made Bree promise she would move the dressers in front of the doors after he left.

Jack listened to the wild winds. He had never heard a storm make such ferocious noises before, and the acoustics of the bunker-like building only magnified them.

Abe's head rolled to the side, and he groaned. Leah looked up at Jack. "Is there nothing more we can do for him?"

"There's only one thing we can do: get him to a hospital. As soon as the weather clears up enough for me to make the trip, I'm going after the PLB again."

Abe drew in a ragged breath that wheezed across his teeth like the draft under the door. His eyes fluttered open and met Jack's. Jack had seen that haunted look before. It was the look of someone waiting to die. Then his eyes closed again.

Jack picked Abe's wallet off the dresser and crouched down beside his bed. "Abe. Listen to me. Open your eyes." Jack opened the wallet and held the photograph of Abe hugging Annabelle in front of Abe's face. "You need to look, Abe. Look at Annabelle."

Abe's eyelids rose slowly, and his eyes filled with tears.

"A princess needs her father. Don't give up. You need to fight. Fight for Annabelle's sake."

Abe's lips pulled back, and he shook his head. "We're trapped. There's no... no way off." His voice was weak and raspy.

Bree reached out and squeezed Abe's hand. "Jack's working on a way. He'll figure out something."

Abe's eyes met Jack's again. The hopelessness was gone, but the desperation that replaced it made Jack's stomach tighten like he'd taken a punch to the gut. "I promised her I'd come home." Abe closed his eyes once more.

"I'll get help," Jack said.

Jack took one last look at the little girl clinging to her father's neck.

He was fighting to save two people now.

43

GHOSTS

Leah spoke into the walkie-talkie. "How you doing, Bree?"

"I'm okay. Abe's sleeping. His fever dropped a little, I think."

Jack walked over to the staircase and sat next to Leah on the steps. The sun had risen, but it was hard to tell through the ice-covered windows.

"Let me know if you need anything," Leah said.

Bree yawned. "I will. I'm going to get some sleep."

Leah clicked off the walkie-talkie and turned to Jack. "Is Ollie still pouting in the kitchen?"

"Yeah. I think we'll have to start rationing our food or he and Harvey are going to wipe out what's left," Jack joked. The lavishly provisioned show had a pantry full of supplies; running out of food was the least of his concerns.

"I'd better go tell Ollie to behave." Leah stood up and stretched. "He's not that bad a guy, you know, once you get to know him." She walked into the kitchen, then almost immediately stuck her head back out. "Jack! You'd better come in here."

He hurried into the kitchen. There was no sign of Ollie.

"I told him not to go, but I couldn't stop him!" Harvey was seated at a table surrounded by several empty bags of chips and cans of soda. He shook his head, his wild hair sticking out all over. "But he said he could kick Eric's ass in his sleep."

"When did he leave?" Jack asked.

"Maybe half an hour ago." Harvey gulped some soda. "He's searching the lodge. I couldn't go with him. I'd be no help in a fight. I've never even thrown a punch."

Jack started for the door, but Leah grabbed his arm.

"You can't go chasing after Ollie and leave everyone else here at risk. He's the one who took off on his own." Leah squeezed his arm. "No one out in that room knows how to fight. If Eric shows up, who would stand up to him? Gavin? Chiri? Cornelius is wily but he's not strong. You said it yourself, there's strength and safety in numbers. Stay here, Jack. All we can hope is that Ollie doesn't find Eric, and once he's blown off some steam, that he gives up and comes back empty-handed."

The walkie-talkie on Leah's belt clicked on. "Leah! Leah! Help!" Bree shrieked.

Jack bolted out of the kitchen and down the hall. The corridor was empty, but he could hear crying from Abe's room. Jack kicked the door just to the right of the doorknob, but with the bureau behind it, the door didn't budge. "Bree! It's Jack! Open up!"

He heard the sound of wood scraping across the floor, and the door opened.

Bree stood before him, cradling her head in her hands, her light-brown hair spilling around her face. The other door was partially open, blocked by the bureau, which had been shoved several inches away from the wall.

Jack guided Bree to sit on the spare bed as Leah ran into the room behind him. Bree's left eye was red and already swelling shut. Her nose was bleeding and her lip was cut.

"What happened?"

"I thought it was Ollie. He was asking for help. He sounded hurt." Bree started to shake. "I know I shouldn't have, but… I only pulled the bureau back just a few inches, and he punched me through the opening in the door and knocked me down. I think I twisted my ankle." She flexed her foot and grimaced. "It caught under the bureau when I fell. He tried to shove the door open, but I kept pushing the bureau against it." Tears streaked her splotchy face. "Then I grabbed my walkie-talkie and called you, and he just ran."

Leah wrapped her arms around Bree's shoulders, and the battered girl broke down. She gulped in air as she sobbed, her small frame shaking with each deep breath.

"Bree." Jack placed a gentle hand on her shoulder. "Did you see who it was?"

Bree squeezed her eyes closed.

"Bree?" Leah's voice was soft. "You said it sounded like Ollie. Was it him?"

Bree shook her head.

"Was it Eric?" Leah asked.

Bree shook her head again. "I didn't get a good look, but… I think it was Charlie."

44

A DAMSEL IN DISTRESS

The punishing wind blasted the rental car from all sides as Kiku drove along the wintry street. Her high beams illuminated the chain-link fence topped with barbed wire that surrounded the quarry. Concrete barriers set a foot behind the fence formed a formidable wall. Behind the fence and concrete, several construction vehicles loomed large in the darkness, covered in snow.

Kiku stopped at the main gate, where a crude, thick metal bar blocked entry. On the left side, a call box was mounted midway up a pole. It wasn't an intercom, just a big yellowed plastic button. Kiku held down the button for several seconds and waited, surprised that there were no motion-detecting lights or vicious dogs.

Seventy-five yards away, a sliver of light appeared as someone opened the door to a trailer on the property. A shadow passed in front of the light. The snow shifted and danced in front of the door for a moment before it shut again.

The construction site was plunged back into darkness. Kiku got out of the car and listened more than she tried to see. The wind howled, the cold stung her cheeks, and the faintest sound slowly grew louder; the sound of frozen gravel crunching under a layer of snow, as an unseen dog raced toward her and the fence.

Kiku took a step back just before the huge Rottweiler flung its bulk against the fence. *They do have a dog.* The fence stretched like a fisherman's net with a big catch. Teeth bared and its eyes rolling back in its head, the dog chomped the air as it danced on its hind legs, eager to reach Kiku.

The sliver of light appeared once again, and a larger shadow exited the trailer.

Kiku made no move to try to calm the frenzied dog. One look at its frothing mouth and wild eyes reminded her of the more barbaric enforcers she had known in the past. *Animals whose muscles control their actions and not their intellect.*

A stream of curses grew closer. A man trudged through the snow, trying to zip up a bulky winter jacket. He was willowy, with long arms and legs, and moved like a spider without grace. Gray hair pulled back into a greasy ponytail blew in the wind as the man shook his head and gaped at the beautiful woman standing on the other side of the gate. He was a dozen years older than the mug shot that accompanied the police report, but Kiku was certain he was Paul Miller.

He stopped behind the barking dog and stared at her with bloodshot eyes. His fly was open.

"Your car break down?" His voice rose with a longing that reinforced her sense of the type of man that stood before her. A type she thought of as human spiders—

though that was unkind to spiders. The way the man dragged his yellowed top teeth over his lip and glanced back and forth between her and her car left little doubt. The man hoped that misfortune had befallen a woman and he could take advantage of the situation.

Kiku, too, would take advantage of the situation. She would go along with his mistaken fantasy. She had no qualms about using deceit to get Paul alone with his guard down. Kiku used *very different* methods to Jack to get answers out of people.

"I got a phone inside." His eyes widened, and he fumbled in his jacket for the key to the gate.

Kiku rounded her shoulders, dipped her chin, and tried to play the part of the damsel in distress.

"I'll let you use it. Warm in there, too." He triumphantly yanked out the key, but then froze.

Some predators have extremely strong survival instincts. Maybe somewhere inside, Paul Miller had sensed just how dangerous Kiku was.

"I really appreciate it," Kiku said meekly.

Paul's eyes darted up and down the street. "Why you out in this blizzard?"

The dog's claws raked the fence, and spit flew from its mouth. It hopped on its back legs, its wide jaws snapping shut with a loud clack.

"I was visiting a friend and took a wrong turn, and my electrical system just shut out. It's always bad in cold weather, I should have had it checked." Kiku wrapped her arms around her chest and let her teeth chatter. "If I can use your phone, my girlfriend can pick me up." She stepped closer and gave Paul a sheepish smile.

Paul's yellow teeth reappeared as his upper lip drew up. He eyed Kiku like she was filet mignon, but whatever perverted thoughts played out in his head were chased off by the dog's vicious barking.

Kiku realized her mistake too late to change course. She had been trying her best to look helpless and vulnerable, yet she had gotten so close to the snarling beast that its stink stung her nose. The chain-link fence separated them still, but most people wouldn't even have dared approach a crazed, musclebound beast like this. Kiku's action had shown that she didn't fear the dog.

And Paul had picked up on it.

He took a step back and put his hands back in his pockets. "There's a convenience store just down the road. They got a phone." He jerked his head left, and his ponytail landed on his shoulder with a damp thwack. "Twenty-four-hour." He turned and started walking away.

"Hold on a second." Kiku glared at the dog, who had stopped barking. "I passed that store. It's two miles down the road."

Paul kept walking, but the wind blew his muttered words back to her as he made his way back to the warmth of the trailer. The words were nonsensical, but she understood the racist chant.

Kiku's canines flashed. In some way her anger burned hotter inward. The Neanderthal had made her, for the briefest moment, feel shame about who she was.

She straightened up and tugged her gloves up tighter on her hands. She repeated the motion twice as she struggled with her own fantasy of pulling out her 9mm Beretta and shooting Paul in both kneecaps. She'd promised that she'd bring whoever was responsible for Alice's family's deaths back alive, but she'd made no such promise with regard to others. Still, Clark would be suspicious, and Jack wouldn't approve.

The trailer's door opened, and Paul whistled for the dog. Kiku watched the beast run back into the darkness.

Trying to play nice complicated things. It was not her style.

Kiku walked back to her car, Paul's racist chant dragging up memories that she'd thought she'd buried long ago… along with her elder sister.

45

HIDE AND GO DIE

Bree slept on one narrow bed, Abe on the other. Abe's face was pale and sweaty, and his hair was plastered to his head, which occasionally lolled from side to side. His body shuddered from head to toe and he groaned.

He's getting worse, Jack thought.

"It's impossible, Jack," Leah whispered. "Charlie's dead."

"They recovered Charlie's body, right?" Jack asked.

"I was a pallbearer. It was an open-casket funeral. I saw him myself. I can assure you, Charlie Parker is dead."

"Well, *someone* hit Bree in the face hard enough to break her nose." Jack crossed his arms. "And that same someone is hunting your crew, picking them off one by one. Ryan is dead. If we don't get Abe to a doctor soon, he's going to be dead, too. Ollie and Eric are missing. And you and I were nearly blown to bits. Who else has to die before you level with me and tell me what really happened last year?"

Leah stiffened. "It was an accident."

Jack waited for her to continue. The depths of her secrecy were unfathomable and beyond frustrating.

Someone in the hallway pounded on the door. "Leah!" Frida called out. "Cornelius is gone!"

Jack yanked the door open. "Come in and tell us what happened."

"We thought Cornelius just went to the bathroom," Frida explained, "but he was gone a long time, so Chiri went to check on him. His gear is gone, too."

Jack turned to Leah. "Stay here with Bree. Don't let *anyone* in. Frida, could you stay here, too? I know it's a little cramped, but—"

Frida nodded. "Of course."

"Wait, Jack. Here." Leah handed him her walkie-talkie. "I've got Bree's. Just in case."

"Thanks."

As Jack left, he was glad to hear the bureau being pushed against the door behind him.

He hurried into the great hall, and Gavin marched over. "I demand to know *exactly* what is going on." He stopped in front of Jack and planted a hand on Jack's chest.

Jack ignored the gesture like it was nothing more than a mosquito landing on his arm. "You and me both, Gavin."

He looked around and, not seeing Chiri, was about to ask where he was when the front door opened and a blast of snow and wind shrieked across the room. Several empty potato chip bags scattered like frightened birds off the table, and the fire in the fireplace roared.

Chiri shoved the door closed. "Cornelius isn't in his tent outside."

"When are you going to untie me?" Wally wailed.

"Shut up!" Jack snapped. "How long has he been gone?"

"Half an hour." Chiri made a face. "Maybe forty-five minutes."

"Did he say anything to anyone before he left?"

"You could see he was starting to freak out." Vicky picked up a deck of cards and started laying out a game of solitaire. "He seemed pretty paranoid. He thinks Eric wants him dead, and he knows Ollie hates him. He's probably hiding in a closet somewhere."

"This is all Leah's fault." Gavin stomped over to the couch and stood beside Vicky. "Wait until—"

"Sit down and shut up," Jack barked.

Gavin glared and thrust out his chin, then flopped onto the couch, jostling Vicky.

"Oh, my gosh, you are such a diva!" she said. "News flash, the cameras aren't rolling! Do us all a favor and go powder your nose or something." She swung her head, and her red hair splashed across Gavin's equally red face.

Gavin leapt to his feet.

"I said sit down and shut up, and I meant it," Jack ordered.

Gavin sat swiftly—but more gently this time—and silently dropped his head into his hands.

Jack looked around the room—at Gavin, Vicky, Chiri, Wally, and Harvey, who'd finally exited the kitchen. "Someone wants you dead, each and every one of you. If you run off like Ollie and Cornelius, you're going to die. Everyone stays together, and we'll all make it out of this mess alive. I'm going to find Cornelius."

"Wait a second," Chiri said. "You *just said* that we shouldn't split up. And now you're going to go out and look for Cornelius alone?"

Jack walked over to the wall, opened the fire extinguisher panel, and pulled out the ax. "Now I've got backup."

46

JUST JACK

Jack stared down the hallway of the first floor. Triangles of dim light shone on the cement in various angles along the bottoms of the doors that were cracked open. His flashlight in one hand and the ax in the other, he moved room by room through the deserted lodge.

He'd performed hundreds of breaches and clears; from cleaning out enemy buildings as a soldier to sweeping houses as a policeman. It was always stressful—opening a door when you had no idea what was waiting for you on the other side. Like playing Russian roulette. The room might be empty, or it might be full of armed assailants with their guns trained on the door. If it was rigged with explosives, opening the door one more millimeter would pull the trigger…

Working alone, the feeling was intensified—like Russian roulette with only one *empty* chamber. A fire team could almost simultaneously check every angle. One man swinging left, one right, one high, and one low, with additional spotters at your back. They used hand signals and touch, a silent language all of their own. With no one to watch his back, Jack had to be looking over his shoulder at the same time he swept the room. Each time he shoved a door open, he pressed his back against the wall and scanned behind him, too. He felt the sweat dripping down under his layers of clothing.

He cleared the first floor. Every room was deserted, and there was no sign of Eric, Ollie, or Cornelius. At the top of the stairs, he paused in the darkened hallway. All the doors were closed, faint strips of light underlining them. He didn't believe in ghosts, but Bree thinking Charlie had hit her wasn't doing anything to calm his nerves.

He tried a door, but the knob didn't turn. He stepped back and froze, his boot ready to kick it open.

Take a second, he cautioned himself. *Rushing gets people killed. If someone's waiting inside, kicking the door open tells them right where you are.*

He decided to check the other doors first. The room directly across the hall was empty. He made sure the next two rooms were clear as well. Then he returned to the locked door.

He wiped the sweat from his hand, dried the handle of the ax, and tucked it under his arm. His boot slammed into the door, shattering the wood around the lock. The door flew open, and the sound boomed in the narrow hallway.

The beam from Jack's flashlight cut through the darkness as he swiveled left and right, revealing an ordinary supply closet. Lining three walls were shelves sparsely filled with boxes, bags, and bottles. Jack stepped back into the hall, listening intently, sweeping his light back and forth. He then took an extra minute in the closet to look for fuses and communication gear, but found none.

The second floor now clear, he headed for the staircase at the end of the building, where he could see his breath in the cold. The whole lodge was chilly with the generator out—except for the great room, kept somewhat warm by the fireplace—but the cement and steel in the stairwell made it as cold as a Siberian gulag. It was also as black as a crypt. Jack tried to walk softly, but his footsteps echoed in the tight space.

Two flights of stairs led to the first floor. At the bottom, to Jack's right, three doors led back into the lodge—one into the first-floor hallway, two into the rooms at the end of the hallway. A short passage to his left led to the exit door.

As Jack's light fanned the passage, a dark smear on the wall caught his attention. Five feet up from the floor, the stain was the width of a thick paintbrush and about a foot long, sparkling when his light reflected off the ice crystals in the frozen liquid; it took Jack a minute to realize it was blood.

On the cement floor, close to the exit, a large puddle of blood had spread. That amount of blood was a *very* bad sign. The puddle was nearly two feet in diameter, running along the base of the wall. Jack knew the average adult had around one and a half gallons of blood. He tapped the edge with the ax handle. Frozen solid.

Jack moved quietly toward the exit door and raised his ax. If someone wanted to attack him, this was the place to do it. The door creaked loudly as he opened it.

The wind blasted inside—it sounded like a freight train bearing down on him. Suddenly losing the ability to hear if someone was charging up behind him, he paused to focus his flashlight so that he could see in that direction. He held the door propped open with his leg and waited. After a few moments, when he felt sure there was no one behind him, he peered through the storm.

The wind had blown the snow away from the side of the building except for a snowdrift about twenty feet from the door.

Jack's heart hammered in his chest. At the base of the snowdrift, he saw two rounded black shapes, a pair of boots, sticking out of the snow.

47

NO HANKY-PANKY

Mrs. Stevens' eyes widened. "How do you make sense out of all that?"

"It's a log file. It looks worse than it is. I was checking out the crew forum where they shared ideas and stayed connected when they weren't on location. I just got to some posts from Mack Carson."

"What are you hoping to find?"

"I want to see if I can figure out who Mack went climbing with. I think it's way too coincidental that Charlie was killed in an avalanche and so was Mack."

"What are all those numbers?"

"IP addresses."

"What's that?"

"Each computer has an IP address," Alice explained. "I can tell where the computer was located for any of the crew members when they posted." Alice stopped scrolling. "That's weird."

"Did you find something?" Mrs. Stevens asked, completely mystified by the rows and columns of digits.

Alice opened up an earlier log of the forum and highlighted Charlie's IP address. "Give me a second." She sat up straighter and felt herself shift into a zone. Like athletes when they let their muscles take over and everything around them slows down, Alice felt in tune with her computer as her fingers glided over the keyboard. Screens flashed and data popped up in windows that she shuffled across the monitor like a conductor, until a collage of information covered the screen. After several minutes she leaned back in her chair, shaking her head.

"What did you figure out?" Not for the first time, Mrs. Stevens reminded Alice of a kid asking, "Are we there yet?"

"Charlie lived in California with his parents. But almost all of his posts for the last two years originated in Boulder, Colorado."

"Vacation?"

Alice shook her head. "No. In between seasons five and seven, Charlie posted almost every day from Boulder."

"Maybe he moved in with someone?"

Alice nodded and highlighted another IP address. "Look at this address."

Mrs. Stevens squinted. "It's the same address, isn't it?"

"It is. But here, it's associated with a post that *Bree* made. There are a dozen more, from both of them. Charlie and Bree were posting from the same IP address. They must have been living together."

"But why wouldn't they tell anyone?"

"They couldn't!" Alice jumped up. "It's in the employee handbook. There's a no dating, no hanky-panky policy for all *Planet Survival* crew. If someone found out Bree and Charlie were dating, one of them would have to leave the show. Even if they were just sharing an apartment, it wouldn't look good to the brass, so they would have to keep mum."

Lady jumped up and pranced over to the door. A moment later, someone knocked.

"Lady's like an early-warning system, isn't she?" Mrs. Stevens said. "Does she do that for me?"

"She moves even faster for you," Alice said with a grin.

Alice opened the door, and Kiku stepped inside. "Hello, Alice. Hello, Lady." She smiled and patted Lady's head.

"Hey, Kiku. Have you met my landlady, Jan Stevens?"

"Very nice to meet you." Kiku gave a slight nod and turned back to Alice. "If it is not an imposition, I was wondering if I may take Lady for a walk."

48

DON'T SHOOT THE MESSENGER

Jack knocked on Abe's door. "Leah, it's me, Jack."

He heard the bureau scraping across the floor and then Leah unlocking the knob.

He was glad they were still taking precautions—considering all he could tell them about the predator that still lurked somewhere very close by was that it had claimed another victim.

Abe lay in bed, unmoving; Frida and Bree sat on the other bed.

Jack asked Leah if they could talk outside. Leah followed him to the room next door.

Jack motioned to the room's only chair. "Please sit down."

She crossed her arms.

Jack sighed. "Ollie's dead."

Leah's legs wobbled, and Jack grabbed her arm and eased her into the chair. She was mute, shaking her head, but as usual, she didn't freak out. Jack wondered what streets she had toughened up on. "He was stabbed in the stairwell at the opposite end of the building. I found his body in a snowdrift just outside the side exit."

"You didn't leave him there, did you?"

"Yes, I had to. Listen, we can't have anyone else taking off on their own. I need you to make that very clear to the others."

"Me? Why not you?"

"I'm going to the weather station. Blizzard or no blizzard, it can't wait any longer. Do you think we can move Abe into the great room? It's important that everyone sticks together."

Leah shook her head. "We can't move Abe. Harvey says he's bleeding internally and if we move him, it might kill him."

"In that case, everyone's moving into Abe's room. You'll sit on each other's laps if you have to."

Leah exhaled, gritted her teeth, and stood. "I'll get everyone in there. Somehow."

"Everyone except Wally," Jack said.

"You're going out with *him*? Jack, no. He tried to kill us! He might have killed Ryan!"

He clasped her shoulders to steady her. There was no time for an argument now. "But there's no way he killed Ollie, is there? He's been tied up the whole time. Which makes him as trustworthy as anyone else around here."

"I guess…" She looked uncertain.

"I'm taking him with me to help search for the PLB. He can show me where it was. We probably have one shot at this—we'll be lucky if we can make it to the weather station *and* back in this storm."

"But that means… it *has* to be Eric. The rest of us were always together when Bree was attacked and when Ollie was killed. It can't be any of us."

"Was everyone all together, every minute?" Jack asked. "Cornelius disappeared. Chiri went alone to look for him. I assume the others went to the bathroom at some point?"

Leah sighed. "Whoever it is, our best chance to survive is with you here, Jack. You stay—I'll go to the weather station."

"No. It's you they need. These people trust *you*, Leah. Keep them together. I need to get moving."

"You're going right this second?"

Jack pointed toward Abe's room. "Can he really afford to wait?"

Leah's forehead creased with concern. "He's so much worse. I don't think he has much of a chance as it is."

"I'm leaving, *now*. You know what to do." He gave her shoulders one last squeeze, and raced down the stairs to get Wally and fight against the beast one more time. This was a rematch Jack needed to win.

49

TRACKS IN THE SNOW

When Jack crested the ridge, he was relieved to find that the worst of the storm had passed. Gusts of ice still pelted their exposed skin, but at least they could walk upright and see farther than twenty feet into the dark-gray sky. And it didn't hurt anymore just to breathe. Of course, this time, instead of being partnered with the good-natured Chiri, Jack was paired up with Wally, who whined and moaned the entire way.

When the weather station finally came into view, the damage was less than Jack had expected. Half the roof on the side of the building next to the propane tank had collapsed, along with the wall on that side, but the rest of the building was still standing.

Wally was less impressed. "This is a total disaster!"

"You have insurance." Jack pushed Wally forward, yelling over the wind. "Maybe you can get upgraded equipment."

Wally craned his neck at the pile of steel jutting out behind the building. "I just installed a new satellite dish up there."

"Go." Jack put his hand against Wally's shoulder and nudged him forward.

Wally planted his feet. "Wait. It exploded, right? What if there are more explosives? *You* go first!"

Jack grabbed Wally's shoulder and half dragged him to the door.

The windows were shattered, and the lingering smell of smoke wafted in the cold air. Jack shoved the door open and peered inside. It was odd to see snow blanketing the floor.

Wally started to walk past him, but Jack blocked his way. "You stay here. Did you have any spare fuses, and where exactly is the PLB?"

"We keep emergency stuff in that cabinet next to what's left of my bed. There are no fuses that I know of. But get out of my way. I need to get some stuff."

Jack shook his head and pointed up. "The roof could come down any minute in this wind. Unless whatever you want is worth getting killed over, you're staying here."

As if to prove his point, a slap of wind blasted more snow into the building. Wood creaked, metal groaned, and though Jack wasn't certain, it did look like the roof leaned even more.

Wally took two steps back and pointed at the ground. "I'll wait here."

Jack stood at the doorway and stared across the threshold. What he'd said to Wally was true: he was taking an enormous chance going into an unstable building that could collapse at any moment. He was used to taking risks, and he even enjoyed it, but there was a difference now: Alice. Ever since she'd accepted his proposal, whenever he put his life in danger, he knew it was *their* life he was putting in danger. If he got killed, the life they would have had together would die with him. And after all the loss in Alice's life, what would losing him do to her...?

He sent up a quick prayer, stepped inside, and trudged toward the cabinet through the snow, which was thigh-deep in places. The swirling drifts had hidden broken windows, and furniture and equipment had been flung far from their original spots. An overturned table had blocked most of the snow from the area in front of the cabinet. He yanked it open and scanned the shelves.

No beacon.

He glared back at Wally and held his thumb down. Wally shrugged.

The PLB has to be here. I'm gonna find it, Annabelle, don't you worry. Jack moved everything inside the cabinet around, while the roof above his head groaned, and dust fell all around him. There were no fuses, either. He wasn't exactly sure of the size and design of the PLB. A small table with a drawer stood a couple of feet away, half covered in snow. As Jack turned to try the drawer and looked back to check on Wally, he noticed something he'd missed on the way inside. He'd been so focused on getting to the cabinet, he hadn't looked at the snow in other areas. But now he saw a trail of shallow depressions, running alongside Jack's fresh boot prints. The blizzard had almost covered them, but not enough to hide what they were.

Footprints.

Someone had beaten him to the PLB.

50

ANYONE HOME?

"Where are you going?" Wally shouted.

"Cornelius's camp is right down there." Jack pointed to the steep hill on the right. At its base, Cornelius's red tent poked out from among the rocks. "I want to check and see if he's there."

Jack didn't say anything about the footprints and the missing PLB to Wally. He may have been tied to a chair all night, but Wally could also be working with someone.

"I'm exhausted. Can we just go back to the lodge?"

Jack pointed to a formation of rocks partially sheltered from the wind. "Rest in there. I'll be back in ten minutes."

Wally moved to the back of the rocks and sat down. "I thought we had to stay together," he snapped.

"If you just shut up, no one will know you're hiding there," Jack advised.

Wally frowned and scooted back into the cold shadows.

The rocks next to the cliff were only dusted with snow, thanks to the gusts and shifting winds that shrieked and swooped around the mountain like angry birds of prey and blew the rocks clean every few minutes. As Jack picked his way down the icy path, his legs burned, and so did his back. It was like walking a balancing beam in constant motion. But each step brought him closer to Cornelius's tent.

Jack called out as he approached. "Cornelius! It's Jack! I'm not going to hurt you." He stepped up to the tent and pulled back the flap.

Two frightened eyes peered out from the back of the tent. Cornelius was crouched low in the darkness, clutching a tent pole with a hunting knife strapped to the end. He pointed his makeshift spear at Jack, his trembling hands making the blade wobble back and forth. "I'll kill you," he growled. "Get back now or I swear I'll run you through."

Still holding the tent flap back with one hand, Jack held out his other hand palm out, like he was calming a frightened child. "I'm just making sure you're okay."

"I'm fine. I got a much better chance against this mountain than I do against Eric."

"Do you really think you're safe alone out here in this blizzard?"

"Yes, I do. Back in the lodge I'm a fish in a barrel. And I don't know who to trust. I'd rather fight something I knows, like a blizzard."

"I can't believe I'm saying this, but I agree with you. And I trust you."

Cornelius eyed him suspiciously. "You do?"

"Yeah."

"Why?"

"Because if you were the killer, you would have found someplace in the lodge to hide, instead of risking your life and running out into a blizzard to stay alive. And I understand wanting to be in your natural element. Look, I don't know who to trust either, so I'm not going to tell anyone you're out here. If anybody shows up, you know that I didn't tell them where you are. Keep your guard up."

Cornelius nodded. "You don't have to tell me twice."

"And try not to snore."

"Are you nuts? You think I'm gonna get a wink of sleep with Eric out there?"

Judging from the white knuckles around his spear and the wild look in his eyes, Jack believed him. "Did you go to the weather station before coming here?"

"I barely made it to my tent—I sure as heck didn't make any side trips. The wind is killer." Cornelius gulped at his choice of words.

"It's getting a bit better. Stay safe."

Jack pulled the flap closed and picked his way back up the slope to the rocks where Wally was hiding.

The weatherman rose wearily. "Tell me you didn't find him dead in his tent."

Jack shook his head. "Cornelius's tent was empty."

51

DIVIDED WE FALL

When Jack and Wally walked through the front door, Wally gasped. Jack jumped sideways and scanned the great room for what had frightened the man.

"They're all gone!" Wally shouted. "They must have gotten the gondola working and took off on us!" He stomped his foot, spun on his heel, and faced Jack. Suddenly, his hands began to shake and his eyes grew as big as doughnuts. "Or m-maybe the killer got them…" He started to bolt outside, but Jack grabbed him by the hood.

"They're all in Abe's room," Jack said. "I told Leah to move everyone there."

Wally yanked his hood free. "You could have told *me* that."

"Consider yourself told. Get moving."

They walked down the hall, and Jack knocked on Abe's door. "Leah, it's Jack."

The bureau slid out of the way, and Gavin opened the door. "Did you get the PLB?"

"No."

"I knew *you* should have gone!" Gavin jabbed a finger in Leah's face. "How do we know that *he* isn't the killer?" He swung around and pointed his finger at Jack. "Everything was fine until he arrived, and now—boom, we're dropping like flies!" His other hand tightened around the ax in his tool belt.

"For one…" Jack stepped forward and placed his right hand over Gavin's, pinning the ax in place. "If I felt like it, I could kill everyone in this room right now."

Chiri moved in front of Frida. "That's probably true, but it's not reassuring."

"I should have worded that differently." Jack held up his hands. "I'm not the killer. I was making a point. If I wanted to kill all of you, you'd be dead by now. And for the record, I would have killed Gavin first."

Soft chuckles rose in the air, along with one loud huff from Gavin.

Bree stood up and winced. Her black eye was now turning purple. "Abe's fever is worse." She limped forward. "He must have an infection, and we don't have the antibiotics he needs. I was afraid he'd lose his leg; now I'm afraid he'll lose his life. We have to do something *right now*, or he'll die. He would've carried any of us down this mountain, with or without a blizzard."

Jack nodded. "I agree. We move to Plan B and get the signal flares ready. The storm is winding down. The first possible break, it's showtime."

Leah put a reassuring hand under Bree's elbow and propped her up. "As soon as the cloud cover breaks, we'll light this place up like the Fourth of July." She smiled.

"Frida and Harvey," Jack said, "come with me. Let's get those flares."

"I can go with you and Frida," Chiri offered.

"Great," said Harvey, opening a new bag of chips.

Jack stepped to the doorway and locked eyes with Leah. "Everyone else stays together."

Leah nodded.

Frida and Chiri followed Jack to the control room. Jack opened the equipment cabinet, pulled out a plastic crate the size of a small cooler, and opened the top.

Chiri whistled low. "Leah wasn't kidding about the Fourth of July."

Inside the cooler were ten flare guns and dozens of flares. "They were going to have a contest where you each had to fire off a flare," Jack said. "The rest were backups for your personal emergency flares."

Frida shook her head. "Even on a good day, it's going to be difficult for someone to see the flares. With this wind, they may not do much at all."

"And even if they see them, they might think it's part of the show," Jack admitted.

"Then why are we doing it if no one is going to pay attention to them?" Frida asked.

"Because someone down there *is* paying attention," Jack said. "My fiancée doesn't like letting me out of her sight. She hasn't been able to reach me for days. I'm surprised she hasn't climbed up here already. But when she sees the flares, she'll get us help."

"*If* she sees the flares," Frida said.

Jack nodded.

"That's why I have a Plan C—the Chiri plan." Chiri looked to Frida, who nodded and smiled. Chiri's chest puffed out, and his cheeks reddened. "It's actually the Chiri-Frida plan. We'll trek down together and get help."

Jack stared at them for a moment, then shook his head. "It's still too risky, with the wind and fresh snow."

Frida stood ramrod straight. "No. We've discussed this. We can't sit by and let a fellow climber die. And, if you will forgive me, we have much more experience climbing in snow than you do."

Chiri took her hand in his. "Nothing is impossible if we work together."

Jack glanced at their hands. He thought he'd sensed something before, but... "Are you two... an item?"

Frida blushed, and Chiri let go of her hand.

"What? Us?" Chiri gave a laugh that was clearly forced. "We can't be. But... I, ah..."

"We'd appreciate it if you didn't say anything," Frida said sweetly. "The others don't know. They might think we have an unfair advantage."

"During the hiatus..." Chiri's cheeks turned crimson. "We started seeing each other."

"Please don't tell anyone," Frida asked again.

Jack shrugged. "My lips are sealed."

"Jack!" Leah's voice crackled over the radio. "HELP!"

52

GIVE ME A NAME

Kiku parked right in front of the gate of the construction site, got out of the car, and left her door open. She didn't bother with the buzzer. From the undisturbed snow, it was evident no one had come or gone.

The thick padlock on the gate was easy to pick. She grabbed the gate, yanked it free of the small snowdrift at its base, and waited. She'd made enough noise that she didn't think she'd have to wait long... and she was right.

The door to the trailer flew open, and the Rottweiler leapt out, kicking up the snow with its claws as it raced toward her.

Kiku waited until it got within twenty yards before she whistled.

The little red rental car rocked on its shocks as Lady bounded out. The enormous King Shepherd let loose a howl that was an unmistakable challenge as it raced past Kiku, straight toward the charging dog.

The Rottweiler scrambled to stop; its paws slipped on the icy ground, and it rolled over twice before changing direction and bolting off with little scared yips.

Kiku whistled again, and Lady stopped as the Rottweiler crawled under the safety of an old pickup truck.

Lady planted her feet and barked three times, her head moving east, north, and west, challenging any other dog to show itself. There were no takers.

Kiku smiled and patted Lady's broad back as they made their way to the trailer.

The door banged off the side of the trailer as Paul Miller kicked it open. He had a tire iron in one hand, and he raised it shakily and leveled it at Lady.

"How the hell—"

"I suggest you put that down so we can have a civil conversation." Kiku and Lady stopped at the base of the stairs and glared up at Paul, who stood with one foot still in the trailer. Lady added a growl. Seeing as he was a convicted felon, Kiku had known the chances were good that Paul would have a weapon like this instead of a gun, but still she watched his hands and not his hate-filled face.

"Are you a cop?"

"No." Kiku eyed the spindly man. He was most likely equal to her in strength, but her training gave Kiku a lopsided advantage. "I suggest you drop the tire iron and walk inside."

Paul scoffed. "You think I'm going to listen to you ch—"

Kiku's left hand flicked out and hit Paul's wrist while she grabbed the tire iron with her right and used the leverage to pivot the tire iron toward his thumb, the weakest part of his grip. As the tool came out of his hand she swung it into a tight arc and down, crushing the steel toe of his boot.

Paul shrieked.

Kiku shoved the man through the door and back into the trailer.

Paul screamed and swore again as he landed on the soiled carpet. "I'm calling the cops, you crazy—"

Kiku leveled the tire iron at his head. "Utter another word and it will be your last. You will not be calling anyone. Ever. Now get up and sit in that chair." Without Kiku giving any direction, Lady stood at attention nearby, ready to spring.

Kiku pointed at an old office chair in front of a computer monitor playing an X-rated video. When she tapped the tire iron into the screen, the monitor cracked and blinked out.

Paul swore again. "I'm suing—"

"Your teeth are not much to look at, and judging by their appearance, you do not value them. Remember, they serve a purpose—chewing. If you want to keep them, close your mouth and answer when spoken to."

Lady stuck her head into the trailer, sniffed, and backed out to wait on the top step.

Kiku's nose wrinkled. The trailer stank of garbage, booze, body fluids, and stale cigarettes. She would prefer to leave, too. "You will not call the police because I will simply say my car broke down and you lured me back here and tried to take advantage of me. With your conviction for rape, who will they believe?"

Paul's eyes darted to the tire iron and he grabbed for it.

Kiku knocked his hand away and backhanded him across the face—splitting his lip. His head jerked back and he stumbled against the chair.

"Sit. Now."

Paul, wiping his hand across his bleeding lip, muttered something and sat down.

"Twelve years ago, you let someone steal a dump truck out of this yard. Who?"

Paul's pockmarked face paled. His bloodshot eyes widened as he searched Kiku's eyes. The unasked questions racing across his face confirmed her suspicions. He knew something.

The tire iron flashed in her hand and landed once again on the steel toe of his boot. She felt the metal flatten even further.

Paul shrieked and thrashed about in the chair.

"Right now, it is toes. Most likely they are not even broken—only slightly crushed. A couple more swings... and they will pop right off."

"Bennie. The guy's name was Bennie. But I had no idea he was gonna—"

Kiku pressed the tire iron down on his boot and leaned against it.

Paul shook his head, and spit flew from his mouth. "I didn't. I didn't. I'd never seen the guy before. I heard about him, but I'd never seen him."

Kiku pressed harder.

"I ain't lying. I'm not. He was supposed to be this badass hitman. But come on—his friggin' name was Bennie. You ever meet a badass named Bennie?"

"Did you speak to him?"

"No. No. Only, like, three words. Big guy. Long black hair. Looked like a lumberjack. I pointed him to the truck and opened the gate."

"Why?"

"Why what?"

"Why target that family?" Kiku thumped the tire against Paul's boot, and he held up his hands.

"I don't know. I don't ask nothin'. I'm freakin' nobody. My cousin only gave me the job here because of my mom. He can't stand me."

Kiku lifted the tire iron off Paul's boot. She'd gotten everything she could from him. "You will not say anything to anyone about our chat." She flipped the tire iron end over end and caught it deftly.

"My cousin is going—"

"Your cousin is Marco DeLaria—'the Wrecker.' Should you tell him that I came here and you told me nothing? Will your cousin believe that? He will do more than mash a couple of toes to find out, and then he will put a bullet in your head. I would like nothing more, so feel free to talk to your cousin at your earliest opportunity."

Paul's stare morphed into a pained grimace.

"I suggest you pry the boot off your foot before the toes swell too much, or you'll still be wearing it weeks from now."

Kiku backed out of the trailer, and Lady fell in line beside her. Kiku flung the tire iron over a pile of cinderblocks. As she walked through the snow, she didn't feel the bitter cold. Her blood was pumping red-hot, and not just because of her interrogation of Paul. Her anger was fueled by the pain her news would bring to Alice.

One would think the tragedy of an auto crash killing your parents and brothers couldn't get any worse.

But it just had.

Someone had put a hit out on Alice's parents.

53

INTO THE STORM

Harvey and Bree were holding Abe down as his body convulsed again and again, racked by spasms. It was horrible to watch as the tall man's back arched high and foam bubbled from his mouth. But it was even worse when, finally, his seizing ceased and his body collapsed against the bed.

Bree covered her face with her hands and sobbed.

Chiri grabbed Jack's arm and the two men stared at each other for a moment. Jack could see the resolve in the Sherpa's face, and he recalled the expert climbing skills he had displayed in the contest.

Jack turned to Leah. "Chiri and Frida are going to descend the mountain and get help."

"In this storm?" Vicky shook her head. "You two have gone mad. You'll never make it. Besides, Abe doesn't look like he's going to last much longer. It's not worth the risk."

Bile rose in Jack's stomach at her callousness.

Gavin put a hand on Vicky's shoulder, leaned in, and whispered, "Let them go. They can get us help, and it's not a risk for us."

Harvey scowled. "I never thought I'd say this, but I really wish there was a camera taping you just then, Gavin. You really are a piece of work."

"Can we tie Gavin up?" Wally asked hopefully.

Leah moved to stand in the doorway. She stared at the floor until the silence in the room grew thick. "I can't allow you to try to make that trip. It's too dangerous."

Frida shook her head. "It's our choice. And it's Abe's only chance. You can light off all the emergency flares you want, but there's no guarantee anyone will see them, or think they're actual calls for help rather than part of the show. Abe is running out of time."

"And technically..." Chiri looked like a mother apologizing before she ripped a bandage off her child's knee. "You can't order us."

"Then I'm *asking* you not to go," Leah said.

Chiri touched his chest. "I'm a Sherpa. It's in my heart and blood to help a fellow climber. I *must* go." His eyes welled up with tears.

"Jack, make them stay," Leah said. "Talk some sense into them."

Jack knew that nothing he said would change their minds. There was a determination in their eyes that he'd seen many times. Soldiers, first responders, and rescue personnel sharing an undeniable bond. It isn't just what they do, it's who they *are*.

"I'll walk with you to the ridge," he said. "If there's a break in the clouds, I'll set off the flares."

Chiri said, "And if there is no break, we'll continue our descent." Frida nodded in agreement.

Leah cast one more pleading look around the room, then lowered her gaze and stepped aside.

Vicky shook her head. "I'm telling you now, you're both going to die."

* * *

The wind had died down considerably, but snow continued to fall, and visibility remained poor when Jack, Chiri, and Frida arrived at the steep slope of the north face.

After what had happened to Abe, all three had inspected every piece of equipment carefully—though Jack was surprised by how little gear Chiri and Frida were taking. Jack stood in front of two people who were about to risk their own lives to save another—and possibly the lives of everyone on the mountain. Pride and fear merged in a dance that twisted his stomach. Words were woefully inadequate.

"We'll send help as soon as our feet touch the base of the mountain," Chiri said, then smiled. "Hopefully that doesn't happen *too* fast."

Frida laughed. She was a good six inches taller than Chiri and had to lean down to kiss him. "I will not let anything happen to you."

"See?" Chiri said. "Things are looking better and better." He winked at Jack and started down the slope.

Jack watched them begin their descent together over the rocks. Just before they zigzagged out of sight, they both looked back and waved, and then they disappeared into the snow.

54

VENGEANCE

As Mrs. Stevens removed a broken cookie from the tin, it slipped from her hand, but it never made it to the floor—Lady snatched it in midair. Returning to the computer with a plateful of cookies—oatmeal raisin this time—Mrs. Stevens rubbed Lady's back, avoiding Alice's disapproving look.

Alice was studying a photo of Bree and Charlie at a picnic. Bree sat in Charlie's lap, and they both wore big smiles.

"They look so happy."

"It's a picture from Bree's sister's Facebook page. Look at their fingers." Alice zoomed in on their hands.

"They were *married?*"

Alice nodded. "Yes. Someone is threatening the crew of *Planet Survival*, and Bree just moved to the head of the suspect list."

"But she looks so sweet. I can't think she'd be threatening anyone, let alone have anything to do with the helicopter pilot's accident. Are you sure about her?"

"Not yet, but she sure has some explaining to do." Alice started closing windows and files. *And so does Brian. Jack is up there risking his life on behalf of McAlister Insurance and Brian is nowhere to be found.* If there was another murder added to this case, it would be Brian's, and it wouldn't be accidental.

Over the last thirty or so hours, Alice had placed five increasingly concerned calls to Brian Strickland, but the office was closed because of the blizzard and his cell phone went right to voicemail.

"Listen, Mrs. Stevens, I have to go up there and let Jack know what I found out. Bree can…"

She trailed off. Her heart had suddenly sped up so fast that her mouth didn't know how to work anymore. She was staring at the log for the crew forum—specifically, Mack's post about going for his dream climb.

Directly beneath it was a post from Bree: *Have fun! Ex 21:24.*

Alice's finger traced the words. But it wasn't the post itself that made Alice's knees start to shake; it was the location of Bree's computer when she sent it.

"Exodus 21:24," Mrs. Stevens said. "I don't know that verse." She took out her phone. "I'll look it up."

Mrs. Stevens' words barely registered. Alice's stomach knotted as she copied Bree's IP address and pasted it into the tracing program. Bree's IP address had changed.

GARMISCH-PARTENKIRCHEN appeared on the screen.

Mrs. Stevens looked up from her phone. "Garmisch-Partenkirchen. Where have I heard that before?"

Alice was still finding it difficult to talk, and impossible to tear her eyes from the damning evidence on the screen. Garmisch-Partenkirchen—a little town in Germany at the foot of the Zugspitze, the mountain where Mack's dream climb ended in his being buried alive in an avalanche.

"Bree wasn't in Colorado when Mack died. Bree was in Germany with Mack."

"But I don't understand… She was with him? Why would she write 'Have fun'?"

"To make the rest of the crew think she was still in Colorado."

"Oh, my." Mrs. Stevens' voice was strained, and her hand shook as she held her phone out for Alice to read. "You should take a look at this."

As Alice read the verse, her own hand began to shake.

Exodus 21:24. *An eye for an eye…*

"I need to get to Jack."

55

GONE-DOLA

Although the wind had died down, to Jack, the storm was beginning to seem endless. Snow continued to fall, and the sky was dark, making it difficult to determine the time of day. *I can't wait for this storm to end. For all of this to end.*

He walked through the front doors of the frigid lodge and headed straight for Abe's room, his rapid footsteps echoing off the walls and his impatience growing with every step. He hated waiting for someone else to do a dangerous job that he could do himself. Not that he possessed anything near the climbing ability of Frida or Chiri—they were in a league of their own—but he shared their drive to take action.

He flexed his dry, chapped hands. When he knocked on the door, he was all revved up and spinning in place.

The bureau scraped, and Leah swore. "Took you three long enough…" Her eyebrows rose in surprise. "Jack? I thought it was Harvey, Wally, and Gavin."

Jack set the flares on the floor and glanced over at Abe, sleeping—or unconscious. Bree gave him a weak smile. He turned his attention back to the distraught, disheveled Leah. "Where did they go and when did they leave?"

Raised voices sounded from down the hallway, and Jack stepped outside to see Wally and Harvey stomping down the corridor.

"You took forever in the kitchen. Pretty selfish," Wally snapped.

"Selfish? I picked up food for everyone." Harvey lifted two plastic shopping bags.

"You said you were going to grab something, not sit there and stuff your face."

"Where's Gavin?" Leah bellowed over their squabbling.

Wally and Harvey stopped short. "He's not back?" Harvey asked in disbelief.

"You two stupid—" Leah started, when Vicky came rushing out of Abe's room. "Where did he go? Did he take his gear?" Vicky asked, her voice rising.

Wally shook his head. "No. He put his jacket on, but he didn't go outside. He said he was cold and—"

"That snake is trying to leave without me!" Vicky started to push past Harvey and Wally.

Jack grabbed her arm. "Hold on."

"Let go!" She struggled like a cornered animal, her eyes wild. "Gavin's leaving in the gondola! I have to catch him."

Jack tightened his grip. "He's not going anywhere without the fuse."

"He found one this morning." Vicky stopped struggling and looked pleadingly at Jack. "In the pantry behind his imported coffee. We were waiting for the wind to die down. But he was supposed to take *me*!"

"Why wouldn't he take everyone?"

"Someone up here is a killer." Her eyes darted suspiciously toward Jack. "And once the killer knew we could escape, they might have just started—I don't know—killing us all."

Jack searched her eyes. She was telling the truth, but...

We turned this place upside down looking for backup fuses. There's no way they just magically appeared behind the expensive coffee that only Gavin is allowed to touch...

He turned to Leah. "It's a trap."

* * *

When Jack, Vicky, and Leah reached the gondola, the motor was humming and the gondola was already starting to move off the platform. Jack broke into a sprint, but he knew he'd never catch it in time.

"Stop the car, Gavin!" Jack yelled. "Stop the car!"

Gavin opened the door and leaned out. "I'll send help back for you! One of you is a killer! This is the safest way!"

Vicky let fly a slew of obscenities and heaved her ax at Gavin. It fell ten yards short and disappeared down the cliff.

"I'll recall the gondola." Leah changed direction and charged for the control booth.

Jack heard arguing behind him and turned to see Wally and Harvey running up. *Idiots!* They were supposed to stay with Bree. Instead they'd left her all alone with Abe. *Probably worried we'd leave them behind.*

Shaking his head, Jack looked at the gondola, still moving. A light pulsing in the gloom above it caught his attention. Jack squinted to see the metal clamp that held the gondola on the cable.

Green lights flashed.

The gondola's connection to the cable was surrounded by avalanche charges, and they were armed.

Jack ran to the edge of the cliff. The gondola was still over the slope. If Gavin jumped now, the drop was just twenty feet. He'd break his legs, but he'd live. If he stayed on the gondola another moment, he'd pass the edge of the slope, and the fall would be a hundred feet or more. "Gavin! There's an avalanche charge on the cable! *Jump!*"

Gavin held up his middle finger. "Nice try, Jack! I'll send help! You have to—"

"*GAVIN!*" Vicky waved her arms frantically and pointed at the clamp. "He's telling the truth, Gavin! I swear! Jump, *now!*"

"Sorry, love, but I just don't trust you!"

But at that moment Gavin's smile faded, and he looked up. He must have heard the warning beep of the explosives as the lights turned red. Either way, when Gavin looked at Jack, it was with a mix of terror and hopelessness.

The charges detonated just as the gondola swung free of the ridge.

The gondola shuddered violently, the cable snapped, and Gavin disappeared down the mountain.

56

PULL OVER

The Charger slid sideways on the snow-covered road as Alice struggled to make the sharp turn. The worried little voice in her ears was now screaming. It was bad enough not hearing from Jack when she'd just chalked it up to the blizzard and faulty technology. Now, when she knew he was trapped on a mountain with a love-crazed killer…

She hit the straightaway and punched the gas. The Charger roared, but the tires spun and the car shimmied sideways. Feeling a little love-crazed herself, she forced herself to slow down. It wouldn't do Jack any good if she got herself killed trying to get to him.

A siren blared, and lights flashed in her rearview mirror. Alice swore under her breath, but she pulled over to the side of the road. The police car raced by her, followed by an ambulance and a fire truck.

The parking lot at the base of the mountain was just ahead. Her chest tightened as she fell in behind the emergency vehicles. She prayed they kept going past it, but when the police car pulled into the gondola parking lot, the pain in her chest spread throughout her body.

Then she saw the gondola station itself and the metal cables that supported the gondola, sagging halfway to the ground.

Alice choked back a cry. *Please, Lord, let Jack be safe. Please.*

The police cruiser stopped in front of a brick ranger station, and the ambulance and fire truck parked behind it. Alice jumped out of the Charger and raced after them into the building.

Inside, a ranger was talking with two people Alice recognized from the *Planet Survival* videos—Chiri and Frida. Chiri's hands were gesturing wildly and the pompoms on his hat danced across his head.

"That's what I'm trying to tell you!" Chiri was saying. "You need to get help up there right now! One man is critically injured and won't last much longer."

Alice clamped her hand over her mouth to trap the scream that was escaping her aching soul. She stood riveted to Chiri's every syllable.

"Two other men are dead," Chiri continued, while Frida nodded vehemently. "Not an accident. They were murdered."

57

CHANCE

Vicky collapsed to her knees. Little puffs of breath escaped her lips, and tears streamed down her grief-stricken face.

Jack jogged along the edge of the cliff, trying to see where the gondola landed and if there was any chance of Gavin surviving the fall. He found a good place to peer over the ledge. The gondola had cleared the slope and plummeted a hundred yards before smashing into jagged rocks. It was hard to tell at first that what resembled a balled-up wad of aluminum foil was the upside-down car, lying on its roof.

Leah reached his side and looked down at the wreckage. "Do you think there's any chance..."

He shook his head.

"We should at least check."

"There's no getting down there without gear. I'll come back with mine."

"No, I'll do it." She glared up at the gray sky. "Whatever his faults, Gavin was still part of the crew."

Vicky was still sobbing and Harvey and Wally helped her to her feet. She pushed the men aside and staggered off. Jack watched her go in the general direction of the lodge.

"First things first," Jack said. "We all need to get back to the lodge. We've left Bree all alone with Abe."

Leah didn't budge, though. Something had caught her attention. She pointed at a spot fifty yards down the slope below them. "Jack..."

He followed the line of her finger to a spot of bright-orange fabric protruding from the snow. A backpack. As Jack squinted, he saw that it was still attached to a body, and the body was lying in a very unnatural position.

"It's Eric," Leah whispered. Her climbing ax slipped from her hand and landed in the snow. "We're all going to die."

Jack stared. He had hoped the killer had been Eric. But Eric was a victim. Which meant only one thing.

The killer is one of us.

58

I DIDN'T EXPECT THAT

Vicky kicked the coffee table against the wall. "I'm not going back into Abe's room. It's freezing in there. If we're going to stay together, let's at least do it by the fireplace." She walked over to the fireplace, chucked a log in, and stared at the flames.

Harvey and Wally apparently agreed, as Harvey flopped down in the recliner and Wally took the couch.

"I'd better go check on Abe," Leah said. Her face was drawn, pale. *She blames herself,* Jack thought.

He gave her shoulder a squeeze. "I'll do it. You stay here." He leaned close to her. "Leah, listen. It's not your fault. None of it. I know you think it is, but it's not."

Leah reached up and squeezed his hand. "Thank you."

Snow fell from Jack's boots as he jogged down the hallway, craning his neck, praying that Abe's door was closed. It was. "Bree. It's Jack."

The bureau scraped against the floor, and the door opened a crack. Bree peered out, then moved the bureau the rest of the way.

Jack stepped inside, and Bree sat in the chair next to Abe's bed, her legs stretched out in front of her. "Did Gavin get the gondola going?" she asked.

Jack walked to the window and stared out at the lightening sky. "Gavin's dead."

Bree put both hands over her face.

"It was a trap," Jack said. "The gondola was sabotaged. It's destroyed."

"We're stuck here," Bree whispered.

"The weather's clearing up. Visibility's going to increase. I'll be able to light off the signal flares soon."

Abe groaned. Bree stroked his forehead. "He woke up while you guys were gone. For a few minutes, anyway. He's not going to last much longer, though. Do you really think help will come in time?"

Jack forced himself to meet Bree's gaze. He wanted to tell her they would be okay and that help was on the way, but he didn't know that. No one could be sure. And he wanted to be careful with his words, in case Abe could hear him. The slimmest hope could sometimes be the difference between life and death.

It had been hours since Chiri and Frida had set off to get help. If they were successful... But the storm was still in full swing when they started. No one else thought their descent was even possible. And now Jack was worried they might be right. He lowered his eyes and stared at Bree's boots and the bits of ice slowly melting on the floor.

"Someone has to come for us sometime, right?" Bree said with a hopeful smile.

Another little chunk of snow fell off Bree's heel and turned to mush. Jack swallowed and forced himself to keep his face neutral, expressionless. Staring at the glistening treads on her boot soles was like figuring out the key letter in a crossword. Suddenly, it all made sense.

Bree was lying.

Her hands were tucked in her jacket pockets. She stared at Jack with the same warm, weary smile teammates might share over a beer after losing a hard-played softball game.

His back stiffened. Plausible reasons Bree could have for going outside flickered through his head. As they did, Jack realized what he was really doing was coming up with counterarguments to any possible alibi Bree could produce.

"Do you need me to go get more snow for Abe, or can you manage?" Jack asked.

Bree flexed her left foot and winced. "I would appreciate if you or Leah could go. My ankle's still bad. I can't walk that far on it yet."

Jack resisted the urge to put his hand on his climbing ax. "I'm sure Leah will do it. We'd all do anything for Abe." He paused. "After all, he's got a little girl at home depending on her daddy to come back to her, right?"

Bree's lip trembled, and she nodded.

"And he's going to buy her one of those little Jeeps for her birthday. What's her name again?"

Bree ground her teeth. Tears were falling now.

"Annabelle—that's it," Jack said. "She's a beautiful girl. Remember how he tried to show me all those pictures?"

Bree wiped her nose with the back of her sleeve. "Change the subject," she muttered.

"I'm sorry it's upsetting." He took a step toward her. "It's just that I can't forget the look of love and pride on Abe's face when he talked about her. That little girl is lucky to have such a wonderful father—"

"Shut up!" Bree pressed her hands against the sides of her head and doubled over. Her tears stained the floor as she rocked back and forth.

"You didn't mean to hurt Abe."

Bree's head snapped up. "What?" she said, as if she hadn't heard him correctly.

"It was you, Bree. Your boots are wet. You went outside so you could detonate the charge on the gondola."

Bree's eyes darted around the room. "*Me?* You think *I'm* the killer? I just walked... Wait, that's why you asked me to get ice? Wet boots don't make me a killer."

"No. But stabbing Ollie does."

Bree wiped her nose and sat up straight. "That's ludicrous. Ollie is twice my size."

"That's why you stabbed him in the back. It was obvious Ollie knew his killer. Whoever stabbed him would never have gotten the jump on him in that hallway unless Ollie let his guard down."

"Ollie knew everyone on the crew. Any one of them could have done it."

"But they didn't. *You* did. You stabbed Ollie, and he must have spun around and broken your nose. That's why the bloodstain on the wall was about five feet up from the floor. That was your blood."

Jack couldn't prevent his hand instinctively moving to the climbing ax on his belt when Bree thrust her hands deeper into her pockets.

He softened his voice. "You didn't mean to hurt Abe. Ollie took Abe's gear."

"It was an accident," Bree whispered.

"Why?"

"Why?" Bree's eyes blazed. "Charlie. *He's* why. He was the most decent man I ever knew, and these bastards got him killed. Gavin was too much of a pampered prima donna to do his own stunts, so Ollie had to do them. You saw it, at the challenge the other day. Ollie took all the risk and Gavin got all the glory." Bree shifted in her chair and leaned forward. Her voice stayed low but intensified. "Ollie was paid extra for the stunts, but it was super hush-hush. If the fans found out, ratings would tank and so would profits, and we'd all be out of a job. It all boils down to money, right?"

"But then Ollie got hurt. So you'd think *then* Gavin would step up and actually do his job, wouldn't you? But no... Ryan, Gavin, and Ollie all ganged up on Charlie and bullied *him* to do the stunt. Charlie was scared out of his mind. He wasn't some macho extreme-sport nut; he was a musician who did sound work for his paycheck. I begged him not to do the stunt, but they told him if the show shut down, the production crew would be fired. That's what did it. He had a huge heart for people. He put these selfish pukes before himself, and what did it get him? Killed. *Buried alive.* And it's all their fault." Tears streamed down her reddening face.

Jack could tell that Bree's hand was gripping something in her jacket pocket. Most likely a knife; probably the same one she stabbed Ollie with. He hoped he could keep her talking and defuse the situation peacefully.

"Why kill Eric?" he asked.

"Because Mr. Know-It-All convinced everyone to search for Charlie in the wrong place! Charlie was suffocating, and only Frida and Chiri were digging where he really was." Her eyes darkened and she started running one hand along her pant leg, smoothing it over and over. "I put myself in the right place at the right time for Eric. I met him at the gondola, before Ollie arrived to take him off the mountain. I stabbed him in the back, and I made sure to puncture his lung. I wanted to guarantee he *suffocated*, so he died experiencing the same pain Charlie felt. An eye for an eye. That's why I smashed the generator. I wanted everyone to lie in the cold and dark, waiting for death to come. That's what Charlie felt. Alone in the dark. Cold. Waiting to die."

"Charlie's death was an accident, Bree. Charlie shouldn't have been bullied to do that stunt, but—"

"That avalanche was not an accident! Do you know what *really* triggered it?" Bree's eyes were wild with rage. "It wasn't the helicopter—it was greed! Ryan and Gavin thought an avalanche in the background of the shot would make the scene more dramatic. More drama bumps up ratings and the bottom line. Ollie and Mack, the helicopter pilot, planted avalanche charges, but they used too many and planted them too close together. They got a much bigger avalanche than they intended, and it ended up coming straight for Charlie."

There was a moment of silence while Jack processed the information, but he had to press on or she'd clam up. "And then Mack died. What happened to him?"

"When the show was on hiatus, I went climbing with him. It was easy to climb ahead of him and set off an avalanche charge." She drew a long, jagged breath. "An avalanche for an avalanche. I made things right."

Jack shook his head. "There's no way to bring Charlie back, so there's no way to make it right. You should have gone to the police."

"I talked to a lawyer. He said the most they would get was manslaughter and that it would most likely be negligent homicide. Nothing would happen to them. They wouldn't spend a day in jail. These materialistic dirtbags took Charlie's life—and mine, too. People need to *pay* for their actions."

"Then your revenge is complete. It's over."

Bree shook her head and pulled a pistol from her pocket.

He hadn't expected *that*. He took his hand off his ax. "I thought there were no guns on the mountain."

"Have you forgotten already? Ollie didn't search my bags thoroughly. I told him I just bought feminine products, and he backed away like a frightened rabbit. Typical male."

"What happens now, Bree?" Jack asked, trying to defuse the situation. "Are you going to shoot me?"

"No. I only want to kill the people who killed Charlie. But I'll shoot you if you get in my way. I have one more to go. Leah. I want her to feel everything Charlie did. I want her to feel all the pain and fear he felt."

"Leah wasn't even on set that day; she was in town."

"You were in the Army, right, Jack? You know the commander is always responsible. Besides, Leah knew Charlie was filling in for Gavin, and she didn't say anything."

"Neither did you."

Bree winced as if Jack had slapped her. The gun in her hand shook. "You're right, neither did I. And I intend to make *that* right, too."

That's why she confessed to all of it. She has no intention of leaving here alive. She's going to kill Leah, then she's going to kill herself.

The door opened, and Harvey took two steps into the room before he saw the gun in Bree's hand.

Bree aimed the gun at Harvey's chest. "Don't move, Jack, or I'll kill Harvey where he stands." She stood. "Hands up, both of you."

Jack and Harvey slowly raised their hands.

"I'm sorry, Harvey," Bree said. "Shut the door, grab that rope, and tie Jack's hands behind his back. Jack, turn around and put your wrists together."

Jack held his hands behind his back and let Harvey tie his arms. Jack kept his arms rigid after Harvey made the first loop of rope, to create slack so he could try to untie himself later. He knew he had to keep Bree talking.

"Would Charlie want you to do this, Bree?"

"Shut up, Jack, or I'll shoot you right now. Take off his climbing belt and tie his arms down, too," Bree instructed Harvey.

Harvey's hands shook, but he did everything she said. When he was done, Jack turned back around.

"I really am sorry, Harvey," Bree whispered through clenched teeth. "You've always been on my side—and you were on Charlie's side, too. He liked you, you know. Don't make me have to kill you."

Harvey stared at the gun, speechless, while Bree waved it toward the bureau. "Move this dresser back in front of the hall door, and move the other one away from the side door. We're going out the back way." Harvey did as he was told.

"Now go to my backpack. In the side pocket are cable ties. Take them out, stick them together, and put them around your wrists." Harvey took out two cable ties, joined them together in a circle, and awkwardly tried to tighten them around his own wrists.

"Use your teeth," Bree said. If it weren't for the gun in her hands and the steel in her voice, she might have been a schoolteacher trying to help a student.

Harvey managed to pull the cable ties tight.

"Don't either of you make a sound, or the others will come and I'll have to kill them all. Keep quiet, and only Leah has to die."

Jack turned to Harvey. "Do what she says."

"Get moving," Bree ordered.

Jack walked into the stairwell first, then Harvey, and Bree prodded them forward to a lone door next to the exit. It opened into the electrical room; a small cement room with a circuit panel on one wall, two metal cabinets against another, no windows, and a metal door. The perfect prison.

With Harvey between Jack and Bree, there was no way to get the gun away from Bree without the risk of Harvey getting shot—and as big as he was, he'd be hard to miss.

"Jack. Walk to the far wall and don't turn around. You too, Harvey."

"Bree, please don't—"

Bree pressed the barrel of the gun against Harvey's ear. Harvey looked like he was about to pass out, gulped in air, and took two unsteady steps forward. Bree stepped back and slammed the door closed, plunging them into darkness. As Jack's eyes lost the struggle to see even the wall he was touching, he wasn't sure if it felt more like a prison or a tomb.

59

CLIFF-HANGERS

Harvey was panting and grunting, his breathing speeding up.

"Harvey, listen to me." Jack nudged the man with his shoulder. "Calm down."

"I am. I'm trying to get my flashlight. It's in my jacket pocket."

"Turn your back to me," Jack said.

Harvey shifted around until Jack could reach back with his fingertips and grab the flashlight from Harvey's pocket. Jack managed to turn it on, giving them enough light to see.

"Harvey, those cable ties are easy to get out of."

Harvey struggled against the plastic ties and shook his head. "I'm not strong enough to break them."

"You don't have to be strong. Just listen to me. You're going to raise your hands above your head and then bring your arms down onto your hips."

"My belly's in the way."

"You'll hit your hips. Just keep your elbows out so you don't elbow yourself in the gut. You have to do it fast and hard."

Harvey nodded.

"Harvey. Look at me." Jack waited until Harvey met his eyes. "Leah's going to die. You've got to put everything you have into it."

Harvey's expression changed. He planted his feet like an Olympic weightlifter readying himself to go for the gold. "Hard and fast," he muttered. "Hard and fast."

Harvey raised his hands over his head and slammed his arms down. His battle cry turned into a shriek, but the plastic ties flew off his scraped wrists.

"Now untie me." Jack turned his back to Harvey.

"I did it!" Harvey said.

"Great. I saw. Untie me."

Harvey fumbled with the ropes for a minute. Jack pushed his hands together to give him slack, but Harvey still struggled.

"Just undo the knot."

"I can't." Harvey plucked feebly at the rope.

"Check the cabinets for something to cut the rope with."

Harvey dumped a box on the floor and found a utility knife.

Pain raced up Jack's arm as Harvey sliced his skin.

"Sorry," Harvey mumbled.

"Cut the *rope* off, not my *arm*."

Harvey yanked the ropes off, and Jack rushed to the door. Not surprisingly, it was locked. Jack scanned the room for something to use on the door.

"Safety laws require the lock to open from the inside," Harvey whined.

"That lock is twice as old as you," Jack said as he began rummaging through the cabinets. "They didn't have safety features then."

Harvey picked up a fire extinguisher. "Can we use this to bash the knob off?"

"No, that only works in the movies." Jack grabbed a wrench and a screwdriver. Using the wrench as a hammer and the screwdriver as a chisel of sorts, he went to work removing the hinge pins from the door. After ten minutes of pounding, he'd knocked all three pins free, and he and Harvey lowered the metal door to the floor.

Jack raced back to Abe's room. Vicky and Wally were standing just outside the door, which was wide open.

"There you are," Vicky said, exasperated. "What the hell is going on? Why is Abe all alone in here?"

Jack ignored her questions. "Have you seen Leah and Bree?"

"Bree called Leah on the walkie-talkie, and then Leah said she had to go and would be right back. She said it would be best if she went alone. I figured it was about Abe, that maybe he had… died. So when she didn't come back after a few minutes, we came up here—and found the door wide open. What's going on?"

"Harvey, fill them in." Jack grabbed Abe's climbing belt, turned, and bolted.

"Wait! She has a gun!" Harvey called after him. But Jack didn't need to be reminded.

* * *

The snowfall had stopped, and Bree's and Leah's footprints were easy to spot. But Jack didn't need the trail to know where they were going.

I want Leah to feel everything Charlie did. I want her to feel all the pain and fear he felt.

Bree was taking Leah to Grandma's Field. Where Charlie died. Bree had a gun. Jack had an ax. He had to find some way to even the odds.

He stopped following the footsteps and took a different trail. He pushed ahead as fast as he could. Cornelius's camp wasn't very far out of the way, and he could use the old man's help. As he stumbled down the slope, his lungs ached and his thighs were on fire. He hoped the hard going was slowing Bree down, too.

When Cornelius's tent came into view below, Jack had to force himself to slow so as not to tumble down the icy slope. His boots slipped on the rocks, and he had to use his climbing ax several times to keep himself from losing his footing altogether.

"Cornelius!" Jack called out as he rushed to the tent. "It's Jack! I need your help!"

He ripped the flap open, and Cornelius shot back to the far side of the tent, his eyes wild and his shaking hands clutching his spear.

"What's the matter with your brain?" Cornelius yelled. "I just peed myself."

"I need your help." Jack grabbed a water bottle and gulped some down. "Bree's the killer."

Cornelius shook his head. "You sure? She's cute as a button."

"Yes, I'm sure! She's going to kill Leah in Grandma's Field. I'm going to cut them off, but I need your help, and we have to move *fast*. You'll have to climb."

Cornelius grabbed his gear. "You've seen me. I ain't much on land, but climbing, I can soar like an eagle."

* * *

Grateful to be on board the helicopter, Alice peered out of the window as they lifted off from the ranger station. An EMT sat on either side of her, a policeman across from her. They hadn't wanted to bring her along at first, but she convinced them she could help. She knew the layout of the mountain and the lodge, and the identity of everyone on set. Besides, once she found out they were going up there, she would have hung from the chopper's skids if she'd had to.

The copter lurched sideways, buffeted by the wind. The pilot lowered the nose and followed the gondola wires up the slope. The pilot turned his head and yelled something back. Alice only heard one word over the loud thump of the helicopter blades: *wreckage*.

The pilot hovered over what looked like a crumpled tissue box. It took Alice's mind a second to reconstruct the image. The mangled blue-and-white stripes straightened out, and she remembered Jack waving back at her as the gondola disappeared up the mountain.

The gondola…

They started moving again, and the pilot pointed straight ahead, toward the lodge. As they approached and hovered, ready to land, a woman with flaming red hair rushed out of the lodge, waving her arms.

* * *

Jack was confident that despite his detour to Cornelius's tent, he had gotten ahead of Bree and Leah, and he figured that Leah was probably slowing Bree down. He glanced back over his shoulder, praying his footprints weren't visible here. The blizzard had swept the north face clean, and only a thick icy layer remained. *This just might work.*

The path to Grandma's Field ran right along the middle of a steep cliff face, about halfway up. It was little more than a narrow ledge, with the rocky cliff soaring up on his left and a hundred-foot drop on his right. A good spot for an ambush.

When he reached a rocky outcropping that could work as a hiding place, he ducked behind it. Bree would be able to spot him before she was on top of him, and he had only the climbing ax to use as a weapon, but if Cornelius could provide a distraction at just the right moment…

It wasn't much of a plan, but it was all he had. He pictured Alice and tried to drive what she'd think about his idea out of his head.

Did Cornelius get into place yet?

He crouched low and waited. His breath came in shallow puffs, but his mouth was bone dry. He grabbed a handful of snow and let it melt in his parched mouth. It tasted good, and his head cleared.

He heard footsteps and cautiously peered out. Leah was still about twenty feet away, and Bree walked ten feet behind her with the gun pointed at Leah's back.

Not yet. Wait till they're a little closer…

"Hey, Bree!" Cornelius shouted from above.

Jack swore under his breath. It was too early.

Bree and Leah both turned their backs to Jack and peered up the cliff at Cornelius, dressed in Jack's *Planet Survival* crew jacket.

"Stop!" Cornelius yelled, lowering his voice and doing his best to sound like Jack.

Jack kept low and crept along the path toward the two women, quiet and fast, sticking close to the rocks.

"You don't understand!" Bree shouted back. She squinted upward. "Cornelius? Is that you?"

I'm out of time.

He broke into a sprint. Hearing the crunch of his boots on the ice, Bree turned, and Jack's long legs covered the remaining distance in five strides. Leah broke off to the side and clung to the cliff face as he lunged at Bree.

She fired her gun and its echo rolled across the rocks.

Jack's shoulder caught Bree just below her sternum, and her breath exploded out of her lungs. He wrapped his arms around her thighs and yanked her legs out from under her. Momentum carried them across the narrow path. Bree groaned as she landed hard on her back with Jack on top of her. The gun skittered across the rocks and disappeared over the edge.

"No! No!" Bree shrieked. She arched her back and struggled to shove Jack off, but he wouldn't budge. *"No!"*

Bree's screams echoed and then merged into a rumble that turned into a roar. Jack cocked his head to the side, praying it wasn't what he feared. He looked down at Bree and saw joy in her eyes as the mountain began to shake with thousands of pounds of moving snow and the deafening thunder became unmistakable.

Avalanche!

Jack yanked Bree to her feet.

Cornelius bellowed down from the top of the cliff, "It's headin' right at ya!" He pointed at the space between them, where the snow on the cliff seemed to be shifting like a living thing, a monster devouring everything in its path.

"Go!" Jack grabbed Leah's shoulder and pushed her forward, casting a glance over his shoulder. Bree wasn't moving. She stood on the path with her eyes closed and her arms out—waiting for the avalanche to take her.

"No, Jack!" Cornelius called out, but Jack was already running back. Though he'd never felt the pull of self-survival as strongly as he did at this moment, and a thousand reasons *not* to rush back into an avalanche flashed through his mind, he shoved them aside as he raced to rescue Bree.

What sounded like a freight train was getting louder, and the ground began to shake.

Bree opened her eyes and bolted away from him, but he grabbed her arm and yanked her into him.

"Let me die!" she sobbed.

"You won't make it!" Cornelius cried.

Jack pulled Bree back with him against the rock face. He tore the rope off her climbing belt and used carabiners to attach it to both her belt and his. Snow was now washing down like a waterfall on top of them both. Jack grabbed a cam, wedged it into the rock, and tethered himself to it. He pressed himself and the squirming Bree as tightly against the rock as he could. The deafening roar of the avalanche drowned out all other sound, a boulder smashed on the path to their left, and Jack's world disappeared in a sea of white.

* * *

Alice raced behind Vicky up the icy path. The policeman lagged far behind them. It wasn't his fault—with his patrol boots, she was amazed he'd kept as close as he had.

Higher up the mountain it sounded like giants were pushing a cart filled with rocks. Alice's eyes searched the slope ahead, and for a moment she didn't believe what she was seeing. It appeared as though the mountain was *moving*. She watched with a mix of terror and awe as a cascade of snow swept down the slope and fell into a valley not a hundred yards away from them.

Vicky swore. "That's the path I was going to take. We'll have to find another way around—" Vicky stopped short, and her hand flew to her mouth. "Oh, dear God."

As the waterfall of snow turned into a trickle and stopped, Alice gasped at what was revealed high above them. Dangling from a rope, two climbers' limp bodies slowly twisted around and around like a watch dangling at the end of a chain.

When Alice recognized the red sweater, she felt as though her own heart had stopped beating.

Jack!

60

HANGING IN THE BALANCE

As Jack and Bree spun in the air above the jagged rocks like a grisly human mobile, Alice prayed Jack was still alive. A rope connected Jack to the cliff above, and a shorter one joined Bree to Jack. Jack was tethered at the waist, so his abdomen was his highest point, with his back arched and his hands and feet swinging loosely.

Then Bree began to move.

She's alive. Please, Jack, wake up.

Bree, hanging head-down, grabbed the rope and tried to pull herself upright, but the motion made them drop another foot and start swinging. Jack, still hanging like a rag doll, banged against the cliff-side.

Alice screamed.

Someone shouted from above. "Bree! Are you hurt?" Leah was on a ledge above Jack, near where his rope was anchored. That must have been where he fell from. Cornelius was higher on the cliff, climbing down with remarkable speed.

Bree managed to get herself into a sitting position, so her head was against Jack's waist. She shook her head. "My arm is broken!" Sure enough, although her left arm was hooked around the rope, it wasn't bending the right way. The look on Bree's face was one of agony.

"I'm going to help. Wait here," Vicky said to Alice. "Even when Cornelius gets down to Leah, the two of them aren't strong enough to pull up both Jack and Bree." Vicky's ax flashed in her hand as she ran to the base of the rocks and began to make her way deftly up. It was the first time she had done anything for anyone but herself in a long, long time.

The rope slipped again, and Jack and Bree dropped another few feet. Bree let out a guttural cry that didn't sound human.

"Hang on and keep still!" Leah shouted to Bree.

Alice watched, feeling helpless. All she could do was pray, and hope to see some sign of life from Jack.

A knife gleamed in Bree's right hand as she raised it toward Jack's belt.

"Stop!" Alice called up to her. "Please, drop the knife!"

Bree relaxed her arm but still clutched the knife in her hand. She looked down the cliff at Alice. "You must be Jack's fiancée."

"I am. Please don't hurt him."

"He stopped me from making it right. Leah's still alive, and it's all *his* fault." Bree's mouth was contorted and her speech was labored.

"Please, Bree." Alice's hands shook as she held them up like a beggar.

Vicky was closing in on Jack and Bree, but if Bree cut the rope...

"We're gonna try to pull you up," Cornelius called down. He had joined Leah, and the two of them had their hands on the rope holding Jack and Bree. Together, they pulled.

Jack and Bree moved up slowly, inch by inch. Then, with a sudden lurch, the rope slipped, and the two of them slid several feet before jerking to a stop. Jack's motionless body spun at the end of the rope, and his head nearly smacked against the rocks.

"Jack!" Alice screamed.

Rocks and snow tumbled down. Leah and Cornelius were trying to brace themselves. "The rope's pulled loose!" Cornelius shouted.

"Bree!" Leah called down. "You *have* to try to climb! Can you use your legs?"

Bree took a long, jagged breath, then shouted, "Let us fall!" She lifted the knife and held it against the rope.

"Bree! Please! *No!*" Alice took a deep breath. She couldn't lose control. Not now. Not when Jack needed her. "Bree. I know you loved Charlie. I know you were married."

"You don't know!" Bree shrieked. "You can't know my pain."

"I do! I'm going through it right now." Tears streamed down Alice's face. "He's the best man—"

"Charlie was."

"He was. Jack is, too." Alice looked at her Jack, her hero, her life; his face streaked with blood. Leah and Cornelius were shouting. Vicky was moving up the cliff, but she wouldn't make it in time.

"What would you do if someone killed him?" Bree's knife pressed against the rope.

For Alice, the world stopped moving. When a huge chunk of snow dropped, it seemed to make no sound. All Alice could think of was Jack and how happy she was whenever she was with him, the future they had mapped out together... At the thought of losing him, it felt like her heart was being crushed in her chest.

Jack's legs twitched, and he lifted his head.

"If someone killed Jack, I'd burn the planet to ash!" Alice yelled.

Bree cut the rope.

DEAD WEIGHT

For a second, everything proceeded in slow motion. Snowflakes drifted down with impossible patience and melted against Alice's hot cheeks. Leah and Cornelius were silent, wide-eyed figures above. Vicky came to a horrified stop. Bree's knife flashed in the wintry air.

Then *Bree* was falling with the snowflakes.

She'd cut the rope between her and Jack, not the rope that attached Jack up above. Bree hadn't killed Jack; she'd saved him.

Her descent seemed to take forever. She hit the snow with a sickening thud, and the world sped up again.

As Cornelius and Leah hoisted Jack up the cliff, Alice ran forward to where Bree had landed. The body lying in front of her looked like a child making a snow angel. Alice knelt in the snow, weeping.

Bree's eyes fluttered open. The snow all around her was melting into crimson. Her breathing was shallow and raspy.

"I couldn't hurt Jack. He was like Charlie," Bree whispered. "A good man." Her eyes looked straight up, fixed on the now clear sky. Blood ran from the corner of her mouth and ears. "And no one else should feel this pain."

Alice held Bree's hand. "I'm so sorry about what happened to Charlie."

Bree's eyes shifted to lock with Alice's. "Me too." Her face twitched, and a faint smile crossed her lips.

THE WINDS OF TOMORROW

Kiku gazed outside, marveling at the storm that raged just beyond the safety of the glass pane. She knew all too well what a harsh place the world could be, though not all storms of life were so visible.

She retrieved her purse and pulled out a cheap, throwaway phone loaded with prepaid minutes that had never been used. She stared down at it for a long time.

In the world in which Kiku lived, debts came in many forms, and all had to be repaid. That was why she was here now: to repay the debt she owed to Jack Stratton for saving her life once. But the favor she was about to request would come at a steep price.

Kiku dialed the number for Takeo Ishikawa.

Her heartbeat sped up and her mouth went dry. It always did when she spoke with the prince of the Yakuza. He was her boss. Twice he'd been her lover. Both times they'd lain together had been consensual. With his power, Takeo could have forced Kiku; it would have cost them both their lives. She would have killed him, and that would have meant a certain death sentence for her.

But he'd asked.

On the other end of the line, the phone began to ring.

The second time they made love, it had been Kiku who asked. That was over a year ago. Now things were... different.

And in Kiku's world, different was *not* good.

"Kiku." Takeo's deep voice was smooth. She pictured him now, his square jaw, his dark hair groomed to perfection. She could see his handsome face with his dark-brown eyes ablaze as he worked to decipher the reason for her call. She ached for him, and that caught her off-guard.

"Good morning, Takeo. I need to request a favor. I need to speak to the record keeper."

"Of course."

Kiku's heart slowed and her mind raced. Information was the most valuable and heavily guarded thing in her world, yet he hadn't hesitated to give his blessing and full access.

Why would he just give me the keys to the vault without knowing exactly what I am looking for?

"Thank you," she said quickly.

"Two weeks from tomorrow, I need to see you."

A feeling of vulnerability washed over her and she instinctively stepped away from the window. It had been months since she'd seen Takeo, and face-to-face meetings with him were rare. Being summoned was not a good thing.

Especially now.

"Certainly." Every thread of her being wanted to try to extract from him the reason for the meeting, but that was something she simply could not do. It would reveal her fear, and Takeo would take a very dim view of her distrust.

Her hope that he might voluntarily provide some detail or reassurance was dashed when he hung up the phone.

Clad only in her silk robe, Kiku returned to the window. The wind howled outside, and the sleet peppered the glass.

She dismantled the phone. The SIM card snapped in her hand.

Across the street, a beautiful maple tree had toppled over. It wasn't meant to survive such a storm. Kiku thought about a more dangerous storm coming her way; the meeting.

She remembered her mother's lullaby and could almost hear her sing.

Ashita wa ashita no kaze ga fuku.

The winds of tomorrow will blow tomorrow.

63

GRAVE DIGGER

Alice entered the apartment carrying a tower of cookie tins and chattering happily. "Mrs. Stevens usually makes only one kind of cookie at a time, but this time she made us seven different batches of cookies! Do you know what that means?"

Jack laughed. "I'll need to buy some new pants?"

"Maybe. But she's agreed to make a cookie cake for us! Your mother thought it was a wonderful idea. Oh, yeah—your mom called once and your dad twice while you were napping earlier. They'll call back later."

"I'm sure they will." Jack sat up on the couch. "It seems everyone is checking in on me. What's a cookie cake?"

"Instead of a regular wedding cake, it's a cookie cake. Stacks of all kinds of cookies piled to look like a cake! These are samples for us to try." Alice's ponytail swayed as she talked excitedly about the first wedding detail she had chosen. "Is that all right? We'll save a lot having her make it."

"Yes, cookie cake is great. As long as we're not having turducken for the main course," Jack laughed. "I *am* looking forward to taste-testing the cookies."

"Very funny. No turducken. Oh, I almost forgot, I confirmed our meeting at McAlister Insurance for next week. It will be with Mr. McAlister this time. Seems that Brian has been reassigned. Did I miss anything while I was at Mrs. Stevens'?" Alice asked, noisily setting down the cookie tins.

Jack got to his feet, leaned against the wall by the window, and stared out. The sky was a crisp blue, and Mount Minuit rose just on the horizon. "I just got off the phone with Leah. Abe's out of the ICU. He'll need a lot of physical therapy, but the doctors think he'll make a full recovery. It's amazing they were able to save his life, let alone his legs."

Alice moved to Jack's side and slipped her hand into his. "You're a good man, Jack Stratton."

Jack kissed her cheek and grinned. "I think that's the third time you've told me that today."

Alice squeezed his hand. "Bree said it too, and I can't stop thinking about her. What she did was so, so wrong, but I understand the pain she must have felt. If anyone took you away from me, I think I'd go crazy, too." Her green eyes darkened, the gold flakes disappearing altogether.

Jack kissed her again. "Just don't hunt them all down and kill them, okay, darling?"

Lady got up and trotted to the door just before a knock sounded. Reluctantly, the lovers unlocked their embrace and Jack limped over to open the door.

* * *

Kiku stood in the hallway listening to the sound of Lady's approaching claws. She had debated with herself for an hour about whether or not to pay this visit. In the end, her promise tipped the scales. The information she held in her hands contained a choice that wasn't hers to make. It was Alice's.

The door swung open and she stepped inside, scanning Jack's bruised face. "Detective."

"Hi, Kiku," Alice said softly.

"I have some information for you." She held out a USB stick.

Alice slowly came closer, reached out, and took it with a trembling hand. "Will this tell me who killed my family?"

"Please sit down." Kiku's eyes locked with Jack's, and he led Alice over to the couch.

Truth be told, Kiku was envious of their relationship. Jack and Alice were inseparable. If one traveled a dangerous path, she knew the other would loyally follow. Their bond had been forged in flames, but that was also now its greatest weakness.

Lady sat at their feet, and Kiku took the recliner. "The information on that device must be kept completely confidential. It's from a very secure source, and there would be personal ramifications for me if any word of it came out. Is that clear?"

"Yes, of course," Alice said. Jack nodded.

"I do not know how much you know about your parents' background, but I found out what I could. The files on that device include a background report on your mother. She immigrated to this country with your grandfather from the Ukraine."

"Kiku, please go slowly. Every bit of information is precious to me. Like golden breadcrumbs. I don't want to miss anything," Alice said softly.

"Of course." Kiku continued at an even pace. "Your grandfather had been a general in their army, and when the Ukraine gained its independence from the Soviet Union, both parties running for president wanted his support. Your grandfather publicly refused them both. He said that in the new Ukraine, the military should stay out of politics." Kiku paused as she recalled the horrific pictures. "Your grandmother was killed in a bombing a week later."

Jack squeezed Alice's hand.

"Your grandfather brought your mother to safety in America. He was among a great number of former Soviet military that scattered around the world. The United States granted him political asylum, but not without strings attached, I am afraid. They enlisted the help of your grandfather in convincing others to come to the United States. The United States government didn't care if these former military did absolutely nothing for the United States directly, as long as they were doing absolutely nothing for the enemy forces too. That was enough of a win for the US."

Jack squeezed Alice's hand. She had grown noticeably paler while Kiku spoke. Kiku noticed it, too, but didn't debate about continuing. Alice needed to know the truth even if it was overwhelming.

"Alice, your mother… assisted your grandfather. She acted in the role of liaison."

Alice shook her head. "I thought my mother helped my father with his flower business."

"She *was* a florist, Alice. I do not want to give you the false impression that she was some sort of spy. On the contrary, she was more of a goodwill ambassador. Included on the USB stick is a field report that she submitted after helping relocate an ex-commander and his family. Her sole concern was for the commander's children and the opportunities they would get here in the United States; she had no interest in any information the commander might have been able to provide the United States government."

"Wait a minute." Alice stiffened and pulled her hand free. "Are you saying my mother was *targeted*?"

Kiku nodded. "Yes. The evidence indicates that it was a well-planned execution by a professional."

"Who was it?" Alice's voice was strained.

"That I do not know. I have a name. Bennie. There is a man I need to speak with who may have more information."

"I want to talk to this man myself."

"I am sorry, Alice. That is not possible. It must be me."

Alice leaned forward and through gritted teeth said, "Then speak to him."

Jack put a cautioning hand on her leg.

"It is not as simple as picking up the phone." Kiku put her feet flat on the floor. "I am sorry for your pain, Alice. I must advise you against taking this path and encourage you to stop here."

"Stop? You just told me that my family was *murdered*, and you expect me to stop looking for the monster that did it?"

Kiku shook her head. "I expect you to ignore all of my warnings, but I hope I am wrong and that you will listen at least to Jack."

"I also need to find out *why* my family was killed."

"Most likely it was to send a message to your grandfather."

"Wait. Is my grandfather *alive*?"

Kiku nodded. "By all accounts, yes. But I cannot confirm that, as I do not know where he is currently."

Alice put her elbows on her knees, and hung her head.

"My apologies," Kiku said, "but I cannot stay. Please look over the information, and I will reach out to you in three weeks' time."

"Three weeks?" Alice stood up.

"You have waited a lifetime, I know. I am sorry to add to that wait, but it cannot be helped." Kiku's dark eyes met Alice's emerald-green ones, which were rapidly filling with tears.

"What if I need to ask you something?"

"You will be unable to do so. I have been summoned. I will be off the grid, as you say." Kiku's stomach tightened. She was not looking forward to what lay ahead.

"Thank you for doing this, Kiku," Jack said.

Alice shot forward, wrapped her arms around Kiku's small waist, and hugged her.

Kiku's breath caught in her throat. True affection was a rarity for her, but she and Alice were a lot alike. Both had had blissful childhoods before their worlds were ripped apart and they had to fend for themselves.

Alice hugged Kiku even tighter. Kiku's arms hovered for a moment awkwardly in the air before she returned the gesture. "You are most welcome."

When Alice let go, Kiku held on to her upper arms. She glanced over at Jack and cast him a look—he picked up on her intent.

"I think you two have something to discuss. Thank you again, Kiku." Jack gave her a tight smile and headed for the bedroom.

Kiku nodded and watched him go. His recent ordeal was evident in his halting gait.

Kiku turned back to Alice and lowered her voice. "As a friend, I say this: stop right here."

"I can't," Alice said, stepping away. "What happened to my family was wrong. I need to make it right."

Kiku rubbed behind Lady's ears but it brought her no comfort. "Do you know what Confucius said about vengeance? Before you go on a journey of revenge, dig two graves. One for your enemy and one for yourself."

Alice met her gaze with an unblinking stare.

With a nod, Kiku turned and walked out the door. As she made her way down the stairs and out to her car, she couldn't get the Confucius quote out of her head.

But it wasn't quite right.

If Alice wouldn't let this go, she wouldn't be digging two graves. She'd be digging three.

One for her enemy, one for herself.
And one for the man who won't leave her side.

THE END

Coming soon…
JACK OF DIAMONDS

THE DETECTIVE JACK STRATTON
MYSTERY-THRILLER SERIES

The Detective Jack Stratton Mystery-Thriller Series, authored by *Wall Street Journal* bestselling writer Christopher Greyson, has over 5,000 five-star reviews and over one million readers and counting. If you'd love to read another page-turning thriller with mystery, humor, and a dash of romance, pick up the next book in the highly acclaimed series today.

AND THEN SHE WAS GONE

A hometown hero with a heart of gold, Jack Stratton was raised in a whorehouse by his prostitute mother. Jack seemed destined to become another statistic, but now his life has taken a turn for the better. Determined to escape his past, he's headed for a career in law enforcement. When his foster mother asks him to look into a girl's disappearance, Jack quickly gets drawn into a baffling mystery. As Jack digs deeper, everyone becomes a suspect—including himself. Caught between the criminals and the cops, can Jack discover the truth in time to save the girl? Or will he become the next victim?

GIRL JACKED

Guilt has driven a wedge between Jack and the family he loves. When Jack, now a police officer, hears the news that his foster sister Michelle is missing, it cuts straight to his core. The police think she just took off, but Jack knows Michelle would never leave her loved ones behind—like he did. Forced to confront the demons from his past, Jack must take action, find Michelle, and bring her home... or die trying.

JACK KNIFED

Constant nightmares have forced Jack to seek answers about his rough childhood and the dark secrets hidden there. The mystery surrounding Jack's birth father leads Jack to investigate the twenty-seven-year-old murder case in Hope Falls.

JACKS ARE WILD

When Jack's sexy old flame disappears, no one thinks it's suspicious except Jack and one unbalanced witness. Jack feels in his gut that something is wrong. He knows that Marisa has a past, and if it ever caught up with her—it would be deadly. The trail leads him into all sorts of trouble—landing him smack in the middle of an all-out mob war between the Italian Mafia and the Japanese Yakuza.

JACK AND THE GIANT KILLER

Rogue hero Jack Stratton is back in another action-packed, thrilling adventure. While recovering from a gunshot wound, Jack gets a seemingly harmless private investigation job—locate the owner of a lost dog—Jack begrudgingly assists. Little does he know it will place him directly in the crosshairs of a merciless serial killer.

DATA JACK

In this digital age of hackers, spyware, and cyber terrorism—data is more valuable than gold. Thieves plan to steal the keys to the digital kingdom and with this much money at stake, they'll kill for it. Can Jack and Alice (aka Replacement) stop the pack of ruthless criminals before they can *Data Jack?*

JACK OF HEARTS

When his mother and the members of her neighborhood book club ask him to catch the "Orange Blossom Cove Bandit," a small-time thief who's stealing garden gnomes and peace of mind from their quiet retirement community, how can Jack refuse? The peculiar mystery proves to be more than it appears, and things take a deadly turn. Now, Jack finds it's up to him to stop a crazed killer, save his parents, and win the hand of the girl he loves—but if he survives, will it be Jack who ends up with a broken heart?

JACK FROST

Jack has a new assignment: to investigate the suspicious death of a soundman on the hit TV show *Planet Survival*. Jack goes undercover as a security agent where the show is filming on nearby Mount Minuit. Soon trapped on the treacherous peak by a blizzard, a mysterious killer continues to stalk the cast and crew of *Planet Survival*. What started out as a game is now a deadly competition for survival. As the temperature drops and the body count rises, what will get them first? The mountain or the killer?

Hear your favorite characters come to life
in audio versions of the
Detective Jack Stratton Mystery-Thriller Series!
Audio Books now available on Audible!

Novels featuring Jack Stratton in order:
AND THEN SHE WAS GONE
GIRL JACKED
JACK KNIFED
JACKS ARE WILD
JACK AND THE GIANT KILLER
DATA JACK
JACK OF HEARTS
JACK FROST

Psychological Thriller
THE GIRL WHO LIVED

Ten years ago, four people were brutally murdered. One girl lived. As the anniversary of the murders approaches, Faith Winters is released from the psychiatric hospital and yanked back to the last spot on earth she wants to be—her hometown where the slayings took place. Wracked by the lingering echoes of survivor's guilt, Faith spirals into a black hole of alcoholism and wanton self-destruction. Finding no solace at the bottom of a bottle, Faith decides to track down her sister's killer—and then discovers that she's the one being hunted.

Epic Fantasy
PURE OF HEART

Orphaned and alone, rogue-teen Dean Walker has learned how to take care of himself on the rough city streets. Unjustly wanted by the police, he takes refuge within the shadows of the city. When Dean stumbles upon an old man being mugged, he tries to help—only to discover that the victim is anything but helpless and far more than he appears. Together with three friends, he sets out on an epic quest where only the pure of heart will prevail.

INTRODUCING
THE ADVENTURES OF FINN AND ANNIE

A SPECIAL COLLECTION OF MYSTERIES EXCLUSIVELY FOR CHRISTOPHER GREYSON'S LOYAL READERS

Finnian Church chased his boyhood dream of following in his father's law-enforcing footsteps by way of the United States Armed Forces. As soon as he finished his tour of duty, Finn planned to report to the police academy. But the winds of war have a way of changing a man's plans. Finn returned home a decorated war hero, but without a leg. Disillusioned but undaunted, it wasn't long before he discovered a way to keep his ambitions alive and earn a living as an insurance investigator.

Finn finds himself in need of a videographer to document the accident scenes. Into his orderly business and simple life walks Annie Summers. A lovely free spirit and single mother of two, Annie has a physical challenge of her own—she's been completely deaf since childhood.

Finn and Annie find themselves tested and growing in ways they never imagined. Join this unlikely duo as they investigate their way through murder, arson, theft, embezzlement, and maybe even love, seeking to distinguish between truth and lies, scammers and victims.

This **FREE** special collection of mysteries by *Wall Street Journal* bestselling author CHRISTOPHER GREYSON is available EXCLUSIVELY to loyal readers. Get your **FREE** first installment ONLY at ChristopherGreyson.com. Become a Preferred Reader to enjoy additional FREE *Adventures of Finn and Annie*, advanced notifications of book releases, and more.

Don't miss out, visit ChristopherGreyson.com and JOIN TODAY!

You could win a brand new
HD KINDLE FIRE TABLET
when you go to
ChristopherGreyson.com
Enter as many times as you'd like.
No purchase necessary.
It's just my way of thanking my loyal readers.

Looking for a mystery series mixed with romantic suspense?
Be sure to check out Katherine Greyson's bestselling series:
EVERYONE KEEPS SECRETS

ACKNOWLEDGMENTS

I would like to thank all the wonderful readers out there. It is you who make the literary world what it is today—a place of dreams filled with tales of adventure! To all of you who have spread word of my novels via social media (Facebook and Twitter) and who have taken the time to go back and write a great review, I say THANK YOU! Your efforts keep the characters alive and give me the encouragement and time to keep writing. I can't thank YOU enough.

Word of mouth is crucial for any author to succeed. If you enjoyed the novel, please consider leaving a review at Amazon, even if it is only a line or two; it would make all the difference and I would appreciate it very much.

I would also like to thank my amazing wife for standing beside me every step of the way on this journey. My thanks also go out to Laura and Christopher, my two awesome kids, and my dear mother and the rest of my family. Finally, thank you to my wonderful team: Maia McViney, Maia Sepp, my fantastic editors—David Gatewood of Lone Trout Editing, Faith Williams of The Atwater Group, Charlie Wilson of Landmark Editorial, Anne Cherry, Ann Kroeker—my writing coach and my consultant Dianne Jones, and the unbelievably helpful beta readers!

ABOUT THE AUTHOR

My name is Christopher Greyson, and I am a storyteller.

Since I was a little boy, I have dreamt of what mystery was around the next corner, or what quest lay over the hill. If I couldn't find an adventure, one usually found me, and now I weave those tales into my stories. I am blessed to have written the bestselling Detective Jack Stratton Mystery-Thriller Series. The collection includes *And Then She Was GONE, Girl Jacked, Jack Knifed, Jacks Are Wild, Jack and the Giant Killer, Data Jack, Jack of Hearts, Jack Frost,* with *Jack of Diamonds* due later this year. I have also penned the bestselling psychological thriller, *The Girl Who Lived* and a special collection of mysteries, *The Adventures of Finn and Annie.*

My background is an eclectic mix of degrees in theatre, communications, and computer science. Currently I reside in Massachusetts with my lovely wife and two fantastic children. My wife, Katherine Greyson, who is my chief content editor, is an author of her own romance series, *Everyone Keeps Secrets.*

My love for tales of mystery and adventure began with my grandfather, a decorated World War I hero. I will never forget being introduced to his friend, a WWI pilot who flew across the skies at the same time as the feared, legendary Red Baron. My love of reading and storytelling eventually led me to write *Pure of Heart,* a young adult fantasy that I released in 2014.

I love to hear from my readers. Please visit ChristopherGreyson.com, where you can become a preferred reader and enjoy additional FREE *Adventures of Finn and Annie,* advanced notifications of book releases and more! Thank you for reading my novels. I hope my stories have brightened your day.

Sincerely,

CPSIA information can be obtained
at www.ICGtesting.com
Printed in the USA
LVHW041045070419
613259LV00003B/648

9 781683 990819